PARTNERS IN CRIME

ALSO BY STEVE HOCKENSMITH

Holmes on the Range Mystery Series

Holmes on the Range

On the Wrong Track

The Black Dove

The Crack in the Lens

World's Greatest Sleuth!

The Double-A Western Detective Agency

Hunters of the Dead

PARTNERS IN CRIME

FIVE HOLMES ON THE RANGE MYSTERIES

STEVE HOCKENSMITH

ROUGH
EDGES
PRESS

Partners in Crime: Five Holmes on the Range Mysteries
Paperback Edition
Copyright © 2023 Steve Hockensmith

Rough Edges Press
An Imprint of Wolfpack Publishing
9850 S. Maryland Parkway, Suite A-5 #323
Las Vegas, Nevada 89183

roughedgespress.com

Paperback ISBN 978-1-68549-407-0
eBook ISBN 978-1-68549-406-3
LCCN 2023947547

CONTENTS

Partners In Crime   1
My Christmas Story   65
Curious Incidents   94
Bad News   135
Can The Cat Catch The Rat?   184

A Look At: Black List, White Death   225
About the Author   227

PARTNERS IN CRIME

PARTNERS IN CRIME

Diana Crowe
328 Franklin Street
Ogden, Utah Territory

Dear Miss Crowe:

I am writing you this letter with the assumption that you await our arrival in Ogden with bated breath. I'm not sure if my breath has ever been bated, but it sounds uncomfortable and perhaps even unhealthy if carried on long enough, and Old Red and I would never forgive ourselves if you did yourself an injury through sheer prolonged longing to see us. So please rest assured and breathe easy: We are still on our way to join you!

Our delay has been my brother's creation—and very much to my surprise. Having you waiting for us in Ogden would be reason enough for Old Red not to dawdle. But you and your father aren't just waiting, of course. Far from it. You're renting an office, filing incorporation papers, and alerting potential clients that the A.A. Western Detective Agency is open for business. Taking all the steps, in other words, that will make my brother's dream of the past year a reality.

We are about to become actual, professional, eligible-to-join-the-union consulting detectives. The very thing Old Red has longed for since I first read him a Sherlock Holmes tale on the cattle trail. Yet it was his idea to take a detour as we headed west to join our new partners in detecting.

"Kansas ain't but a hop, skip and a jump thataway," he announced not long after we passed through Omaha.

He was staring miserably southward out the window of a Pullman car at the time. As you well know, "staring miserably" is his primary occupation when riding on a train, so this came as no shock to me. Not like what he said next.

"If we got off at Lincoln we could get horses and be down in Peabody in a couple days."

"Indeed we could," I said. "And why the hell would we want to do that?"

"'Cuz I ain't visited Peabody in nearly 10 years, and you ain't been there in more than five."

"True. Which I always took as a sign that neither of us cared to go. Along with the fact that you never once brought it up before."

"Well, we ain't never been this close before."

I cocked an eyebrow and began counting silently on my fingers.

"Yeah, all right," Old Red said. "We been close a few times. But not with money in our pockets and the freedom to spend it."

"And you want to use that freedom on a trip to *Peabody, Kansas?*"

My brother shrugged. "A fella only gets one hometown."

"And when the hometown's Peabody the fella runs away and never looks back. If the fella's you."

Old Red grimaced. "I didn't 'run away.'"

"No. You galloped."

My brother glared at me a moment, then went back to staring miserably out the window.

I'd not only touched a nerve, I'd given it an extra poke out of spite. Shame on me.

I followed Old Red's gaze southward, across the broad, flat, yellow Nebraska plains toward Kansas. Two hundred-some miles that way was the farm we'd grown up on, and Peabody a little ways beyond it. All our family was down there, dead though not necessarily buried, floods doing what they do. What was there for us now?

Land we no longer owned. A hometown that wasn't a home. Old "neighbors" we no longer even knew.

Old neighbors...

Not all of them would be old. I could think of one exactly my own age, in fact.

A little smile came to my face.

"You know what? If it means that much to you, fine," I said. "I'm game for a jaunt to the old haunts."

Old Red turned away from the window. "Yeah?"

"Sure. Only I don't see why our jaunting has to be on horseback. The Atchison, Topeka and Santa Fe will get us there a lot faster."

My brother's face fell in a way that told me he wasn't just angling to get to Peabody. He wanted to get *off* the trains.

Me, I don't love train travel, but I love saddle sores even less.

I gave him a "Take it or leave it" shrug.

He took it.

"Fine," he said. "But once we're there I'll want at least two full days to stretch my legs."

"Of course, brother. I wouldn't dream of rushin' you."

Old Red gave me a quizzical look—clearly wondering what reason *I* might have to dawdle around Peabody—but he didn't push his luck by asking questions.

A couple days later (trains aren't always *that* much faster than horses, you know) we were pulling into Peabody. The country around it hadn't changed much. ("Oh, gosh—look," I said. "They still have grass." Then later: "Oh, gosh—look. They still have cornfields." Then later: "Oh, gosh—look. They still have cows." "Oh, gosh—look," Old Red finally said. "You're still a fool.") The town had definitely grown, though, with as much brick to it now as clapboard. I didn't spot any electric or telephone wires, but I did see other signs—a spiffy new firehouse, a bicycle shop, a bowling alley—that Peabody wasn't going to let the rest of America toddle on toward the 20th century without trying to keep up.

"Oh, gosh—look," I said as we approached the station.

My brother glowered at me.

I pointed at a crowd gathering by the platform.

"Someone must've told 'em we were comin'," I said.

There was no brass band, no bunting, no signs saying "WEL-COME BACK, BOYS!" But the small mob—perhaps fifty men, women and children, supplemented by half a dozen dogs— was clearly waiting for *someone* on the train. I tried giving them a jaunty wave through the window, but no one paid me any mind. They didn't seem to be watching the passenger cars at all, in fact. It was the baggage car they were fixed on.

As Old Red and I stepped down onto the platform, carpetbags in hand, a murmur of excitement went through the crowd. Which had nothing to do with us. The baggage man had opened the side door of his car.

"You see it?" a man nearby asked.

"I'm not sure," said another, craning his neck.

"How big will it be?" said a little girl.

"Big enough to sit on!" her brother laughed.

Their mother shushed them.

"Pardon me, ma'am," I said, stepping toward the lady. "What's all the fuss—?"

She shushed me, too.

"Don't make me miss it," she said without looking at me.

"Here it comes!" another woman cried out.

The baggage man had begun pushing a crate toward the door. It was a little more than waist high, with the words "FRED. ADEE & CO., NEW YORK" stenciled on the side.

The crowd cheered.

"This is a big day for Peabody," an old man said, wiping away happy tears.

Another old man gave the crate a dismissive swipe of his withered hand. "It'll never work."

I was about to ask him *what* would never work when a thickset, mustachioed gent in a brown overcoat stepped up to us.

"You two staying in town?" he asked.

"We thought we'd—" I began.

The crowd cheered again. A man had hopped into the baggage car waving a piece of onion skin paper—a receipt, it seemed. He was either the proud owner of a big box of something from Fred. Adee & Co. of New York or was fetching it for whoever was. My money would've been on the latter based on his unshaven face and frayed cap and working man's denim overalls. (See? My brother's not the only one capable of making deductions.)

The stout fellow with the mustache jerked his head to the side, and Old Red and I followed him away from the train. He didn't look back at the crowd, but there was something about the way he walked—with a swagger that was almost a strut—that suggested he was very aware of all the eyes nearby.

He didn't lead us far before stopping and swinging around to face us again. Maybe twenty yards down the platform—not enough to make much difference in the noise. I took that as another sign he was putting on a show.

"You were saying?" he growled at me.

"That we do indeed plan to stay in Peabody for a bit, Roy. It's nice to see you again, by the way. You just filling in for Marshal van Doorn today, or have you moved up in the world?"

The stout man—one Roy Bewley—peered at me, puzzled.

I swept off my bowler and gave him a grin.

Bewley gazed up at the flaming red hair atop my head. After a blink and a sideways glance at Old Red's equally fiery mustache, he nodded in recognition. He didn't, however, return my smile.

"Well, well. Otto Amlingmeyer, back in Peabody. And this must be your brother. Gunnar, wasn't it?"

"Gustav," Old Red said.

"Right. Of course. Well, well, well."

Bewley—the town marshal now, it seemed, for who else would be getting so nosy with apparent strangers fresh off the noon train?—looked us up and down again. We made an odd pair, I'm sure. My slight, pucker-faced brother in his Stetson and duster and boots, looking like a small-time rancher who's just found out the price of beef has dropped for the fourth time that month. And beside him big, friendly me filling out a tailored suit with such manful panache I would've looked right at home in a fashion plate, should there be one large enough to contain me. The only indication we were family was the red hair we shared and our habit of looking annoyed with each other.

"I heard you two were Pinkertons or something like that," Bewley said.

"Something like that," said Old Red.

He offered nothing more, being allergic to explanations unless it suits him. So I hopped back in.

"Actually, we just turned down jobs with the Pinkertons to pursue a more exciting opportunity. We're partners in a new detective agency outta Ogden, Utah. We're on our way there now."

Bewley's already less-than-friendly expression turned skeptical.

"On your way to Utah to start a detective agency…via a southbound train to Peabody?"

The look on his face told me it wasn't just our sense of direction he doubted. I guess Old Red and I have some work to do to look like entrepreneurs or capitalists or captains of industry or whatever you want to call it.

"As long as we were in the general vicinity we thought we'd swing by and see the old homestead," I said.

"And how welcome we do feel," my brother grumbled.

Bewley frowned at him. He wasn't that much older than us— early thirties to our twenties—and when I'd known him he'd just been the nice-ish fellow who worked at the lumber mill and occasionally pinned on a badge when Marshal van Doorn needed a deputy. In the intervening years, it seemed, he'd perfected the air of impatience, suspicion and vague (or often not so vague) disdain that is the full-time lawman's stock in trade. (At least the full-time lawmen Old Red and I cross paths with.)

"Dirk van Doorn died last month, so I'm acting marshal," he said. "Times are hard, and we get a lot of vagrants and trouble-makers passing through the area. There's the Doolin-Dalton gang and the Give-'em-Hell Boys and all those outlaws down in the Indian Territories. Outlaws it's my job to watch out for now. A couple professional 'detectives' ought to understand that, if they know their business at all."

"Of course, Roy," I said. "I'm sorry to hear about Marshal van Doorn, but I'm sure you're filling his shoes splendidly. Congratulations on the new job...and please don't let us keep you from it."

Another man—a drummer of patent medicines, I knew, him having attempted to interest my brother in a cure for rheumatism —had gotten off the train at the same time as us. He stood at the edge of the crowd watching as the crate from Fred. Adee & Co. was scooched out onto a buckboard. I held a hand out toward him and gave Bewley a "Have at it" look.

Bewley glared back at me a moment before heading off to harass someone else.

He did *not* grace us with a "Welcome back."

"Roy Bewley, the town marshal," Old Red said with a snort. "Figures."

"You don't think he's the man for the job?"

"Oh, he might march around lookin' tough well enough." My brother shook his head. "But god help Peabody if there's actual deducifyin' to be done."

Before I could reply—to say the only mystery I expected to encounter in Peabody was why we were there—another man separated himself from a plump lady in a mink-collared coat and approached us, hand outstretched. He was a slender gent of fifty or so, dressed, like the lady and the marshal, in an overcoat to ward off the mild mid-November chill.

"Well, isn't this the day for auspicious arrivals!" he said. "Otto

Amlingmeyer! After all these years! And surely this must be your brother Gus with you."

He gave my hand a hearty shake, then attempted the same with Old Red. My brother thwarted him with a loose grip and droopy wrist.

"Mr. Dishane, ain't it?" Old Red said.

"That's right. I'm surprised you remember me. We probably haven't laid eyes on each other in ten or twelve years."

"Oh, I ain't likely to forget *you*."

Dishane kept smiling, but his eyes were wary.

I hadn't known the man well. He was a businessman about town, with his manicured fingers in a variety of financial pies, and what gentleman of that stripe has much time for farm boys or granary clerks (both of which I'd been when I was around)? I'd had but one protracted interaction with him, and that had been the last. It was my last memory of Peabody, in fact.

Not long after the flood that swept away my mother and sisters and aunt and cousins, Richard Dishane took me under his wing for a time. Just long enough to help a shocked, distraught boy put his family affairs in order and get word to his illiterate ranch hand brother in Texas that he needed collecting. Take out what my mother owed the bank on our land—not to mention Mr. Dishane's fees for acting as advocate and go-between—and there was just enough left for a ticket to Dodge City and a sandwich on the way. More like half a sandwich. After I signed everything over, Mr. Dishane kindly walked me to the station and waited with me till the train came…no doubt to make sure nobody happened along who'd talk me out of it.

As that train rolled away, I'd waved goodbye to Richard Dishane and Peabody, Kansas, and mud-mud-mud in all directions and a hell of a lot of dead Amlingmeyers. I waved goodbye to my boyhood, too. And my innocence. And any desire to spend another minute in the middle of Kansas.

Now here I was. Back again. And as Dishane's eyes flicked back and forth from my brother to me, I could tell he was wondering if it was him we'd come to see.

It wasn't, of course. But I didn't feel any particular need to set his mind at ease.

"You still in the real estate business, Mr. Dishane?" I said. "Helping folks get a square deal for their land?"

Dishane gave me what was supposed to be a modest shrug. "Oh, I dabble. Insurance is my main line now."

"Insurance? That makes sense," Old Red muttered. Meaning, I'm sure, that it would be just like Dishane to jump into a booming new business a lot of people saw as a slick flimflam.

Dishane chose to take it another way.

"Indeed—the farmers and businessmen around here could certainly use it. Just one bad turn is all it takes to go from riches to rags, as you well know. Why, if only your family had taken out a policy, you might have been able to...well."

My brother's unfriendly glower had quickly flared up to a full-on scowl.

Dishane cleared his throat and changed the subject.

"Peabody's not the same town it was when you two left." He turned and nodded at the buckboard with the crate in the back just as the fellow in overalls gave the reins a gentle snap. "Modernity has arrived."

"They ship 'modernity' from New York in a big box?" I said.

Dishane gave that a hearty (and unconvincing) chuckle. "Actually, they do, Otto. And I'm proud to say the final destination is my home."

The crowd parted to let the wagon through, then fell in behind as the workman steered his two-horse team toward the street.

"Congratulations," I said to Dishane.

(I wasn't sure what the proper thing to say is when someone tells you they just got a shipment of modernity. Not that I was especially inclined to say the proper thing to Dishane. "Congratulations" just popped out.)

"Thank you," Dishane said. "And what is it that brings you back this way? Business or pleasure?"

"Both," said Old Red.

The word was firm, terse. Implying that our business would be a pleasure—and that we wouldn't be telling Dishane anything more about it. For now.

Which was sheer malarkey. But Old Red had seen an opportunity to make Dishane sweat, and he'd taken it. Petty, perhaps, but rather enjoyable.

"I see. Well…best of luck to you," Dishane said. "If you gentlemen will excuse me."

He was wearing a gray wool fedora, and he touched the brim and moved off to take the lady's arm again and follow the wagon.

"Yeah," a man passing nearby called to us. "He tell you how much he paid for it?"

I shook my head. "The thing off the train? We still don't even know what it is."

Several people in the crowd laughed as they strolled off after the Dishanes.

"That," said the man, pointing ahead at the crate, "is going to be Peabody's first indoor toilet."

"The pipes came last week," another man added. "It's all set!"

"Dick Dishane's finally got himself a throne!" yet another man threw in.

That got more laughs. Everyone was so excited you would've thought they'd been waiting all week to sit on Dishane's "throne" themselves.

"What do you say, brother?" I said. "Shall we join the throng and take in the spectacle?"

"Nah. We seen them things before."

"Done more than see 'em. What a worldly pair we have become."

Marshal Bewley was still talking to the drummer by the steps down from the Pullman, but he clearly wasn't giving it his full attention. He'd seen us making conversation with Dishane, and now every few seconds he'd glance our way looking even less welcoming than before.

And he wasn't the only one giving us looks. Several of the townspeople were staring, now that they'd noticed us. Many seemed vaguely familiar to me, and I assumed the vice versa was true.

News of our return would surely spread around town soon enough. It would've been the day's hottest gossip if a toilet hadn't stolen our thunder.

"To the hotel then?" I said.

Old Red nodded. "Yeah. Be good to get us a room. Gettin' so many stares I feel like a monkey in the zoo."

"I've often noted the resemblance."

My brother rolled his eyes and fell in behind the crowd. A little beyond the station they swung left while we kept on straight, heading south down Walnut Street. (Unlike many American towns, Peabody has never bothered with a "Main Street." Maybe that would seem too uppity.)

"Methodists got 'em a new church," I pointed out.

Old Red just grunted.

"One of the Mullers opened a taxidermy shop."

Old Red just grunted.

"They repainted the library."

Old Red just grunted.

"The hotel burned down."

"Well, shit," Old Red said.

We stopped and took in the scorched rubble up ahead. Not only was the Peabody Grand Hotel gone, so were the bakery and haberdashery that had once bookended it.

"Now I'll never know if that hotel really was grand," I said.

"It wasn't," said Old Red, though as far as I knew he'd never set foot inside the place either. Maybe he was trying to help me feel better. There's a first time for everything.

"Are you gentlemen looking for a place to stay?" someone said.

I guess standing there gawping at the ruins of the hotel with carpetbags in our hands was a bit of a giveaway.

We turned and found ourselves facing what felt like the only man in town who hadn't been at the station awaiting Dishane's new water closet. His voice was more than familiar. It was like the sound of thunder or wind or the singing of birds. Something you heard so often when young it became a part of you. Something you'd still be able to hear clear as day even were you struck deaf.

"Oh my goodness," I said. "What's this 'gentlemen' talk? Don't you know the Amlingmeyer boys when you see 'em?"

The old man slowly approaching us—tall and stoop-shouldered and stiff-legged—squinted, then grinned.

"And here I thought I'd never see you two again," he said. "Otto. And Conrad."

"Gustav," Old Red corrected gently.

Old Pastor Vogel had been around Peabody long enough to have known our brother Conrad. Long enough to have comforted our *Mutter* after smallpox took Conrad and our *Vater* both.

"Of course," the old man said. "I'm sorry."

I waved the apology away. "We been gone quite a while. Even someone as remarkable as me is bound to fade from memory sooner or later. Otto here...well, I'm not surprised it's 'sooner.'"

The reverend shook his head, grinning again. "You haven't changed."

"And who'd want me to?" I said. I shot a look at my brother. "Don't answer that."

He didn't. He was going to ignore me entirely, in fact.

"What happened to the hotel?" he asked Vogel.

The old man shrugged. "A fire. It happened about two weeks ago. They never did figure out how it started. The Steins—that's the owners these days—they hope to rebuild in the spring if they can scrape the money together."

Old Red snorted. "They didn't buy insurance from Dishane?"

Vogel shook his head. "Unfortunately, no."

"Then this'll make good advertisin' for him," I said, nodding at the broken beams and fire-blackened plaster strewn about where the hotel once stood.

The reverend shrugged again. "I suppose so."

"Where are out-of-towners stayin' in the meantime?" Old Red asked.

"Here and there. Plenty of people are letting rooms these days, times being what they are. In fact, that's just what I was going to mention when I first saw you standing here. Do you remember Mrs. Gunther? From church?"

"How could I forget her?" I said.

I almost added an explanation: "I still see her in my nightmares every night." But I let that part go without saying it.

Mrs. Gunther had taught Sunday school for years. Suffice it to say "the Amlingmeyer boys" had not been her prize pupils.

"She's been taking in boarders ever since Mr. Gunther passed," Vogel said. He lowered his voice and leaned in a little closer, though there was no one around to eavesdrop. "There wasn't much of an estate."

My brother showed he understood with a silent nod.

"Nice of you to wander the streets drumming up business for a parishioner in need," I told the reverend. "What's your percentage?"

The old man looked horrified.

"That was a joke," I said.

"Oh. Of course." Vogel chuckled dryly for a moment—a very short moment—then shook his head. "You really haven't changed."

He made that sound unfortunate.

"We'd be happy to give Mrs. Gunther our business if she'll take it," Old Red said. "She still live on Pine Street?"

"That's right. Why don't I walk you over? Help you get reacquainted?"

"Thank you, Pastor," I said. "That's very kind of you."

It also struck me as rather ambitious. The Gunthers' house was five blocks off, and Vogel looked unsteady enough to make five *steps* less than a sure thing. But I wasn't going to say no. Once Mrs. Gunther realized it was us on her doorstep I didn't know if she'd greet us with open arms or reach for something to throw.

We passed the time waiting to find out by inquiring after the people we once knew there. The pastor's answers weren't cheery.

The Brandts—wiped out by diphtheria.

The Herrmanns—cleaned out in the latest bank panic and moved back east.

The Roths—only half wiped out by diphtheria...with suicide, food poisoning and tetanus from a rusty nail taking the rest.

The Fischers—still living above their barbershop on Locust Street! Score one for Peabody!

The Kaisers—diphtheria again.

By this point I was tempted to ask Vogel what he'd done to upset his Boss, for it sure looked like the Lord had a grudge against St. Paul's Lutheran Church and its dwindling membership. I figured the pastor wouldn't see the humor in it, though.

"What about our old place?" Old Red asked. "Who ended up on it?"

Vogel gave my brother a nervous look, as if this was one update he'd prefer to skip.

"The Winters," he said.

My brother snorted out a bitter chuckle. "I'm surprised ol' Klaus had enough money in his mattress for that."

The Winters had been our neighbors, you see, and everyone around knew about Klaus. He was the sort of farmer you hear rumors about all the time: the kind who don't trust banks and keep all their cash in coffee tins buried in the back forty. He was all-around sour to boot, with a reputation for being hard on his family, crusty to his neighbors, and beyond hard and crusty—cruel even—to his animals. He had a particular dislike for me by the time I left town, which I held as a point of pride. I figured if the meanest man in the county *liked* you, you were doing something wrong.

"How are Emmeline and Romy?" I asked.

I quickly added "And Mrs. Winter?" so as not to seem overly occupied with thoughts of ol' Klaus' daughters. Though I was. Emmeline was half the reason I'd let myself get talked into coming back at Peabody—and more than half the reason Klaus Winter hated me.

Vogel shook his head sadly, and for a second I feared I was about to hear that the diphtheria had struck again.

"Romy and Emmeline are all right, I suppose—though you

know their father can be a difficult man," the pastor said. "Mrs. Winter was sent to Osawatomie two years ago."

Old Red and I nodded without comment.

Osawatomie's a little town about a hundred miles east of Peabody. Folks don't go there for picnics.

It's where they built the Kansas State Insane Asylum.

"Is that what brings you here again?" Vogel asked. "An interest in your family's land?"

And getting it back? he didn't add. Because he didn't have to. It was clear enough that was the "interest" he meant.

Old Red didn't feel the need for any games with his answer this time.

"No," he said. "Ain't our family's land anymore. We're just here to…"

His words trailed off, and after a few quiet steps he blew out a breath and shrugged.

"Visit," he said lamely.

"You know how my brother enjoys socializing," I said.

Vogel furrowed his already prodigiously wrinkled brow. If there was one thing he should have remembered well about Old Red it was how quiet and distant he'd been even as a boy. Just in case he'd forgotten, my brother reminded him now—by saying nothing for the rest of our walk.

That left all the gabbing to me. Of course, I'm the man for the job, so I didn't mind filling the pastor in on our post-Peabody adventures when he changed the subject to us. Our recent triumph at the World's Columbian Exposition had made the Kansas papers, albeit in a garbled form that spread the credit too thin amongst too many, and I was more than happy to set the record straight (something I also plan to do in my next book). I finished just in time for our turn onto Pine Street and the last short stretch to Mrs. Gunther's door.

Mr. Gunther had been a carpenter and wheelwright, and the home he'd shared with his wife and a son now long dead from typhus was small but sturdy-looking. Which described Mrs. Gunther, too. She'd always had a certain stump-like solidness to her—low to the ground but, boy, just try to move her. Her hair was more gray, her face more pinched, but she still looked like she could ride out a tornado just by planting her feet and telling it to get off her lawn.

"Look who's back, Wylda," Pastor Vogel said to her when she opened the door. "And in need of a room."

Mrs. Gunther grunted. "Fritzi's boys, hm? Didn't think I'd ever see them again."

"Nor we you, ma'am. So what a pleasant surprise it is to find ourselves at your doorstep," I said.

Mrs. Gunther grunted again and gave us a long, appraising look. Me she didn't seem to take issue with, but Old Red's duds got a frown out of her. (You know how respectable Kansas folk feel about cowboys. Most of the whooping and hollering is a thing of the past now that the cattle trails are fading away, but there are plenty of bullet holes still around to remind people how things used to be.)

"This is a decent Christian house," she said. "No drinking."

"Why, ma'am," I said. "We know Kansas is a dry state—and we wouldn't think of befouling your home with liquor even if it weren't."

Mrs. Gunther thought that rated more than a mere grunt, so she favored me with an outright snort.

"I've heard that before," she said.

Old Red had already taken off the Stetson the woman so clearly disapproved of—presence of a lady, you know—and now he placed it over his heart.

"Mrs. Gunther—on my mother's grave, we won't touch a drop while we're under your roof."

"Well…you didn't have to drag poor old Fritzi into it," Mrs. Gunther said. But she stepped aside and let us in.

Soon afterward, Pastor Vogel said his goodbyes—inviting my brother and me to Sunday service the next day before heading out. We couldn't very well say no with Mrs. Gunther already giving us the evil eye, so it was agreed: In the morning we'd get a chance to see if the pews in St. Paul's Lutheran Church were as uncomfortable as we remembered them.

Soon we were settling into the little spare room at the back of the house, and I asked Old Red if we'd gotten in the door on a technicality.

"You know *Mutter* don't have a grave," I said. "We never found her, and there wasn't any money for a coffin and headstone even if we had."

"I wasn't tryin' to be tricky," my brother grumbled. "I was just gettin' tired of luggin' this bag around. It's not like I'd want to dig up a drink around here anyway." He jerked his head at the door—and Mrs. Gunther somewhere beyond it. "Can you imagine what she'd do if she caught us sneakin' a snort?"

I shivered. Since taking up detecting we've faced rustlers, train robbers, Chinatown "hatchet men," a ghost (sort of) and every variety of murderer the good Lord could dream up and send to Earth for his own inexplicable amusement. And none of them put a chill in me like the thought of my old Sunday school teacher smelling liquor on my breath.

"Well, now that we've lined up a bed and can put down our bags, please tell me we're going somewhere," I said. I looked around at the drab, cramped room—the one Mrs. Gunther's son Stefan had died in twelve or so years before—and shivered again. A picture of the boy in his coffin hung on one wall just in case one somehow worked up the nerve to attempt a good mood. "If we end up hanging around in here much longer I'm gonna need to hunt down some booze no matter what Mrs. Gunther might do to us."

"I saw Dan Pownall still has his livery on Eighth Street," Old Red said. "Let's go see about gettin' mounts for the day."

"And riding out to…?"

My brother shrugged. "Where do you think?"

"The old place…?"

I considered the reception we were likely to get from Klaus Winter and almost shivered yet again.

Then I considered the reception *I* might get from his daughter Emmeline and smiled.

"Yeah," Old Red said, seeing the look on my face, "I thought so."

"I don't know what you're talkin' about."

But the smile didn't leave my face for quite a while—not until my brother said we were being followed. We'd told Mrs. Gunther we'd be out for a bit—"Don't come back with bottles in your pockets," she told us—and headed north up Pine Street. There were more houses in town than there used to be, but they still weren't packed together wall to wall like in Chicago or San Francisco. So when I glanced back to see who was behind us, the man —and, yes, he clearly was following us—had no convenient corner to duck around. All he had for cover, in fact, was a shrub. It was only about half as tall as he was, but he stepped behind it all the same, turning to stare blankly westward as if contemplating the majesty of America's manifest destiny from here to the Pacific. That gave me a good look at his profile, though he was forty or so yards behind us.

"Well, how about that?" I said. "I think it's Randy Thompson."

Randy had been a classmate of Old Red's…in the few months Old Red had been able to go to school. He was never a classmate of mine because, like my brother, he'd already dropped out to work by the time I got to the schoolhouse.

"Looks like," my brother said.

"Didn't you and him get in trouble together a few times?"

"A few."

Randy kept gazing resolutely westward—though I could tell he was side-eyeing us as we carried on up the street. He was wearing a misshapen cone of a hat, and even from a distance I could see his coat was worn and discolored.

"Now there's a man who looks like he has a bottle in his pocket," I said.

"Don't—"

"Hey, Randy!" I called back to him. "If you want an auto-graph, all you gotta do is come up and ask!"

"—stare," Old Red finished. Then he sighed.

Randy turned his back to us, though he didn't leave his bush.

"Now we can't follow *him*," my brother said.

"Follow him? Looks like all Randy could lead us to is wherever they hide the whiskey these days."

"No," Old Red said in that low, slow, growly way of a man speaking through gritted teeth. "He could lead us to whoever slipped him a couple dimes to keep an eye on us."

"Oh."

I let a few steps go by in silence, then looked back again. Randy had stepped out from behind his bush and was carrying on after us.

"Never mind, sir!" I shouted to him. "I thought you were someone else!"

Randy ducked behind a hackberry tree.

"Sherlock Holmes got Doc Watson, and I get you," Old Red said, shaking his head. "Sometimes I do wonder if we can actually make a livin' at this."

"I hate to point it out, brother, but Chicago aside there's close to zero evidence we *can* make a livin' at it. When our money runs out I suggest we try our hand at barbering. Payin' mysteries can be thin on the ground, but every town's got heads to cut."

That shut Old Red up. More so than I'd intended, in fact. His mouth puckered under his mustache and didn't unpucker for a single word until we reached the livery.

I'd touched a nerve again. Of course, it doesn't help that my brother has so many raw nerves every conversation's a game of hopscotch to keep from treading on one. And they seemed more raw than ever since coming back to Peabody popped into his head.

Mr. Pownall, the liveryman, was a townsman and a Baptist, so he wasn't someone our family crossed paths with much back in the day. I knew him best of all the Amlingmeyers, in fact, because I'd had dealings with him while clerking for the local granary. He paid his bills on time and never tried to shortchange me—something that couldn't be said of all the townsmen and Baptists (or the farm folk and Lutherans and Methodists and Presbyterians)—so he was all right in my ledger book. He recognized us on sight when we walked in, chatting with us (mostly me) amiably about our recent experiences in Chicago before getting down to business and renting us mounts and tack. When we were ready to go, he walked us out to the street—noticing before he could say goodbye that we were being watched.

"You need something, Randy?" he said.

Randy—who was staring at us from the other side of Eighth Street—didn't have anything to hide behind this time, so he just stuck his hands in his pockets and sauntered off whistling something by Sousa.

"Now that's how you do it," Old Red said under his breath.

"You think he's improving?" I said, surprised. "He may as well be wearing a sandwich board that says 'I AM FOLLOWING YOU.'"

"I wasn't talkin' about Randy."

I followed his gaze and saw that, indeed, he was looking at someone else: a broad-shouldered man directly across the street who was taking in the chickens, hogs and sausage in a butcher shop window. Unlike Randy he was dressed respectably enough, in a new-ish coat and homburg hat.

"You think he's watchin' us, too?" I said. "I don't see eyes in the back of his head."

"The ones in front'll do the trick just fine...thanks to our reflection in that window."

"Oh ho. Neat trick. Someone's been readin' the *Police Gazette*."

I looked at Randy again. He'd stepped behind a lamppost, still whistling.

"You figure that fella and Randy are...you know?"

"'You know' what?" said Old Red.

"Don't make me say it."

My brother just stared at me.

"In cahoots," I sighed. "You know I'm tryin' to sound less rustic."

"I can't help you with that. As for them fellas watchin' us... ain't enough data to say."

Pownall was still with us in front of the livery, and he was eyeing us now with an expression that suggested we should be sent to the insane asylum to keep Mrs. Winter company.

"Is this normal for you two?" he said.

"Well, I wouldn't call it 'normal," I said, "but it sure does happen to us a lot."

Old Red nodded at the man across the street. "You know that fella who's so interested in sausage?"

"Sure," Pownall said. "Looks like Pete Tobolski."

My brother and I looked at each other. He shrugged, I shrugged. The name wasn't familiar.

"He moved to Peabody maybe three, four years ago," Pownall explained. "Sort of a jack-of-all-trades. Roofer, plasterer, paper hanger." Pownall cleared his throat and scratched the back of his neck. "He's started being Roy Bewley's deputy when he needs one, too."

Old Red and I looked at each other again.

"Ah," he said.

"Ah," said I.

Poor Deputy Tobolski. He could be living it up watching a toilet get installed with the rest of Peabody, but no. His boss Marshal Bewley had him watching us.

"We bumped into Bewley at the train station," Old Red said to Pownall.

"I'd say he bumped into us," I threw in. "And not gently."

My brother carried on as if I hadn't spoken.

"He told us he's been actin' marshal since last month. When's the town gonna make it permanent?"

"In a few weeks," Pownall said. "There'll be a special election on December sixth. Most folks like Roy well enough. He does things pretty much how Dirk van Doorn did. Keeps things quiet. You know how it is—there's always a few people talking loud about 'reform.' But it should be a cakewalk for Roy…unless a surprise contender sweeps in to try and snatch it from him."

The liveryman gave us a questioning look.

"What, us? In politics?" I laughed. "Nah. We're just gettin' goin' as detectives." I jerked a thumb at Old Red. "And can you imagine what would happen if he went around tryin' to kiss babies? The poor little things wouldn't stop cryin' till Christmas."

Pownall chuckled politely. But my brother went on ignoring me. He was more interested in Tobolski and, further up the street, Randy. He gave each a long, openly curious look of the sort they were so studiously *not* giving us. Then he announced that it was time to go.

We said our goodbyes to Pownall, swung up into our saddles, and set off for Ninth Street—and the road east into the country-side—at a trot. We watched to see if Tobolski would stay on us, but either he couldn't find a horse fast enough or he was sticking to the marshal's jurisdiction. He didn't follow us out of town. (There was no question about Randy. He obviously wasn't the type to mount up and give chase. He'd content himself with lurking behind hitching posts and shrubbery till we were back inside city limits.)

Familiar as I am with my brother's ways, I knew to get any question-asking in quick, before he could spur up to a gallop and leave me and my questions behind.

"So—" I said.

Old Red spurred up to a gallop and left me and my questions behind.

I spat out a curse, dug in my heels, and galloped after him.

The road was the same as I remembered. If there was anything different about the fields to either side there'd be little way to tell, them lying fallow now with winter coming on. So the only thing new-ish across that broad, flat expanse was the barbed wire running along the different spreads. There'd been some before. There was lots now.

The land hadn't changed, and maybe the people hadn't. But the lines between them were more clear than ever.

After about twenty-five minutes of riding the road took to bending in the way that told me our old home was near. Soon my brother slowed his mount to a trot and turned left up the lane that had once led to the little house we'd grown up in. I could see it led to a different house now—far larger and nicer and sturdier than the crude one floodwaters had so easily busted to pieces. A horse was tied to the railing that ran along the front porch, and it glanced back at us placidly as we rode up.

I knew better than to expect Klaus Winter to greet us so serenely, especially showing up out of the blue like we were. So I gave the house a halloo and put a smile on my face and tried to look all-around unthreatening. There was a flutter of movement at one of the windows, and a moment later the front door flew open.

A figure burst outside screaming.

"Jesus!" Old Red said, jerking back in the saddle.

The horses, equally startled, cut loose with profanities of their own, albeit in horse.

I managed to keep my wits about me even as the figure charged straight at us, still screaming. After a dozen or so steps the shriek became words.

"Oooootto! Otto Amlingmeyer!"

The figure—and a lovely figure it had become—threw her arms wide.

I slid down off my horse just in time for those arms to wrap around me.

"Emmeline," I managed to wheeze.

She was squeezing me so tight it was a wonder I didn't end up spread across her gingham dress like jam.

"Otto! Otto! Otto! Otto!" Emmeline Winter said, giving a little hop with each "Otto!"

I had no choice but to hop along. She trod on my toes with every landing, but I didn't mind.

I glanced over at my brother, meaning to give him a gloating "See how *some* Amlingmeyers affect the ladies?" look. But he was gazing off toward the house.

I looked that way, too, half expecting my next hop to be back into the saddle—so I could race out of range of Klaus Winter's shotgun. Fortunately, it wasn't Emmeline's father who'd stepped out onto the porch. It was her sister Romy and a young man scowling so fiercely it took me a moment to recognize him though I'd known him more than half my life.

"Romy," I said. "Christian."

"Hello, Otto," Romy said with a smile.

The young man said nothing. Without a smile.

"Christian Neuhaus?" Old Red said.

Neuhaus nodded.

"Gustav," he said.

My brother shook his head in wonderment, obviously stunned that the willowy blonde lad he'd known ten years before—part of the big brood of our neighbors to the west—had grown into this taller, broader (and very unhappy looking) man.

I looked down at Emmeline, who was still stuck to my front tighter than a tick.

"Uhh…I assume your father ain't around?"

"He went over to see Christian's father. Collecting rent," Emmeline said into my chest. "The Neuhauses have been renting our old place from us ever since we moved over here."

"Regular musical chairs."

"Well, some things haven't changed."

Somehow Emmeline managed to squeeze me even harder (and I managed not to snap in two). Then she finally let loose and stepped back.

"I can't believe it." She gazed up at me with a dreamy look in her eyes. "You came back."

"What for?" Christian snarled from the porch.

"'What for?'" I repeated as if only a lunatic would ask such a thing. "Who could stay away from this?"

I swept a hand out toward the farmland around us—but gave Emmeline a smile that said I was speaking of her.

"We read about you two in the newspaper," said Romy in her limp, wan way. She was the younger of the sisters—probably eighteen or nineteen now—and though she could almost match Emmeline for looks she'd never had near the same spark. It was as though Emmeline hogged it all when she was born and hadn't left any for whoever might come along behind her. "It said you caught a murderer at the Exposition in Chicago. Beat King Brady and some other famous detectives to him. Won some kind of crazy contest doing it, too."

"How much of that's true?" Christian asked, his tone implying that he already knew the answer: none of it.

"All of it!" I said. "Why don't we get the ladies in out of this chill and we'll tell you about it. I can see you're anxious to get all the details, Christian."

I would say Christian stared daggers at me, but it seemed even sharper than that. He was staring pitchforks.

"Hold on now," Old Red said. "We ain't here to intrude. I was just hopin' for a look around the place…*if* it was all right with Mr. Winter."

"Well…" Romy said.

"Oh, he wouldn't mind!" said her sister.

All of us knew better, of course, but Emmeline didn't give anyone time to say it.

"You all go in and let Gustav start telling the story," she continued. "I want to show Otto what's in the barn. We've got a brand new J.I. Case combine, Otto. You always were awful interested in combines, weren't you?"

"*Awful* interested," I said.

Of course, in reality I find farming equipment more awful than interesting, but I wasn't going to argue. The barn—and visiting it alone with Emmeline—sounded intriguing indeed.

I hitched my horse to the porch railing beside Christian's swaybacked nag, then turned to offer Emmeline my arm.

She grabbed my hand and began dragging me away from the house.

"Uhh…wait up," Old Red said. "I think I'd like a look at this new combine, too."

Emmeline started dragging me faster.

In all we had perhaps eight seconds alone together in the barn. Emmeline made the most of it, laying a kiss on me that was a far cry from the hesitant pecks we'd exchanged years before. I didn't have time to ask whether she'd been practicing with somebody or had simply been reading the kinds of books it's supposed to be illegal to send through the mail. Old Red barged in before I could get my tongue back inside my mouth and wave away the steam coming from my ears.

"Golly, yes—that is quite a combine," he said.

Emmeline had kicked the door shut behind us, but now Old Red opened it as wide as it would go. Emmeline took a step away from me as the sunlight flooded in.

My brother strolled past us and began walking around the large, boxy, ungainly looking machine. If you've never seen one, these days they're a bit like a slightly shrunken riverboat, complete with what appears to be a paddlewheel on one side and assorted pulleys and pipes affixed willy-nilly around the rest. This one looked like it would need a team at least ten strong just to drag it out the door, and indeed a horse further back in the barn whinnied as if worried we were there to make him do just that.

"Oh, quiet down, Horatio! I'm not here to see you!" Emmeline called out. She looked back at me and explained. "Horatio's my special favorite. I give him a little sugar when I'm in the mood."

She winked, then turned toward my brother.

"There's sponge cake in the house if you're hungry, Gustav. Romy and I made it this morning."

"Thank you. Maybe later," Old Red said as he carried on around the combine.

He was so intent on playing chaperone he forgot to be bashful around a young lady in his usual blushing, stammering way.

"I must say," he continued, "I'm surprised to see something as fancy as this contraption in Klaus Winter's barn. Forgive my sayin' so, Miss, but as I recall, your father had a reputation as quite a skinflint."

Emmeline brayed out a bitter laugh. "Oh, he'll spend money

if it suits him. And only him. You know, he even bought insurance for that dumb thing and the team that pulls it. And look at me! Still stuck in faded gingham like an old ragdoll!"

She ran her hands over her dress, supposedly putting its shoddiness on display but actually, I knew, showing off what lay beneath.

"Faded gingham it may be," I said, "but an old ragdoll you are not."

Emmeline rewarded me with a sultry smile.

"Insurance, you say?" Old Red said. "From Richard Dishane?"

Emmeline nodded, still smiling, oblivious to the bitterness in my brother's voice. "Yeah, Dishane. He's sold insurance to a lot of people around here the last few years. Every time there's a fire it's good news for him. More customers! Me, though—I can't understand why anyone would put out good money because they're worried about what *might* happen when much better things to spend it on are standing right in front of them."

"I see what you mean," I said, giving what was standing right in front of me—*her*—a long, appreciative, head-to-toes-and-back-again look.

Emmeline's smile widened.

"Just like Dishane to profit off other people's fears and misfortunes," my brother grumbled.

Emmeline kept her eyes locked on me as if she didn't even hear him.

"You know, you and Romy oughta figure out where your dad hides his money so you can borrow some for new dresses," I told her, trying to keep things light. "I bet he's got such a pile now it barely fits in his mattress. Or did he decide if he can believe in insurance he can finally believe in banks?"

"After all the runs this year? Ha! He'll *never* trust banks. He'll never trust anybody. But that's all right. Who's to say we haven't figured out his hiding place already…?"

Emmeline waggled her eyebrows at me.

"I'll say it!" I laughed. "'Cuz if you *did* know where the old man's stash was you'd have already used it to get the hell away from him!"

Emmeline laughed along with me.

Old Red didn't. He wasn't even paying attention to me and Emmeline as we flirted away. He was staring off at nothing, seemingly still stewing on Richard Dishane.

"Pretty good deduction there on my part, wouldn't you say?" I said to him.

"Oh. Yeah. Right," he said (though of course he hadn't heard my deduction at all).

"Say," Emmeline said to me, eyes lighting up, "what about *your* money? The newspaper said you won a bundle in Chicago. What are you gonna do with it?"

I told her about the detective agency we're starting with our new partners in Ogden—admittedly making it sound like the whole thing was my idea and I'd be more or less in charge. My brother was gracious, for once, and didn't jump in with embarrassing amendments.

It turned out he didn't need to.

"The paper made it sound like you're the brains behind it all," Emmeline said to Old Red. "Called you 'the Holmes of the Range.'"

He finally remembered to blush and go bashful. "Well...I do most of the deducifyin', it's true."

He retreated to a harness hung to the barn wall and pretended to inspect it.

"You know, I've read some of the stories that doctor wrote about Sherlock Holmes," Emmeline said. "I'd say you've got some pretty big shoes to fill, Gustav."

"I couldn't agree more," my brother muttered, fiddling with the harness straps.

It was obvious he didn't intend to turn around until the subject was changed from himself. Which gave Emmeline an opportunity.

She seized it—and me, grabbing me by the lapels and pulling me in for another smooch.

"Your detective agency need a secretary?" she said when our lips unlocked.

"Oh, absolutely! But we need customers first."

"I'd be a good secretary, Otto. I'm good with spelling, good with numbers, good with…lots of things."

Emmeline batted her eyes.

"I'll keep you in mind," I said. "That I guarantee."

Old Red cleared his throat but didn't turn around.

"Uhh…so…how big a team does your father need for this combine of his?"

Emmeline couldn't answer him. Not with her mouth pressed hard against mine again.

Old Red sighed.

Some chaperone he was. For which I was grateful.

"Emmeline," someone moaned.

To my surprise, it wasn't me.

Emmeline finally released me, and we all turned to find Romy joining us in the barn.

"Twelve horses," she said to Old Red. "I wondered why Emmeline didn't answer you." She glanced at her sister and shook her head. "I shouldn't have."

"All right, Mr. 'Holmes of the Range,'" Emmeline said. "If you're so good with 'deducifying,' tell me: Why is Romy such a wet blanket?"

"Oh…n-now…that's not the kinda thing I usually…I mean, I w-wouldn't want to say that…w-well…" my brother stuttered.

Here we were alone with two pretty young ladies with no mystery to solve, so naturally he had to go all shy and retiring on me. I was tempted to complain about this—pointing out who the real wet blanket was—when Old Red peered past Romy and let that "alone" part truly sink in.

"Where's Christian?" he said.

"Oh, he went home," Romy told him.

"Did he now?"

Old Red cocked an eyebrow at me.

Christian was going back to the Neuhaus place...which also just happened to be where Klaus Winter was.

Now I assure you, fleeing irate fathers is not something I make a habit of. It sure seemed like the time to start, though. We were uninvited, unsupervised and—because what could go wrong in the midst of an innocent sojourn to our childhood home?—unarmed. If we wished to remain unscathed, we'd beat a hasty retreat.

Emmeline knew it, too.

"When will I see you again?" she asked me.

"I don't know. We haven't made up our minds how long to stay. We got folks waitin' for us in Ogden..."

"And you've got someone waiting for you here."

Emmeline grabbed me by the lapels again and pulled me in for one more kiss.

I couldn't see Romy and Old Red, of course, yet I was certain a lot of head-shaking and eye-rolling was going on. The kiss lingered quite a while, though. Emmeline released me about two seconds before I would've passed out.

Our next farewells were more demure—tipped hats as Old Red and I turned our rented mounts toward the road. Then we were off.

"You never told me you and Emmeline was sweethearts," my brother said once we had the Winter sisters far enough behind us.

"I wasn't entirely sure we were. It kindled up not long before I had to leave. I had no idea the flames of passion still burned that hot."

Old Red gave me a look so sour you could throw a cup of sugar in it and make lemonade. "Them flames'll up and burn us both if we ain't careful."

He nodded at a speck in the distance: Christian Neuhaus pushing his old farm nag homeward as fast as it would go.

"Am I rememberin' wrong," my brother said, "or was he always a little shit?"

"You're rememberin' right. Ah, what happy memories we've stirred up."

"Yeah, well...that's enough stirrin' for one day, I reckon."

Old Red gave his horse a "Yeeha!" and galloped off. By the time Christian could tell Mr. Winter the Amlingmeyer brothers were sniffing around his property—and his daughters—we were halfway back to Peabody.

About a quarter mile outside town, Old Red surprised me by slowing his horse and swinging it south, off the main road that fed into Ninth Street. Instead we cut through brush and trees—the autumn leaves a muted but beautiful bouquet of browns and reds and oranges—until we hit the little mill on Doyle Creek. Then we turned west again, riding into Peabody at its southeast corner.

I didn't have to ask what we were doing. Ninth Street was the town's front door. Old Red was choosing to come in the back.

Still, a thinking man wouldn't have to watch the front door or the back to know where he could spot us sooner or later. We'd have to go to Dan Pownall's livery to return our horses. Yet neither of our former shadows were there when we rode up.

"You think Tobolski and Randy are out watchin' Ninth Street for us?" I asked my brother as we swung down from our saddles.

"That'd be a guess," said Old Red.

Sherlock Holmes disapproved of guessing, of course, so he does, too.

I started to lead my horse into the livery, but my brother turned toward a kid lingering in front of the butcher shop across the street. He was a nine-ish lad in knee socks, coat and cap who seemed as prone to hypnosis by lamb chops and hog heads as was Pete Tobolski.

"Hey, kid!" my brother called out. "Kid!"

The boy turned around.

"They get Mr. Dishane's water closet to work?" Old Red asked.

The boy shrugged. "I dunno."

"Well, they even get it hooked up enough to give her a try?"

The boy shrugged again. "I dunno."

"All right. Just wonderin'."

My brother headed toward the livery.

"You really that curious about Dishane's commode?" I asked him.

"Nope. More curious to know if that boy's been hangin' around here the last couple hours or at Dishane's place waitin' to hear a flush along with every other kid in town."

"Ahh. And seein' as he *ain't* been at Dishane's...?"

"Then there's been some subcontractin' goin' on. Only question is who done it."

After we'd squared up with Pownall and stepped back outside, Old Red got his answer.

Pete Tobolski, part-time deputy, was back in his spot in front of the butcher's shop.

"Yeah...I figured it was him," my brother said, steering us west along Eighth Street.

"Oh? And how'd you do that?"

"You saw the state Randy Thompson's in. You think he'd split so much as a nickel with a lookout if he could save it for hooch?"

"I suppose that makes sense. Still...seems to me there's a fine line between deductions and guesses sometimes."

Old Red glowered at me. "The line's about as fine as the Grand Canyon. One's built on fancies, the other on facts."

"I think it's more that they're guesses when I say 'em and deductions when you do."

"Feh," my brother growled.

I smiled, "Feh" being (in my humble opinion) his white flag of surrender when I've won an argument.

I threw a casual glance over my left shoulder, toward the other side of the street. Tobolski was about thirty yards back, heading west with us.

"Dammit, this is silly," I said. "Let's just break a law and get it over with. How do you feel about public indecency? I could stop behind a tree and pretend to pee."

"What the hell are you talkin' about?"

"Don't you figure Tobolski's lookin' for a chance to arrest us for somethin'? It's startin' to make me jumpy waitin' to see what it'll be. You got any cigarette makin's on ya?"

"Why? You don't smoke."

"No, but I can litter. There's gotta be an ordinance against that."

"Oh, shut up."

Just in case I wasn't inclined to cooperate, Old Red gave my mouth something new to do: He stopped us in front of a diner. Evening was upon us, as was the stomach rumbling that comes with it for me, and Mrs. Gunther had helpfully informed us earlier that we could expect nary a crumb from her larder. So I gave my brother no arguments as we headed inside. I just felt bad for Deputy Tobolski if he hadn't had his dinner yet. I was tempted to send him out a plate of crackers, but Old Red wouldn't let me.

We got a few stares from some vaguely familiar faces while we ate, but I didn't spot anyone who rose to the level of an old acquaintance. Whatever speculating folks were doing about us, they politely kept it to a whisper. So most of what we overheard stuck to another subject.

Move over, London. Step aside, Paris. Out of the way, New York. A new metropolis has arrived, and its name is "Peabody."

Dishane's toilet worked.

When we stepped back outside I half expected to see celebratory fireworks lighting up the sky. But no—there were just the usual stars peeping past wispy clouds aglow in the light of the new-risen moon.

Old Red and I pulled our coats tight around us and set off for Mrs. Gunther's…studiously ignoring Pete Tobolski thirty yards behind us. He, in turn, studiously ignored Randy Thompson thirty yards behind *him*. (I didn't look back and stare, but I thought I heard a little stagger to Randy's footsteps. He may have lost us for a while, but he obviously had no problem locating liquor.)

"If someone starts followin' Randy we'll officially have ourselves a parade," I said out of the side of my mouth. "It's not even the invasion of privacy that bothers me so much. It's the inefficiency. I know we're barely actual professionals at this point, but even I'd know better than to…what?"

Old Red was shaking his head at me.

"'You see but you do not observe,'" he said, quoting You Know Who.

"Not true. I *see* a runty little know-it-all, and I *observe* him to be a pain in the ass. Argue with that deduction."

"Oh, stop it. We got bigger fish to fry…startin' with that 'inefficiency' you was moanin' about. Seems to me it ain't inefficiency at all. It's information. You was wonderin' earlier if Tobolski and Randy are in cahoots—"

I winced. "That word sounds even worse when you say it."

My brother acknowledged that with a frown but managed to keep to his point.

"If they are *workin' together*, why would Tobolski need Randy? Randy ain't helpin' with the trailin', staggerin' along back there like he is. And when Tobolski needed someone to keep an eye on the livery, it wasn't Randy he turned to. It was some kid."

"So you're sayin' they ain't workin' together."

"No. I'm sayin' if they *are* workin' together there's only one use I can think of for Randy right now. Somethin' that boy couldn't or wouldn't do."

"Trip and fall on us? Breathe on us? I don't see any other way Randy could help if Tobolski decides to arrest us for some bullshit thing."

"Oh, he could be plenty of help. Not with the arrestin', though. With the justifyin'."

I let that sink in a second. It was starting to get a bit unnerving walking along the deserted nighttime street hearing two sets of footsteps behind us in the dark. When I realized what Old Red meant, the "a bit" before the "unnerving" was gone—replaced by "pretty damned."

"He's a witness," I said. "Ready to swear he saw whatever he's told to."

We were on a quiet stretch of Elm Street by then, Mrs. Gunther's place still two blocks away on Pine. I looked around at the small homes dotting either side of the street. It being November all the windows were closed, and no one was lingering on the porches when they could be inside staying warm by a fire.

"They've just been waitin' till no one's around who'd tell a different story than Randy," I said. "And here we are."

"Maybe."

"Maybe?"

"Or..."

"Or?"

"The opposite."

"What do you mean 'the opposite'?"

"I mean, maybe Randy's not along to be a 'witness' when Deputy Tobolski tries to pull somethin'. Maybe he's along to be a witness *in case* Deputy Tobolski tries to pull somethin'."

"Meanin'...he's protectin' us?"

"Oh, I have no idea. This is all guesswork. Normally I'd keep it to myself, but we got us a decision to make."

"We do?"

"Sure. Whether Randy and Tobolski are in ca—...partnership or not, there's a good chance somethin's supposed to happen out here. So...do we run?"

"Ah. I see. Not very dignified."

"True. But—"

Whatever might have come after that "But," I wasn't around to hear it.

Dignity be damned. I'd already taken off up the street.

My legs being a good stretch longer than my brother's, I managed to keep my lead for nearly a block. But as usual with him, Old Red made up in hustle and grit what he lacks in other regards, and by the time we had Mrs. Gunther's house in sight he'd taken the lead.

I looked back as we closed in on the front door. All I could make out was a blur behind us in the dark. *Someone* was still after us, but either they weren't as speedy as we or they were far more dignified. Or they'd simply dropped back to keep to the shadows.

Whatever the reason, we had a moment to catch our breath when we finally reached Mrs. Gunther's porch. Or so I thought.

I'd barely had two seconds to huff and puff when the door swung open.

"Why are you two tearing through the neighborhood like a couple savages?" Mrs. Gunther blared at us.

"Why, we were just excited to see you again, ma'am," I said.

"*Ohhh*," the lady groaned in that way that indicates the words she *really* wants to use are ones she's not even supposed to know exist.

Still, she stepped aside to let us hurry inside—though she didn't look happy about it.

"Well, it's about time you got back," she said as she closed the door behind us. "We go to bed at a respectable hour here, and we expect guests to do the same."

I wasn't sure if she was using the royal "we" or if she was including her husband and son even though they'd called it a day on life long ago.

I glanced at the lady's grandfather clock and tried not to wince.

Apparently, the "respectable hour" to go to bed in Peabody these days is eight o'clock, for that's what time it was. I wasn't the least bit tired, but I also didn't feel like trying to convince Mrs. Gunther to stay up past her bedtime reminiscing by the hearth. So there was nothing for it but to wish her a good night and retire to Stefan's room.

I could tell Old Red was itching to take a peep out the front window before we went—looking to see if Pete Tobolski or Randy Thompson were still lurking about outside—but it was obvious that would agitate the lady. (I could hear it already: "What are you looking for? Who's out there? Did you do something? I knew you two were trouble!") So he resisted the urge, added his own good night, and followed me to the back bedroom.

It actually wasn't so bad being trapped inside at a respectable hour, for I had work to do: chronicling our recent experiences at the Columbian Exposition for my publisher, Urias Smythe. My manuscript—perhaps a quarter done at the moment—has the working title *World's Greatest Sleuth!* but I'm well aware of what'll happen when Smythe gets a hold of it. It'll show up in print as *Cowpoke Crimebusters Battle the Midway Murderer!!!* or something like that. Oh well. If that sells more copies it means more free publicity for the A.A. Western Detective Agency, right?

Of course, there was no writing desk in dear departed Stefan's cramped little room, so I had to scribble away scrunched up on the bed, my notebook propped on my knees. My brother had turned in in his long johns, his pillow over his head to block out the scratching of pencil on paper, but every now and then he'd heave a sigh to let me know I was keeping him up.

"Just let me get to the end of this chapter," I finally told him.

There was a quick, hard *rap-rap-rap* on the wall directly behind my head.

"Keep it down in there!" Mrs. Gunther yelled.

Old Red turned over and removed the pillow from his head so we could give each other incredulous looks.

The old lady's hearing was even sharper than her tongue.

"Stop sighing so loud," I told my brother in a whisper.

"Shut up," he whispered back. And the pillow went back over his head.

I returned to writing. It turned out to be a long chapter, and I was still trying to hurry it along to the end like a drover pushing cattle when Old Red let go with another sigh.

"All right," I whispered, lowering my pencil. "I'll call it a night…as long as you answer one question before I turn down the light."

My brother muttered something into his pillow that I chose to interpret as "Why certainly—what would you like to know?" (though it sounded more like "Oh for god's sake…").

"Why?" I said.

Old Red sighed again—but he took the pillow away and said, "Why what?"

"You know why what."

"Do I?"

"Yes, you do. Why bring us back to Peabody when we've finally got us a new home to go to?"

"We ain't got a new home yet."

It was my turn to heave a sigh. "You know what I mean. Yeah, we still gotta find a place to live in Ogden, but the town—that's gonna be our home now. We'll be settled. At last. With our own business and partners and friends. Things we can build on. So…"

I waved a hand at the room tight around us (and the picture of dead Stefan I'd turned to face the wall).

"…why are we here?"

"I don't know," Old Red said. It came out like a groan. "I been thinkin' on it, and…well…maybe it's that—"

There was another *thump-thump-thump* on the wall behind my head.

"I CAN STILL HEAR YOU!" Mrs. Gunther roared.

"Ain't the time for talkin'," my brother said, and he ducked back under his pillow.

"Apparently not," I grumbled.

I got up, put my notebook away, and started stripping down to my union suit.

"GO TO SLEEP!" Mrs. Gunther shouted just in case we hadn't got the message.

I thought silence was a wiser reply than "HOW ARE WE SUPPOSED TO SLEEP WITH ALL YOUR HOLLERIN'?" So I just turned down the light and slipped under the covers again.

I didn't think I was tired, but I guess I nodded off pretty fast, for the next thing I was aware of was the old lady's voice again.

"WAKE UP!"

I bolted up straight, let fly with "Make up your mind, dammit," then was instantly overcome with terror at the thought of what would happen if Mrs. Gunther had heard me. Fortunately she was pounding on the door when the words popped out, and her own knocking blotted out what I'd said.

I stumbled to the door and opened it just wide enough to peek out while keeping most of my flannel-wrapped self safely out of sight.

Mrs. Gunther stood before me wearing a frilly housecoat and a chilly frown. She had a lamp in her hand, the flame turned down low.

"Was one of us snorin' too loud?" I asked her.

"Yes, but that's not what the problem is," Mrs. Gunther said.

Now that the door was open I could hear a distant, muffled voice coming from beyond her.

Someone was shouting outside, at the front of the house.

"Christian Neuhaus wants to see you," Mrs. Gunther said.

"What time is it?" Old Red asked from the darkness to my right.

"Midnight."

"Oh my," I said.

Midnight is *not* a respectable hour for company—obviously I knew that even without the old lady's scowl to tell me.

"Just give us a moment," I said.

I shut the door and turned the gas back up, and Old Red and I threw our clothes on as quick as we could.

"Why would Christian Neuhaus come lookin' for us at midnight?" I said as I buttoned up my shirt.

"Why do you think?" Old Red replied.

I knew what he meant. And he was right. When we joined Mrs. Gunther by the picture window in her little parlor—where she'd gone to peep out at the front yard—we could hear Neuhaus' ranting more clearly...and could hear, as well, just how *unclear* most of that ranting was.

"Cuh bon, Amblingamayer...I know you can 'ear me in there! Get ouch 'ere an' fie me, you big sumama bitch!"

Kansas may be a dry state, but Neuhaus had found a way to wet his whistle. With about a gallon of whiskey, it sounded like.

I glanced at the grandfather clock near the window and saw that it was indeed midnight—twelve oh five, to be exact. Neuhaus wasn't hollering *that* loud—I doubt he had the strength for it with so much rotgut in him—but the nearest neighbors couldn't have missed it. I could only hope they were enjoying the show.

"There's someone out there with him," Mrs. Gunther said. "I think it's his brother Karl. He's drunk, too, the way he's swaying."

She spun toward me and Old Red and put her hands on her hips.

"Well?"

"I aina fraida you 'detectiffs'!" Neuhaus shouted outside. "'Homes of a Range.' Ha!"

"Well, what, ma'am?" I said.

"What did you do? Why are they here?"

"We didn't do anything," Old Red said.

"We did bump into Christian when we visited the old farm this afternoon," I added. "He was there paying a call on the Winter girls, and—"

Mrs. Gunther snapped up straight and cut loose with an "Oh ho!" as if all was explained.

She pointed a withered finger at the door. "Get rid of them."

"I'll give you somefin to deteck! A boo rie up yer ass!" Neuhaus yelled. "Ol' man Winter gave Emmamaline holy hell cuzza chu! And now yer gonna get it from me!"

"You tellem, Chrishuh!" his brother threw in. "Nobody asked them two ta come back and…oh…ohhhhh…"

From the sounds outside, it was obvious that whatever Karl Neuhaus had been drinking earlier was now to be found splashed upon Mrs. Gunther's front lawn.

"*Get rid of them*," Mrs. Gunther said again.

"All right. I'll try," I said. I took a reluctant step toward the door. "But—"

My brother shot out a hand and grabbed me by the arm.

"No," he said as I stumbled to a stop.

"*No?*" said Mrs. Gunther.

Old Red shook his head. When he was sure I wasn't going to start moving again, he let go.

"Not us," he said.

"You think the lady should go and get rid of 'em?" I asked.

"They'd be more inclined to listen to her than us. But no. I think she should ask Pete Tobolski to do it."

"Peter Tobolski?" Mrs. Gunther snorted. "How would I do that? In case you haven't noticed, I don't have a telephone, and I'm certainly not going to get dressed and wander around town looking for him or Roy Bewley in the middle of the night."

"You don't got to do any wanderin', ma'am," my brother said.

"Just open the door a crack and call for Pete. He's out there somewhere."

Mrs. Gunther scowled at him skeptically.

"We did notice him in the neighborhood earlier," I assured her. "When we were on our way back here after dinner."

"And you honestly think he'd still be lurking around in the dark all these hours later?" Mrs. Gunther said.

"Yes, ma'am. I do," Old Red said. "What harm could tryin' do?"

Mrs. Gunther snorted again.

My brother just looked back at her placidly. He stayed rooted to the spot, so I did, too.

"Otto Ambalamayer!" Christian Neuhaus wailed. "Come ouch, you cowder!"

(I assume he was calling me a coward.)

"Shameful," Mrs. Gunther spat.

She marched to the door and jerked it open. Frigid night air flooded into the house, and the temperature felt like it dropped ten degrees in a second.

"Peter Tobolski! Peter Tobolski, are you there?"

"Wha'?" said Christian.

"Ohhhh," moaned Karl.

"Peter Tobolski!" Mrs. Gunther shouted again. "If you can hear me, you come out this instant and send these boys home!"

"Where's Otto?" Christian said to her.

Karl kept moaning.

Mrs. Gunther harrumphed.

Old Red stepped up behind her and cupped a hand to his mouth.

"It don't look good for Roy, Pete!" he called out. "This kinda thing happenin' with his deputy just standin' back doin' nothin'! Gonna make folks wonder if he should be town marshal after all!"

Mrs. Gunther put her hands over her ears and swiveled to glare back at my brother. "Are you trying to deafen me?"

"Not at all, ma'am," Old Red said. "I want everyone who can to hear this."

"Hey! You! Gooshtaf!" Christian said. "Send out that big dumb brother of—!"

"All right, all right," someone cut in outside. "That's enough of that, Neuhaus."

I didn't recognize the voice, so I moved to the doorway to peer past my brother and Mrs. Gunther.

It was a dark night—crescent moon and clouds—and only a thin, dim band of light was escaping from the house. So it was hard to make much out in any detail. But I could see two figures in the yard, one standing (though swaying), one on all fours over a dully glistening puddle. The Neuhaus brothers. Another figure was striding toward them, this one sturdy-looking, steady on his feet, wearing (I could tell as he drew closer) an overcoat and homburg hat.

Old Red had been right. It was Pete Tobolski.

"Well!" Mrs. Gunther exclaimed. "Good! You give those boys a stern talking to, Peter!"

"Yes, ma'am. Absolutely," Tobolski said. "Get up, Karl. You two need to go."

"But I uz gonna whup Otto's—!" Christian started to protest.

"*Shut up*," Tobolski snapped. He was close enough now to grab Karl by the arm and start yanking. "This is over."

"Watch out, Pete," Karl groaned as Tobolski hauled him to his feet. "I gotch upchuck all over me."

"Really!" Mrs. Gunther huffed. She shooed me and Old Red away from her and started to close the door.

"Come on, come on," Tobolski was saying impatiently as it shut. "Let's get you back to your horses…"

"Interestin' that—" my brother said.

Mrs. Gunther cut him off.

"I won't stand for it!"

"Nor should you," I agreed.

"It is completely unacceptable!"

"It sure is," I said.

"I never should have let you two tramps in the door!"

"Oh," I said.

"I don't care if you are Fritzi's boys—get your things and go!"

"Now, ma'am, this really wasn't our fault," I said.

"GET…OUT…NOW!"

Well, what do you say to that? Other than (given the wild-eyed look the old lady was giving us as she said it) "All right, we're goin'—don't start throwin' things." Which is what I *did* say.

A couple minutes later, we were out in the cold with our carpetbags in our hands and the door slamming shut behind us.

I looked over at Old Red.

"Welcome home," I said.

My brother said nothing. He was slowly scanning the dark street before us. Lights were on in a few houses up and down the block—neighbors clustered behind windows to take in the entertainment outside—creating lonely little patches of illumination in the gloom.

"If you're looking for someone steppin' out to invite us in for the night, I think you're gonna be lookin' a long time," I said.

"Stop shouting out there!" Mrs. Gunther hollered from the other side of the door.

Poor woman. Her hearing's so good every mouse fart must sound like a cannon going off.

"We'd better go," I whispered…even though I had no idea where we might go *to*.

We started toward the street. Which made sense, of course. It's where a person would naturally go to do their leaving. But after a few steps, my brother angled off sharply, seemingly headed for a big, fat-trunked sycamore at the edge of Mrs. Gunther's property.

"If there's something you need to do I suggest we sneak around back to the outhouse," I said.

"Oh, there's something I need to do," Old Red said. "But it ain't that."

His gaze was locked on the tree.

I gave it a long, careful look. It remained a tree.

After a moment, though, I noticed a little wisp of silvery vapor coming from one side to shimmer for a second in the dim glow of a street lamp beyond at the corner. Either the tree was breathing or someone behind it was.

I knew what that meant. At least this time he wasn't trying to hide behind a daisy or an ice cream cone or something. He was properly out of sight, except for his breath. We rounded the tree, and there he was.

Asleep, his back against the trunk, hands clasped on his chest, shapeless hat upside down on the ground beneath his drooping head.

"Oh my god, Randy," I said. "You're gonna freeze to death doin' that."

Randy Thompson jerked awake kicking his legs and goggling his eyes.

"I'm moving! I'm moving!" he said, snatching up his hat and pushing himself to his feet. "Don't worry! I'm going ho— oh. Hello, boys."

It had taken him a moment to realize he wasn't being rousted off a bench.

"Hello, Randy," Old Red said. "It's been a while."

"Yeah…haven't seen you in all of three or four hours," I added.

"What's going on out there?" someone shouted from a neighboring house.

"Never mind us—we're leavin'!" I called back.

"All of us," Old Red said to Randy. "Together."

He held out a hand toward the street.

Randy just stared back at him.

"Oh, come on, Randy. Walk with us," I said. "At least now you won't have to hide behind any bushes."

Randy sighed, nodded and started toward the street.

"So," my brother said as we joined him, "how are your folks?"

"Well, thanks for asking, Gus. It's nice you remember 'em," Randy said, looking surprised. He'd been expecting a different question. "They got taken together five years ago."

"Diphtheria?" I asked.

Randy shook his head sadly. "Canned ham."

"Ah," I said.

You got to watch out for that canned ham.

We stepped into the street, headed back downtown. I was impressed with the steadiness of Randy's steps. I'd have thought a man passed out behind a tree would need a few minutes to wake up before going for a midnight stroll. He looked used to it, though.

"You still in the old house on Olive Street?" Old Red asked him.

"No. I…lost that a couple years ago. I kinda bounce around town now. It depends on how much money I've got…and who feels like putting up with me."

"Where you stayin' these days?"

"I rent a closet from Stu Fackler."

Old Red and I both looked over at Randy. He kept marching along, eyes straight ahead, no hint of a smirk on his round, unshaven face.

He wasn't joking, and "a closet" wasn't just colorful language.

Randy Thompson lived in someone's closet.

"Where else could a feller find to stay warm this time of night?" my brother asked him.

"You mean 'stay warm'?" Randy said, miming the lifting of a glass to thirsty lips. (It was a motion he could mimic well through much practice.) "Or 'stay warm'?"

He wrapped his arms around himself and tilted his head and made snoring sounds.

"I'm curious about both, actually," Old Red said, to my surprise.

"Staying warm" the liquid way usually isn't of much interest to him.

"Well, for the fun one…" Randy began with a smile.

The smile vanished as quickly as it had appeared.

"I'm sorry, Gus. But I'm not sure I should be talking to you two," Randy said.

"That disreputable, are we?" I said.

Randy looked pained. We were getting to the question he didn't want to be asked. So he changed the subject.

"Say, fellas—what are you doing out here in the cold anyway?"

"You missed it," Old Red said. "Mrs. Gunther kicked us out."

"What? What for?"

"We forgot to say our prayers before turnin' out the light," I said.

Randy gaped at me. He really had slept through the whole thing.

"Christian and Karl Neuhaus showed up wantin' to fight Otto," my brother explained. "I think Christian's jealous 'cuz we went out to our old place today, and Otto and Emmeline…well, they were mighty excited to be reunited." Old Red waggled his bushy eyebrows in a very un-Old Red sort of way. "Pete Tobolski happened along just in time to run off the Neuhauses, but Mrs. Gunther don't appreciate drunken farm boys makin' a scene on her doorstep. So me and Otto got the heave ho."

"*And* we forgot to say our prayers before turnin' out the light," I added. "I'm sure that didn't help."

"Oh. Well. That hardly seems fair," Randy said.

My brother shrugged. "I stopped expectin' 'fair' a long time ago. Which leaves us walkin' the cold, dark streets of Peabody after midnight with nowhere to…"

He wrapped his arms around himself and snored just like Randy had a moment before.

"Any suggestions?" he asked.

"Sure. If Dan Pownall has empty stalls he'll let fellas he likes sleep in the livery for four bits. Just go around the back to the tack room. That's where he sleeps. Knock gently, though. He sleeps with a shotgun."

"Thanks, Randy," Old Red said.

We were coming up on the corner of Pine Street and Sixth, and Randy nodded off to the left.

"I'd better toddle off to my closet," he said. "It's been real nice seeing you boys. You take care of yourselves."

He started to veer away from us.

"Hold on," my brother said. "There's one more thing I'm wonderin'."

Randy turned back with obvious reluctance—so obvious I figured he'd just whip around and hightail it if Old Red asked that question he didn't want to answer.

"Who ended up buyin' your parents' house?" my brother asked instead.

Randy relaxed and smiled. It was a strained smile, though. Relieved but sorrowful.

"Oh. That. Dick Dishane bought it from me. Then he turned around and sold it to some Swedes pretty quick. That's who's in it now."

"I see," Old Red said, nodding. "Well, so long, Randy. Be seein' you."

Randy lifted his lumpy sack of a hat. "Good night, gentlemen."

And now he did whip around and hightail it, making his escape before my brother could ask him anything else.

"He never did tell us where to—" I lifted my arm and took a long drink from an invisible mug. "—'stay warm' the other way."

"The where don't matter."

"Speak for yourself. I like that kind of warmth."

Old Red glowered at me.

"Someone's already tried to get us into trouble once tonight. We ain't strollin' from that straight into the lion's den," he said firmly. "What matters is knowin' the place exists."

"Well, of course the place exists...wherever it is. Even a tight-ass town like Peabody's gonna have a blind pig nearby. When I left it was just south of town, on the Brandts' land."

My brother's irritation turned to surprise. "Emil Brandt let someone sell liquor offa his spread?"

I nodded. "Had a nice, cozy shack tucked away in the cottonwoods. Got so crowded with Lutherans of a Saturday night it's a wonder there were any in the pews come Sunday morning. Yet it didn't make Mr. Brandt's tithing one penny bigger. Or so *Mutter* told me. The deacons *will* talk, you know."

"Damn. The things I missed when I hit the trail…"

"Oh, it was all fun and games right up to the flood."

Old Red winced, then looked away, at Randy as he toddled off up Sixth Street. He'd picked up speed as he went, moving with admirable fleetness for a man who'd been sound asleep ten minutes before. He was in a hurry to get somewhere—and to get some*thing*, I figured. The kind of something that comes out of a bottle.

When he reached the next corner—Elm Street—he zipped right.

"North," Old Red said.

Not south, in other words. Not toward the illegal watering hole I'd heard of as a boy.

"Pastor Vogel did say the Brandts got wiped out by diphtheria," I pointed out. "Maybe whoever took over their land actually believes in prohibition. *Someone* in Kansas must other than Mrs. Gunther."

My brother just gave that a grunt, then started off up Pine Street again. He seemed talked out—unsurprisingly, since under normal circumstances there's not much talking in him—and nothing more was said until we reached Dan Pownall's livery.

Randy had been right: Pownall was around back in his tack room, and when he answered my gentle knock he had a shotgun in his hands. Old Red let me explain the situation—in a simplified, streamlined sort of way—and I guess Pownall liked us enough (or was hard-up enough for customers) that he accepted a buck for two stalls in the barn. He even threw in a couple horse blankets for the night free of charge. Who needs the Waldorf when you've got Pownall's Livery & Feed Stable?

"Brother…" I said as we settled in for the night.

"Don't say it," Old Red growled from his stall.

"How do you know what 'it' is?"

"I don't have to know to know I don't wanna hear it."

"Maybe I was about to wish you sweet dreams."

"No, you weren't."

"Yeah, you're right. What'd be the point?" I took a big sniff. "All we're gonna dream of in here is horseshit."

"Well, let's get to it then."

"But, brother—"

"*Later*," Old Red snapped. Then he added with a sigh, "I'm tired, Otto."

"Fair enough. It's been quite a day."

I snuggled in under my horse blanket and closed my eyes.

"Sweet dreams," I said.

There's no harm in trying, right?

Old Red didn't bother replying this time. Maybe he'd already gone straight to the dreaming, but I doubted it. More likely he was chewing on who wanted us gone and what they'd spring on us next and how long we should stick around to find out. That's certainly what *I* was chewing on…until I remembered the highlight of the day: getting chewed on by Emmeline Winter.

The dreams were indeed sweet after that.

They didn't last forever, of course—what dreams can?—for come morning Pownall opened the doors onto Eighth Street to let in the morning light and signal that he was open for business. It was the Sabbath, but the demand for horses and stalls and feed never rests, so neither do liverymen (except at night snuggled up with a shotgun). Old Red and I got up slowly and brushed the straw out of our hair and pulled fresh clothes from our carpetbags.

"Where's the nearest pot of hot coffee?" I asked Pownall once we were wearing something that didn't smell of horses and what comes from them.

"About fifty steps'll get you to Pappas's Diner. Right on Sycamore."

"Fifty steps?" I groaned, putting both my hands to my stiff, sore back. "I *think* I can make it…"

"And where's the nearest drink?" Old Red asked.

Both Pownall and I turned toward him in surprise.

"You mean…drink-drink?" Pownall said. "Like…not coffee?"

My brother nodded. "The nearest drink-drink."

"Well, that'd be off Ninth Street. 'The Place,' they call it. Little house tucked away behind the old stockyards. I can't speak to the selection—I've never been inside myself—but it seems to keep its customers satisfied."

"Oh, I don't care about the selection," Old Red said. "I don't *want* a drink-drink. I was just curious."

"He's a curious fellow," I told Pownall.

Pownall gave us a long look that indicated we were both curious in his book.

"So," I said to my brother as we began the first of our fifty steps to coffee, "now you know where the locals go for their on-the-sly drinkin' these days. Why'd you bother askin'? I don't see how it matters now."

"'You can see everything. You fail, however, to reason from what you see,'" Old Red replied. Or I could say Sherlock Holmes replied, for of course they were his words.

"No, I can't see everything," I said. "I haven't had my morning coffee. It's a wonder I can see you walkin' next to me, let alone reason anything."

If Pownall hadn't awakened us a few minutes before we'd have been jarred out of our stalls now, for a clanging cacophony suddenly started up that made me jump.

It was the ringing of church bells. The local denominations must've worked out a truce on them until some specified time, for the second one began off to our left another kicked off to our right, with more literally chiming in ahead and behind us seconds after that.

"Good thing we weren't at 'The Place' last night," I said. "I'd hate to be listenin' to this racket with a hangover."

We rounded the corner onto Sycamore—the coffee I needed so desperately now a mere twenty-five steps away—and almost plowed headlong into Marshal Roy Bewley and Deputy Pete Tobolski.

All four of us stopped short and eyed each other warily.

Bewley and Tobolski, I noted, were in their Sunday best— topcoats over suits and ties, homburgs on their heads—with one notable bit of ornamentation: They each had their badges pinned prominently to their lapels. Being practically a professional now I also noticed the way their coat pockets bulged on one side, the weight of something within pulling the wool down to the right on each man's hip.

In other words, they were packing.

Bewley looked down sourly at the carpetbags my brother and I held in our hands.

"Not leaving town are you?" he said.

"You beggin' us to stay?" I said incredulously.

Bewley gave me his best lawman scowl. It wasn't bad, though I thought he needed to work on his eyebrows. They didn't tilt in toward his nose enough.

I had the wisdom to keep this critique to myself.

"I'm *ordering* you to stay," he said. "So you can talk to the sheriff when he arrives from Marion."

"You want us to give him some tips on catchin' crooks?" I said.

(As you know, I don't *always* have the wisdom to keep unhelpful comments to myself.)

"I want you," Bewley replied slowly, "to answer his questions about the barn that was burned down last night…on the Winters' farm."

Old Red and I glanced at each other, a silent "Well, *damn*" passing between us.

"What makes you think we'd have anything to say about it?" my brother asked Bewley, though the answer seemed obvious.

"The Winters' farm," of course, used to be the Amlingmeyers' farm, so the barn that had burned down was the very one we'd toured with Emmeline and Romy Winter the day before. The one that was home to a fancy new combine and a big team of horses to pull it. If anyone suspected we'd come back to Peabody to settle old scores, it might seem like we'd taken a look at the place and decided to start there.

But that wasn't the problem, it turned out. Or not all of it anyway.

It was much worse than that.

"Witnesses saw two men ride out from town, set the fire, and ride out again," Bewley said.

Old Red and I glanced at each other again, and the words that passed between us weren't just silent. They weren't fit for print.

We thought we were taking a little nostalgic detour before beginning our new lives in Ogden. But now the detour was getting a lot bigger—to include the Kansas State Penitentiary.

"What time did this happen?" my brother asked.

"You work all that out with the sheriff," Bewley said. "He'll be here by noon. If you try to get on a train or hire horses, Pete and I will hear of it. And stop you."

The volume of Bewley's words rose and rose as he spoke, so that by the time he was done he was practically shouting. He wasn't afraid we couldn't hear or understand him, though, him being all of two feet from us. It was the townspeople within earshot—folks watching from further up the sidewalk and door-ways across the street and passing buggies—that he was speaking to. Performing for, really. Stump speeches and glad-handing will only get you so far when you're running for town marshal. Much better is an opportunity to show off what a tough cuss you are with lawbreakers...the supposed lawbreakers, unfortunately, being us.

"You should've left the past in the past," he barked. "Don't leave town."

He looked over at Tobolski and jerked his head to the side, and the two men stepped around us—though the deputy made sure to not *quite* clear my shoulder as he went, bumping me back a step.

"Excuse me, Pete," I said. "I should watch where I'm goin'."

Tobolski and Bewley just carried on up the sidewalk and stalked around the corner.

"Feh," Old Red spat.

"I agree completely."

There were still townsfolk gawking at us up and down the street, so I gave them the customary signal that the show was over:

I took a bow. No one applauded, though most of our audience did at least stop staring.

"Oh, don't be a clown," my brother said.

"Why not? Looks like we're center ring in a circus, thanks to you. If we hadn't switched trains the other day we'd practically be in Ogden. Now who knows when we'll get there...and if Colonel Crowe and Diana will still wanna be partners with a couple barn-burners."

"Yeah, well...wasn't no way to see all this comin'."

"How about a way out of it? You see that? 'Cuz I don't... other than makin' like hoboes and sneakin' out of town in a boxcar."

Old Red looked at me sharply, then nodded, eyes going glassy. He brought up his right hand and ran his fingers over his mustache a moment, lost in thought. The bells were still clanging away all around Peabody, and an especially loud *gong* from the south jerked him out of his reverie.

"First," he said decisively, "we get our coffee."

"Good start."

"Then," he went on, "we're goin' to church."

I was hoping he was joking (not that my brother jokes). Just in case he wasn't, I tried to delay things by following our coffee at the diner with eggs and bacon and fried potatoes and toast. And more coffee and more coffee and more coffee. If I was lucky, I could keep Old Red stuck there till we missed the morning service. If I wasn't lucky, I figured I'd need the coffee to keep me awake.

I wasn't lucky.

"Why are we doin' this?" I asked as we neared the white-washed limestone building on Division Street that I remembered so well. "If you want to pray away our troubles you can do that from anywhere. I assure you God doesn't give any special favor to prayers he gets from in there. If He did, my life up to now would've looked a lot different."

"Pastor Vogel invited us to come, remember?" Old Red said. "I'm takin' him up on it. Don't you think it's what *Mutter* would want?"

I shot my brother a glare for dragging our dear old mother into it. I kept my mouth shut, though. What I wanted to say shouldn't be uttered within five miles of anything holy.

I grimly accepted my fate and carried on into St. Paul's Lutheran Church.

Now, lest you misjudge me, let me assure you I am not hostile to religion. It's churches that give me the willies. Specifically sitting inside them stifling in a stiff collar and Sunday suit. And for me St. Paul's added to its air of smothering solemnity with a thick coating of bad memories. Amlingmeyers and Ortmanns (our *Mutter's* people) could once fill two pews with no help, but now it was just me and Gustav left. Even the man who'd comforted us over our first family losses—Pastor Vogel's predecessor, Pastor Kracht—was not only dead, I'd watched him roll up his eyes, foam at the mouth and keel over in the very pulpit we'd soon be sitting before. If that doesn't give a fellow a permanent case of the heebie-jeebies I don't know what will.

As if that weren't enough to send a shiver down my spine, the looks we got inside were of the sort usually reserved for weevils in the cornmeal. There was Mrs. Gunther giving us her well-honed evil eye on the left, Marshal Bewley (beside Mrs. Bewley) doing the same on the right, Richard Dishane (beside Mrs. Richard Dishane) glowering back at us from a pew near the front, and the whole Neuhaus clan looking ready to throw their hymnals at us from a pew near the back (though Christian and Karl were so obviously and thoroughly hungover I'm sure they'd have missed). Even the choir appeared to be readying a rousing chorus of "GET THE HELL OUTTA HERE!!!" accompanied by a blast from the equally hostile organist.

For sheer, sizzling-hot hatefulness, though, none of them could match Klaus Winter. The old man—as unnervingly burly as I remembered him, but stoop-shouldered and wrinkled now—was in a pew on the left, Emmeline and Romy cowering beside him. When he saw me and my brother come in, he started to rise to his feet, fury flashing in his pale blue eyes. Emmeline grabbed his wrist and pulled him back down—not without risk to herself, for

his fury was instantly redirected at her. Despite all my bad memories of St. Paul's, at least I'd never seen anyone slapped inside
before, but for a moment it looked like I finally might. Romy whispered something to the old man that seemed to help him restrain
himself—"Not in here" or "Let the sheriff deal with those two" or
something like that, perhaps—and he turned his back on us.
Emmeline let him go, dared one quick, tortured glance at me,
then turned away, as well.

Some lovers are star-crossed. Some get crossed-up by a barn
burning. I was crushed to find myself one of the latter.

The rest of the congregation took all this in with an air of
silent, seething displeasure, and when Old Red and I slipped into
one of the last pews the family already seated there scooched
away and squeezed together like sardines to put as much space as
possible between us and them. I guess when God sent down His
lightning to smite us they wanted to be as far off as they could
manage.

Our backsides were barely on the wood when the organist
launched into the prelude and we were hopping to our feet again
along with everyone else. Pastor Vogel came up the aisle from
behind us and made his way to the altar and kicked things off as I
remembered: "In the name of the Father, and of the Son, and of
the Holy Ghost." Old Red and I were out of practice, but we
managed to get our "Amen" out at the right time.

"Beloved in the Lord," Pastor Vogel intoned, gaze moving
slowly across the congregation. "Let us draw near with a true
heart and confess our sins unto God our Father, beseeching Him,
in the name of our Lord Jesus Christ, to grant us forgiveness."

His eyes settled on Old Red and me.

There's supposed to be a little silence in the service at this
point—maybe all of five seconds of it—but Pastor Vogel let it
stretch on for what felt like an hour. My brother and I didn't take
the opportunity to do any beseeching for forgiveness, though. Not
that I didn't have a few things I could confess—wistful but impure
thoughts upon seeing Emmeline again, say. But that's not what the
pastor was angling for, so I kept my mouth shut. I noticed Mrs.

Gunther swiveling to look back at us pointedly, and I gave her a smile and held out a hand toward the pulpit, encouraging her to share *her* sins. Perhaps she didn't have any, because she just scowled and turned around.

"Our help is in the name of the Lord," Pastor Vogel sighed, finally moving on. Each time his gaze fell on Old Red and me after that it was with palpable disappointment, as if he'd given us our last shot at salvation and we'd blown raspberries and skipped off arm in arm with Beelzebub.

I don't know what denomination you might claim, but I assume you're familiar enough with church services to picture the various recitations and readings and standings and sittings that followed. As I remembered so well, the pew was hard and the singing bad. The epistle of the day was from Corinthians, and though inscrutable to me as epistles so often were I did detect perhaps a dig at the Holmes of the Range and his Watson of the West. ("For it is written, 'I will destroy the wisdom of the wise, and the discernment of the discerning I shall thwart.' Where is the one who is wise? Where is the scribe?") The sermon took on a softer tone, being a reminder to the faithful to heed Jesus's words in the Gospel of Luke: "Judge not, and you will not be judged; condemn not, and you will not be condemned; forgive, and you will be forgiven."

The faithful weren't buying it. That was obvious from the stares and glares we got every time "sin" and "wicked" and "misdeeds" came up.

Old Red ignored it stoically. I tried to do the same, but I had to wonder again what we were doing there—not just in St. Paul's but in Peabody. Our future as partners in a detective agency awaited us in Utah, yet we'd come to Kansas instead…and perhaps thrown that future on the pyre in the process. If my brother was going out of his way to get in good with God at a critical moment, that would be a first for him. Yet I also didn't think —love our dearly departed mother though he did—that he'd subject us to a long morning of sneering sanctimony just to honor her memory. It was so bad I almost looked forward to getting grilled by the sheriff afterward…and presumably hauled off to the hoosegow right after that.

Then it got even worse.

Having survived the sermon and the offertory we'd at long last reached the General Prayer—which meant *my* prayers were answered and the service was almost over. Pastor Vogel asked God to ensure the health and prosperity of the president and the Congress and the governor and the legislature and "all our judges and magistrates." (Why the Sanitation Department and the dog catcher were excluded I don't know.) He asked also for special blessings on "all who are in trouble, want, sickness, anguish of labor, peril of death or any other adversity." And he invited those in need of special supplications and intercessions to share their woes and receive the support and prayers of their fellow congregants. This was usually the cue for ten seconds of silence or perhaps an announcement on the order of "My great-aunt in Emporia has taken to bed with lumbago and the piles. Please keep us in your thoughts." But that's not what we got this day.

A dozen rows ahead of us, on the opposite side of the aisle, a tall, broad, stoop-shouldered figure arose.

"No, Papa. Don't," Emmeline pleaded, trying to tug him down.

Klaus Winter jerked his big, withered hand away and turned his back to the altar.

"I ask for your prayers…and your righteous rage," he said to the congregation in his stiff, German-accented English. "A great wrong has been done to me by evil-doers with the gall to walk in and sit with us in this holy place this morning. Last night…"

To my surprise tears welled up in the old man's pale eyes. I'd have thought him about as capable of crying as a hickory switch.

"…my horses were run off and my barn burned to the ground along with everything still inside," he went on.

Rather than sink down beneath our pew—what I was tempted to do—Old Red suddenly sat up straight, eyes alight.

"My beautiful new combine—many of you here have seen it —was lost, along with…so much more," Winter continued, voice cracking. "All because of spite. Resentment. A sick, twisted desire for revenge in two un-christian hearts."

He'd been moving his gaze up and down the pews as he spoke. But now he fixed it firmly on me and my brother, and it went so white-hot it was a wonder the tears in his eyes didn't sizzle and turn to steam.

"Let us demand justice!" he said. "And let the spawn of Satan go to Hell where they belong!"

There were gasps and mutters as Winter turned away and plunked himself back down beside a horrified-looking Emmeline.

Up in the pulpit poor Pastor Vogel seemed to be at a complete loss, his mouth as oval-wide as his eyes yet no sound coming out. Obviously he'd never been so thoroughly upstaged in a service, and he didn't know what to do about it.

Which is why he just kept gawping impotently as Old Red stood up and cleared his throat. I couldn't blame the pastor for that, as I was doing it myself.

"I'm gonna ask for a special intercession, as well," Old Red said. "And it starts with folks hearin' me out."

The murmuring throughout the church grew louder, with one voice in particular—Marshal Bewley's—cutting through the rising racket.

"Amlingmeyer..." he said.

"Sit down and shut up," or something like it, was clearly coming next.

Old Red cut him off.

"Everything Mr. Winter just said is true...just not in the way he meant."

The ruckus around us got even louder, and Bewley stood and growled out another "Amlingmeyer..." Fortunately for us he was trapped in the middle of his pew—four people to his left, his wife and four more people to his right—or he might've stormed over and thrown handcuffs on us (assuming he brought some to church). It was fortunate, too, that his deputy, Tobolski, apparently wasn't a Lutheran, and none of the other men in the church appeared anxious to hop up and help out in his absence.

"I don't see why you should object to my takin' part in the service, Marshal," Old Red said mildly. "It's only 'cuz of you that my brother and I are here."

The general hubbub faded. People wanted to hear this.

"Surely you coulda taken me and Otto into custody this morning. Held us for the sheriff to question about the Winters' barn," Old Red said. "Yet you didn't. Instead you just told us the sheriff was comin' and that things look mighty bad for us and we shouldn't leave town. Almost as if you hoped we *would* get spooked and skedaddle. That'd seem to settle who set that fire. Except, of course, you already know we *couldn't* have done it…'cuz of the trap you and Mr. Dishane set for us last night."

"Oh, now this is beyond the pale!" Dishane barked out. "Roy, are you really going to just stand there and let this rascal slander good citizens *in church?*"

Before Bewley could respond beyond a furious scowl directed our way, Old Red pivoted to the left.

"Mrs. Gunther—you can confirm where my brother and I were at midnight," he said. He jerked a thumb at the Neuhaus clan bunched up in their pew to our right. "That's when Christian and Karl showed up drunk as skunks to challenge Otto to a fight, right?" (Old Red ignored the cries of indignation this elicited from Mr. and Mrs. Neuhaus. Christian and Karl just hung their heads lower.) "Funny that they knew where we were stayin'. Someone must've told 'em. And funny, too, that after we refused to set foot outside—and get ourselves arrested for disturbin' the peace, no doubt—Pete Tobolski should show up to steer the Neuhaus boys straight back where they came from. He said that's what he was gonna do, remember, ma'am? 'Let's get you back to your horses.' Well, how did he know where their horses were?"

Mrs. Gunther didn't say anything or nod. But the expression on her face—intrigued rather than outraged—was confirmation enough that what my brother was saying was true. And seeing that was enough to intrigue a lot of other folks, too.

"Now, it's really no mystery where two liquored-up farm boys would've left their horses," Old Red said. "'The Place' I hear it's called. The nearest blind pig." He offered up a small, apologetic smile. "That's slang for an illegal drinkin' establishment, ladies. There was always one somewhere around when I was a kid. The Place is a little different than those old ones, though. It's on Ninth Street. Inside city limits, not outside town. That means there's gotta be…let's say an understandin' between the owner and the law in Peabody."

The murmurings rose up again, and Marshal Bewley turned this way and that trying to find the quickest route out of his pew.

"This has gone far enough," he said.

Yet no one moved to let him out—not even his wife. Everyone was watching Old Red.

"Of course, as is the nature of such arrangements, that they were *in cahoots*—" My brother glanced down at me ever so briefly, as if saying "See? Nothing wrong with using that phrase at the right time." "—doesn't mean they trust each other. Which is why, say, a wannabe lawman up for election might worry that this partner's thinkin' of replacin' him when another possible candidate suddenly shows up in town. And why a businessman with under-the-table interests might worry that said lawman's tryin' to turn reformer on him when he's seen greetin' a couple newly famous investigators at the train station. So they'd have men watchin' these visitors—and watchin' the others' watchers. Surely some of you saw that little parade through Peabody yesterday. Not the one for the Dishanes' water closet, but the one for us. I know for certain Dan Pownall saw it, if anyone insists on a witness."

The mutterings from the congregation hadn't died down, carrying on like a low rumble beneath my brother's words. But one comment in particular—from Mrs. Dishane—caught my ear.

"Richard…why are people looking at *you*?"

Indeed, several of the parishioners—the male ones who hadn't needed anyone to define "blind pig" for them—had been throwing unhappy looks Dishane's way. Regular visitors to "The Place," I assumed, displeased to have their Saturday nights alluded to come Sunday morning.

"You're imagining things," Dishane snapped at his wife.

"Now all this watchin' and plottin' ended up doin' me and my brother a big favor," Old Red pressed on with such confidence you'd have thought he was the one behind the pulpit, not Pastor Vogel. He may be a shy, tight-lipped fellow most of the time, but —as you saw recently in Chicago—he knows how to stand up and command a room when there's deducing to work through. "Steerin' the Neuhaus boys at us at midnight gave us what's called in our line an alibi. Proof we were a certain place at a certain time. It gave the Neuhauses an alibi, too, though it hasn't seemed to occur to anyone that they need one. Marshal Bewley told us this morning that witnesses saw two men ride up to the Winters' barn at midnight, set the fire, and ride out again. Now if you take that at face value, those two riders could be Christian and Karl as easily as me and Otto…if we weren't all at Mrs. Gunther's house at that exact same time. But that's not even the most telling detail about the fire. The one that told me who set it. It didn't come from Marshal Bewley. We all heard it just a moment ago from Klaus Winter himself."

Moving as one, everyone in the church turned to look at old man Winter. He'd been sitting twisted around to scowl back at Old Red, but now he swiveled his hateful gaze left and right at his neighbors.

"What? You think I would burn down my own barn? Destroy my own machinery? After all my work to buy it?"

"I'm not sayin' you would or wouldn't, Mr. Winter," Old Red said—though in a way that clearly put him in the "would" camp. "I did learn you're insured yesterday, which surprised me. Your barn, your combine, your team—all covered by a policy Mr. Dishane there sold you. Which is what told me who done it. Anyone who knows you knows you don't give a…a *hoot* about your animals. Drive 'em till they drop and whip 'em after that—that's the Klaus Winter I remember. So let's say you did see an opportunity—two convenient scapegoats back in town—and you decided to collect on that insurance. Or let's say those two scapegoats ain't scapegoats at all, but 'the spawn of Satan' out for revenge for old wrongs, just like you said. Well, either way…why spare the team?"

Once again, there were mutterings all through St. Paul's. I barely heard them this time, though. Suddenly there was a ringing in my ears as if I'd stuck my head inside the church bell when it was gonging away earlier that morning.

I now knew what was coming next, and I didn't want to hear it.

"According to Marshal Bewley, witnesses saw whoever set the fire drive off the horses before the barn went up," Old Red said. "*Witnesses*. More than one. Well, who was in any position to supposedly see all that? There's only one house within a mile of that barn. Were there a couple someones inside who'd be more soft-hearted about horses? Someones who know Klaus Winter don't believe in banks and is gonna get the insurance payout in cash and stash it right there on the farm until he can get a new combine? Someones who could maybe use that money to escape a hard, cruel man who's made their lives so miserable it drove poor Mrs. Winter to the state insane asylum? Someones, to sum up, with a reason to do it and the chance to do it and a story about two men ridin' in from town to do it that sure does look like a lie. Give that a little thought, folks, and you'll stop pointin' fingers at me and my brother."

Old Red started to sit down, then rose up again.

"Amen," he said.

"Hallelujah," I added.

Not that I was feeling particularly joyous. Yes, there was a sense of relief as the congregation turned as one yet again to stare accusingly at someone other than us. It just broke my heart that the someone—the *someones* Old Red had spoken of so convincingly—should be Emmeline and Romy Winter.

I stared at them, too. Romy was still facing forward, toward the pulpit, but I could see her shoulders shaking. She was crying.

Emmeline was looking back at me, a mischievous but tremulous smile on her pretty face. I don't know what that smile was supposed to mean.

No hard feelings, maybe?

Ain't I naughty?

Oops?

Whatever it might've been saying, it was also, for her and me, *goodbye.*

"You fool!" her father raged at her, and she turned toward him.

That was the last time I saw her face.

"I knew you'd been getting into my money, so last week I moved most of it again!" Mr. Winter went on. "To the barn! Eight thousand dollars you two burned up!"

Romy's shoulders shook harder, and her head drooped.

I thought I heard Emmeline laugh.

It was hard to say, actually, for that low, steady murmuring throughout the church suddenly exploded into a roar.

Mrs. Dishane was yelling at Mr. Dishane. Mrs. Bewley was yelling at Marshal Bewley. Mrs. Gunther was yelling at the Winters. The Neuhauses were all yelling at each other. And the rest of the congregation, swept up in the moment, seemed to be yelling at no one in particular.

It was utter, deafening chaos from one end of the church to the other. You would've thought we were Baptists.

Up in the pulpit, poor old Pastor Vogel was yelling at everyone. "Quiet, please! Quiet!" I think he was saying. It was impossible to tell without any quiet.

Old Red turned to yell at me. (He wasn't mad or anything. It was just the only way to be heard.)

"Think we should leave?"

"What—before the benediction?"

"You think we're gettin' a benediction?"

I looked around St. Paul's Lutheran Church. Not only was the yelling continuing, Mrs. Neuhaus was now beating Christian and Klaus with her Sunday hat. The organist—perhaps thinking music might soothe the savage breast, as they say—launched into "Nearer, My God, to Thee." Only a couple choir members joined in, though. The rest were too busy yelling.

"Hell, no," I said to my brother. "Let's go."

We picked up our bags, scurried out of the chapel, and—

without even needing a single word of consultation between us—rushed straight to the train station.

Goodbye, Peabody, Kansas.

Hello, the rest of our lives.

It actually took us a couple days to get back on track with our journey westward. It was the various connections and delays that gave me time to write this letter, in fact. While I've scribbled away, Old Red passed the time gazing out the window and sucking on peppermints. I haven't asked him if he regrets our detour or found whatever it is he was looking for. But maybe I don't need to ask.

Our little homecoming was a disaster no matter how you slice it, and we've spent the days after our escape either on or waiting for the thing my brother hates most in the world, other than my jokes—trains. Yet he's been in an uncommonly pleasant mood, for him. We don't travel with much baggage—just our beaten valises—but somehow it feels like Old Red has even less now. In the good sense.

Perhaps before facing our future he had to take one last look at our past. And the look we got would certainly convince anyone that the future is the place to be.

We're almost there now. Another couple hours, and we'll be in Ogden.

Obviously, there's no use posting this letter at this point. Soon, I'll have the pleasure of placing it in your hands personally, Miss Crowe.

My brother and I are about to place ourselves in your hands, as well. I can assure you on both our behalves—despite the delay getting there, there's no place we'd rather be.

Sincerely,

O.A. Amlingmeyer

A little north of Salt Lake City

November 14, 1893

MY CHRISTMAS STORY

Urias Smythe
Smythe & Associates Publishing, Ltd.
175 Fifth Avenue
New York, New York

Dear Mr. Smythe:

Season's greetings to you, Mrs. Smythe and all the little Smythelings! I hope my stories have helped you put a few extra presents on the tree for them. All my brother and I could afford to exchange last year were pats on the back and an extra helping of beans for our "feast," so the money you've sent my way for my stories will make Christmas 1893 a merrier one indeed.

Thank you also for sending along the latest *Smythe's Frontier Detective*. (And what a pleasure it is, I must say, to finally have a permanent address it could be sent *to*.) The issue was a real rip-snorter, as usual, and it was a thrill to see me and Old Red—or at least the rather, shall we say, *embellished* versions of us your illustrators favor—gracing the cover once again. You might want to remind said illustrators, however, that my brother is neither nine feet tall nor as strapping as a stevedore. Quite the opposite, in fact.

I appreciate, however, that they have, by way of compensation, made me twelve feet tall and as muscle bound as Samson before he saw the barber. Our cowboy attire remains as colorful as ever, I see, but at least this month the red-and-white Stetsons, vests and boots at least make us look like a pair of Santa's less-heralded helpers. His reindeer wranglers, perhaps?

I read your accompanying note about next year's Christmas annual with the utmost interest. I reckoned I couldn't help you out with a story, though, as Old Red and I tend to have the kind of yuletide that's memorable less for cheer and miracles than deprivation and boredom. We haven't had a family to celebrate with in nearly six years, and in that time our Christmases have been spent (one might say *endured*) pinching our few remaining pennies as fiercely as Ebenezer Scrooge so that we wouldn't starve before the spring round-ups. Fond as they might be of my brother and me, your readers probably wouldn't derive much holiday merriment from "A Grub-Line Drifter Christmas" or "The Miracle of the Abandoned Shack" (the miracle being that we found it before we froze to death).

Fate, however, stepped in yesterday to supply the very holiday tale you sought—which is why this is shaping up to be a twenty-page letter rather than a Currier & Ives card. I don't know if my Christmas story will bring much (in the words of the old song) joy to the world. But...well, you asked for it.

As you know, Old Red and I moved to Ogden, Utah, last month in order to establish a private investigation firm with our new partners, Colonel C. Kermit Crowe and his daughter Diana. It's been slow going. The Double-A Western Detective agency has a name and an office and not much else. There are, as yet, no clients, no cases, no work. Colonel Crowe has been getting the word out to his old contacts with the government, railroads, express companies and cattlemen's associations, but so far this has netted us many best wishes for success and not a single contract.

The resulting hours of idleness have been as much blessing as burden for me, as I've been able to spend many of them in the company of the lovely Miss Crowe. She's provided invaluable assistance as I set up housekeeping for my brother and myself, and I've made the most of her generosity and womanly wisdom. (By "made the most" I mean I've milked it for all it's worth. I recently dragged Miss Crowe to no less than four department stores in search of the perfect bed warmer, and at the end of the day I convinced her that we still hadn't seen a decent one and would have to try again the next morning. After sharing breakfast at a restaurant I wanted to try with her, of course. Sometimes I amaze even myself....)

My brother, meanwhile, descended into such a mood as to make the aforementioned Scrooge look positively jolly. You might think having a warm, snug winter for once would slip a smile beneath his big nose, but no. A permanent frown resided there instead.

The first problem was tedium. "My mind rebels at stagnation!" he'd say, quoting his hero, Sherlock Holmes. "Give me work!"

The second problem was "The Final Problem." Or "The Adventure of the Final Problem," to be more exact. (I'll admit that I'm not always thrilled with the new titles you give my stories. "The Black Dove" I find evocative and mysterious, for instance, while "Range Rider Dicks Smash the Chinatown Terror!" is...let's just say *less so*. But I appreciate that you don't feel the need to stick "The Adventure of" in front of everything, as Dr. Watson's publishers have taken to doing. It seems so obligatory I wouldn't be surprised were it to extend to everything the doctor puts to paper: Should I receive a Christmas card from the man I'd expect the inscription to read "The Adventure of the Season's Greetings!")

Old Red and I knew that "The Adventure of the Final Problem" was coming and the gist of the tale it told, of course, but that didn't lessen the impact on my brother when we got our hands on the December *McClure's* and learned at long last the particulars of Mr. Holmes's passing. When I was done reading out the story, my brother muttered Doc Watson's own words—"the best and wisest man whom I have ever known"—before adding a few of his own.

"So...no more Holmes stories for now."

"For now?"

Old Red pointed at the magazine spread out on my lap. "We've seen the like before. Just 'cuz someone says a feller's dead don't make it so."

"John Watson ain't just any someone," I said. "And Sherlock Holmes, amazing as he might have been, wasn't Jesus Christ. Leave the miracles to the carols, Brother."

This, I'm sure it will not surprise you to learn, earned me a glare hot enough to cook a Christmas goose. Old Red stomped from the boarding house parlor room in which we'd been sitting, threw on his coat, plopped his white Boss of the Plains upon his head, and left me alone by the fire to stew in regret. Here we were at the holidays, missing more keenly than ever our *Mutter* and *Vater* and sisters and brother and all the other dead Amlingmeyers we'd never see again. And when my brother held out hope that a friend, of sorts, might somehow return to us from the void that had swallowed our family, I'd told him to "leave the miracles to the carols."

I felt unworthy of so much as a lump of coal. If Santa filled my stocking with anything after that, it would be the gift that horses bestow so freely upon the streets of every city.

I didn't see Old Red again until the next morning, when he came down for breakfast with the other boarders looking as ireful as when he'd stormed out of the house. Our landlady, Miss Derringer, has already learned not to turn to my brother for meal-time pleasantries—or pleasantries of any kind at any time—and has made more than one caustic comment about his less-than-elegant taste in attire. (He doesn't have to slap brands on strays anymore, but he still dresses like he might be asked to any second.) So she tends to direct her conversational gambits my way instead, as she did this particular morning.

"USUALLY I'D HAVE A TREE IN THE PARLOR BY NOW!" she boomed at me as I took a seat beside Old Red, who'd positioned himself as far from Miss Derringer as possible.

The other boarders gathered around the table—all of them railroad middlemen of one stripe or another—jumped.

Miss Derringer leaned toward me expectantly, coffee cup in one withered hand, ear trumpet in the other. (We've had older and crankier landladies before, but never one so profoundly deaf.)

"OH?" I replied.

"WHY, YES! BUT ANNIE TELLS ME THERE'S NOT A PINE, FIR OR SPRUCE TO BE FOUND IN TOWN!"

"OH?" I said again. I turned to Annie, Miss Derringer's maid, who was bringing a plate of fried potatoes in from the kitchen.

"That's right," Annie said. "Every one within a dozen miles has already been—"

"DON'T MUMBLE, WOMAN!" Miss Derringer said.

Annie stifled a sign and put the plate on the table.

"EVERY ONE WITHIN A DOZEN MILES HAS ALREADY BEEN CHOPPED DOWN AND SOLD OFF!" she shouted. "THE LAST ONES WERE SELLING FOR TEN DOLLARS EACH!"

"SHAMEFUL!" Miss Derringer proclaimed.

Most of us at the table knew to nod in agreement even as we began piling potatoes and ham and scrambled eggs on our plates. But one of the newer additions to the household shrugged and said, "Supply and demand."

"WHAT WAS THAT?" Miss Derringer snapped, slamming down her coffee cup and shooting a glare at the heretic. "SPEAK UP, YOUNG MAN!"

"I SAID IT'S SIMPLY A MATTER OF SUPPLY AND DEMAND!" replied the "young man" (who was portly, balding and well north of forty).

Miss Derringer aimed her ear trumpet at him like it was the muzzle of a musket.

"AND WHAT IS *THAT* SUPPOSED TO MEAN?"

"HE MEANS IT'S JUST BUSINESS, MA'AM!" I translated. I threw in "AS HE SEES IT" to keep myself out of the line of fire.

Miss Derringer scowled at the "young man." If her ear trumpet had been loaded she would have pulled the trigger.

"CHRISTMAS TREES AREN'T 'JUST BUSINESS'!" she said. "THEY ARE A TRADITION—ONE ANY GOOD CHRISTIAN SHOULD BE ABLE TO PARTAKE IN WITHOUT BEING GOUGED BY AVARICIOUS OPPOR-TUNISTS!"

"HEAR, HEAR!" I said as I sawed away at a slice of ham.

"Kiss-ass," Old Red muttered.

"Yes, of course, you're right," said the gent who'd set our land-lady off, his pudgy face blushing bright red.

"E-NUN-CI-ATE!" Miss Derringer barked at him, banging a little fist on the table with each syllable.

"YES! OF COURSE! YOU'RE RIGHT!" the man repeated.

He attempted to remove himself from the conversation by becoming utterly absorbed in his work: the prodigious over-buttering of a biscuit. Another boarder—an old veteran of the breakfast battles that could erupt if one said the wrong thing—stepped in to give his comrade cover as he made his escape.

"BELIEVE ME, MISS DERRINGER, THE UNION PACIFIC RAILROAD AGREES WITH YOU WHOLE-HEARTEDLY!" he said. "ARRANGEMENTS HAVE BEEN MADE FOR A CHRISTMAS SPECIAL THAT WILL BRING DOZENS OF TREES TO OGDEN ANY DAY NOW!"

"WHEN?" Miss Derringer said.

The railroad man cleared his throat.

"ANY! DAY! NOW!" he roared.

My brother winced with every word.

"Like trying to eat in a damn lumber mill," he sighed.

"I HEARD YOU, MR. TURNBULL! THERE'S NO NEED TO BELLOW!" Miss Derringer blared back at the railroader. "I WANT TO KNOW WHEN 'ANY DAY NOW' IS!"

Mr. Turnbull looked like he deeply regretted entering the fray.

"WHEN THE BOXCAR IN FARMINGTON IS FULL!" he replied.

"OH HO! MEANING DECENT PEOPLE HAVE TO

WAIT FOR HEAVEN KNOWS HOW LONG SO THAT THE UNION PACIFIC RAILROAD CAN MAKE MAXIMUM PROFIT WHEN IT FINALLY DEIGNS TO LET THEM HONOR A PRECIOUS CHRISTIAN HOLY DAY!"

Miss Derringer returned her glare to the "young man," who looked like he wanted to finish his meal beneath the table.

"'SUPPLY AND DEMAND'!" she spat. "EXTORTION IS WHAT IT IS!"

"FEAR NOT, MA'AM!" I said. "AFTER TODAY YOU SHALL BE TREE-LESS NO LONGER, AND YOU WILL NOT HAVE THE UNION PACIFIC OR ANY OTHER CAPITALIST TO THANK FOR IT!"

Miss Derringer sat back and widened her eyes. "OH? AND WHO WILL I HAVE TO THANK?"

"MY BROTHER!" I said.

Old Red froze, a forkful of fried potato halfway to his opened mouth.

"HE JUST VOLUNTEERED TO RIDE OUT AND FIND YOU THE MOST BEAUTFUL CHRISTMAS TREE YOU'VE EVER SEEN," I went on. "'YOU SUPPLY THE AXE, I'LL SUPPLY THE PINE,' HE SAID."

My brother put down his fork and swiveled in his seat to scowl at me.

"YOU'LL HAVE TO FORGIVE ME FOR SPEAKING UP ON HIS BEHALF, MA'AM!" I said. "YOU KNOW HIS VOICE DOESN'T CARRY!"

Miss Derringer favored Old Red with a small smile.

"YOU ARE A TRUE GENTLEMAN, MR. AMLINGMEYER!" she said. She looked him up and down, her smile stiffening. "DESPITE APPEARANCES!"

After that, we were able to eat in peace—though I knew I'd be paying a price for it.

"You big-mouthed, fat-headed idjit!" Old Red raged at me in the parlor a little later.

The other boarders had dispersed to their railroad paper-pushing, while Miss Derringer was out taking her morning constitutional (which consisted of being rolled around the block by her manservant Claypool while seated in a wicker wheelchair).

"Now, now, brother...where's your Christmas spirit?" I said.

"I ain't got none! Not if it means freezing my ass off trying to find some grumpy old maid a shrub!"

I shook my head and clucked my tongue. "Such an un-Christian sentiment. What would *Mutter* say?"

At the mention of our mother, Old Red clamped his mouth shut and spun away to face the fireplace. I'd said the wrong thing again—poked at the wound in danger of opening up every year around this time.

"Look at it this way," I went on quickly, trying to bury my mistake under a heap of words. "You yourself have been grousin' about bein' bored. 'My mind rebels at stagnation!' Well, here's something useful to do. Plus it'd give us the chance to try one of the local liveries and get some ridin' in. And we oughta get the lay of the land hereabouts, don't ya think? Ogden's our HQ now. We need to learn what we can about it before the sleuthin' work starts comin' in. Why, it's all clay for bricks, to put it as Mr. Holmes might. Data—and a foundation for the Double-A Western Detective Agency."

My brother snorted and kept his back to me. But after a moment passed with no sound but the crackling of the fire, he spoke.

"So you wasn't just tryin' to push this tree thing onto me? You'd be comin', too?"

"Of course, I would! And I'll let you in on a little secret, brother: It'll be fun."

"Well...I reckon there's no gettin' out of it," Old Red grumbled. But when he turned toward me again, I do believe there was actually a smile hiding behind his bushy red mustache.

An hour later we were riding out of town, my brother on a rented pinto, me on a sturdy chestnut Morgan. Behind me, rolled up in a blanket, was an axe brought to us by Miss Derringer's man Claypool.

It was a day so perfectly Christmasy it could tempt Dickens to rise from the grave and reach for a pen. The air was crisp and cold, but there was no wind to bite through one's coat, and though the snow was heavy for a time it soon slowed to a lazy dusting of fat, fluffy flakes that drifted down on us like powdered sugar sprinkled over a batch of fresh-baked spice cookies.

We ambled south beside the ice-crusted Weber River and the railroad tracks along it, aiming to swing away and leave both behind once we were far enough from the city limits to give us a shot at spotting a suitable *Tannenbaum*. The trees we passed were beautiful, but—being exclusively boxelders, cottonwoods and bigtooth maples—couldn't have been accommodated indoors by a parlor room any smaller than the Mormon Tabernacle. All that remained of whatever young pines or firs that had been in the vicinity was the occasional sad little sawed-off stump jutting up out of the snow.

About two miles south of Ogden, river and railroad curve to the east, and Old Red and I began searching for a spot to ford and begin our tree hunt in earnest in the flat grassland in the opposite direction. Our competitors had already picked clean the city outskirts and mountain foothills behind us, our logic went, so these two young men were heeding Horace Greeley: We would go west.

Now, the Weber is more creek than river around Ogden, but none of us (I'm including the horses) was anxious to get wet on such a day. A little splashing we could handle. A good soaking would turn us into icicles. So as we moseyed over the rocks and frozen mud along the bank we kept our eyes on the water, looking for broad, flat shallows where the crossing would be easy. Despite the blow of reading of Holmes's death the day before, my brother seemed to be enjoying the ride—he hadn't cut loose with a single sigh, grumble or snide aside since we'd mounted—so I did the one thing I could to preserve this rare good mood as long as possible. I kept my mouth shut.

We were about forty yards from a particularly sharp bend of the river when Old Red suddenly sat up straight in his saddle and turned away from the water. Up ahead, I saw when I followed his gaze, was a small figure swaddled in what looked like three coats, five scarves and six knit caps. It was a kid, seven or eight years old, toddling along the embankment that bordered the railroad tracks. When he spotted us, he stopped and waved his mittened hands over his head. (Or as close to over his head as he could get them. He had on so many layers it seemed to take all his might just to lift his arms away from his sides.)

"Hey!" he called to us. "You two got guns?"

"Yeah!" I shouted back, for Old Red and I had left Ogden heeled lest we run across wolves or a cougar or such with nothing to fight with but snowballs. "There some kinda trouble?"

The boy swiped an arm at us stiffly.

"This way! Hurry!"

He turned and tottered off the way he'd come.

"Whadaya think that's all about?" I started to ask Old Red. But he was already giving his mount a "Yah!" and charging up the embankment. I dug in my heels and followed.

When we reached the top, we saw the boy waddling toward two figures on the ground about a hundred yards off. They were stretched out flat in the snow, unmoving, between the tracks and the ridge overlooking the river.

I reined up and scanned the horizon, looking for a who or what that could have laid two people out like that. There was nothing to see but snowy fields and distant, cloud-shrouded mountains.

Old Red had trotted on ahead, but slowly, his left hand taking the reins while his right slid back toward his holstered forty-five. I tugged off my gloves and stuffed them into my sheepskin coat before continuing on after him. If there was going to be gunplay, I didn't want to be caught out in the open barely able to jam a finger through the trigger guard.

The boy looked at us, waved for us to keep coming, then turned back toward the figures in the snow.

"Ammon! Sariah! Look!" he shouted. "I found somebody!"

He got an answer in two-part harmony.

"Shut up, Gideon!"

The voices were high-pitched, but one more so than the other.

Those weren't corpses by the tracks. It was a very alive boy and girl around the same age as our new acquaintance "Gideon." They wriggled forward through the snow to peep warily over the edge of the embankment. Whatever had the kids spooked, it seemed, was down by the river.

The two on their bellies pushed themselves up and walked over to join their friend. As they brushed the snow from themselves, I could see that their clothes were drab and worn, with mismatched patches here and there. I know poor farm kids when I see them, for I'd spent my first decade-plus as one myself.

"…hibernate in caves, not on river banks, you blockhead," the boy—a gawky lad of perhaps twelve—was saying to Gideon as Old Red and I rode up.

The girl was a couple years younger but just as gangly, and looking at them together and hearing how the eldest spoke to the youngest I instantly knew these three were siblings. (I was the baby of the brood myself, you might recall, and though I was doted upon by my sisters, my brother Conrad was even harder on me than Old Red. "Blockhead" would qualify as a treacly term of endearment compared to the things he used to call me.)

"What's the trouble, kids?" I said.

The older boy—Ammon, I was guessing—jerked a thumb at the ridgeline behind him. For the first time I noticed something flat and rectangular lightly covered with snow there: a sled. A hatchet was sitting atop it.

"We were out looking for a Christmas tree," the boy said, "and we spotted a bear and—"

"*I* spotted it," the girl—Sariah—interjected.

Her brother ignored her.

"—we think it might be dead but if it's alive we thought we could shoot it and sell the meat in town—"

"*I* thought we could shoot it and sell the meat in town," Sariah said.

Ammon kept plowing on.

"—but we don't have a gun so we sent our little brother to find someone who did—"

"*I* sent our little brother…," Sariah began.

Ammon raised his voice so much he was loud enough for even Miss Derringer to hear.

"—AND WE'LL SPLIT THE MONEY WITH YOU IF YOU HELP US."

Old Red and I both looked nervously at the ridge. If there was a live bear beyond it, it sure was a sound sleeper.

I swung down out of my saddle.

"Gideon," I said, "would you be so good as to hold our reins for us?"

Your average youngster, in my experience, is thrilled to be asked for such small favors by men who, like Old Red and myself, look like cowboys. (As you know, I've taken to dressing like a gentleman in town, but any time I'm atop a horse again a three-piece suit and bowler just seems silly.) Gideon was no different than most boys. He waddled forward to take my reins with a grin and an excited "Yes, sir!"

My brother dismounted, handed over his reins, then pulled out and cocked his Colt. The cylinder turned smoothly, moving a live round under the hammer. I unholstered my forty-five and did as Old Red had. The previous winter we'd nearly been killed by wolves of two varieties (canine and human) because our guns had frozen solid. We weren't going to give a bear the same opportunity now.

"That's all you got?" Sariah asked, giving our Peacemakers a dubious look. "No rifles?"

"Missy," my brother said, "I came out here lookin' for a tree, not trouble."

He stomped off toward the ridge.

"Don't worry. Bullets are bullets," I told the girl. "These'll do."

But I knew she had a point. If a grizzly charges you, you want a buffalo gun to stop him with, not a peashooter.

"Y'all wait here," I told the kids.

I resisted the urge to add, "Or better yet, why don't you wait about half a mile thataway?" Why spook them? And anyway, they had our horses. If Old Red and I ended up an early Christmas dinner for a bear, at least they could ride off before they were made dessert.

I turned and followed my brother. Like him, I got to crouching and creeping when I reached the other side of the railroad tracks. We ended up sprawled in the snow beside the sled just as Ammon and Sariah had been a couple minutes before.

We snaked up to the ridge and peeked over the side. The hillside beyond was steep and pocked with boulders and snow-covered brush.

"There," Old Red whispered, pointing off to the right.

About twenty-five yards from us, halfway down the hill, a big ball of black fur was wedged between two pole-like, white-barked trees. It looked like an animal all right, but the way it was hunched over, half-hidden under fresh snow, made it hard to tell what kind.

"YA SEE IT?" Gideon called to us.

Old Red and I winced.

The big ball of fur didn't.

"Yes," I said. "We see it."

Yet still the furball remained motionless.

Old Red pushed himself up to his hands and knees and took a long look at the hillside.

"There," he whispered. "Snowfall's almost covered it up, but not quite."

He pointed at a wide line cutting through the snow. It moved at a diagonal down the slope, starting about twenty yards to our left and ending to our right with the black whatever-it-was.

"A trail," I said. "Which means that ain't just an old bearskin coat down there."

"Well, it could be. It's just that the bear might still be in it."

I sighed. "Any chance we could just wish him happy holidays and get back to lookin' for the right tree?"

"We could move along, sure." Old Red jerked his head back at Ammon, Sariah and Gideon. "But I don't think they would."

I sighed again. "No, I don't guess they would."

I looked over at my brother. He was peering down at the dark shape in the snow with a fixed, narrow-eyed intensity that told me it wasn't just the kids who wouldn't leave well enough alone. His curiosity had him hooked. Which put me on the hook, too.

"Alright, then," I said. "Get ready."

I slid my Colt into its holster and began gathering up a handful of snow.

"Now ain't the time for a snowball fight," Old Red said.

"I beg to differ," I replied. "Now is precisely the time for a snowball fight."

I started packing the snow tight, then gathered up more.

My brother nodded brusquely, grasping my plan, then drew a bead on the furball.

When I had the snow I was holding so round and firm it could've passed for a baseball, I got up on my knees and whipped it at the thing down the hill. It splatted against its dark fur.

"Bull's-eye," I said. "Ain't lost my touch."

The mound of hair did not get up to throw a snowball back. It didn't react at all.

"Dead?" I said.

"Sure looks it," said Old Red.

He got to his feet and headed down the incline. I drew my forty-five again and went with him. Ammon and Sariah crossed the tracks to watch us as we picked our way slowly, carefully down the slope.

"Remember," the girl said. "Whatever it is, we found it."

"Thank you for your concern, young lady," I threw over my shoulder. "If it hops up and tries to eat us we'll be sure to send half of it your way."

"What's happening?" Gideon called out. "I can't see a thing!"

"Nothin' new to see yet!" I called back.

But that wasn't true for long. As Old Red and I drew closer, we got a better view of the shape beneath the snow. It stretched out a few feet to either side of the hairy hump visible from the ridge. All in all, the thing looked to be nearly six feet long.

A chill went through me that had nothing to do with the frigid air or the snow we were wading through.

"Well, merry goddamn Christmas," I said under my breath, for I now assumed I knew what we were approaching.

I stopped and holstered my Colt, letting Old Red have the honor of unveiling the now-obvious. He walked the last few feet without me, knelt beside the body, and pulled it away from the trees it was jammed against.

"What the hell!" I cried, instinctively snatching my gun back out again.

I'd been expecting the blue-tinged skin and ice-crusted clothes of a frozen corpse. What I saw instead was more shaggy hair and a black, grotesquely grimacing face topped by two long, curling horns.

There was a shrill shriek behind us, and I glanced back thinking I'd see Sariah staring down at the thing's ghoulish features in wide-eyed horror.

I was close. It was Ammon who had his mittens pressed to the sides of his face and his mouth hanging open.

Sariah took a couple steps down the hill and leaned to the side to get a better look.

"Dang," she said. "That is *ugly*."

"What is it? What is it?" Gideon yelled in the distance. "Come on, guys! Tell me!"

"It's...it's...a monster!" his brother stammered.

My initial shock had worn off by now, and I shook my head and re-holstered my gun.

"No. It ain't no monster," I said. "Not exactly."

Sariah took another step down the hill. "What do you mean 'not exactly'?"

"It's a Krampus," Old Red said. He swiveled to give me an astonished look of the "Will wonders never cease?" variety. "A dead Krampus out in the middle of nowhere."

Sariah continued down the hill.

"What's a 'Krampus'?" said Ammon, cautiously following his sister.

"He's sorta like Santa's helper," I explained. "Only he ain't nice. Instead of bringin' good children presents, he whips the bad ones or even drags 'em down to h——...uhh, the opposite of heaven."

Sariah glared at me. "Don't treat us like we're stupid. We know there's no such thing as Santa."

"What did you just say?" Gideon called from up above.

"Nothing!" Sariah shouted.

She stopped a few yards off and went back to glowering at me. Ammon stepped up beside her, but his gaze was glued to the body.

"It's a legend. A tradition," I said. "Around Austria and Bavaria and them parts, the night before the feast of St. Nicholas is *Krampusnacht*. Men dress up like the Krampus and go around town scarin' folks. It wasn't anything we ever did—our people was strictly German Lutheran—but we used to have neighbors who had them a Krampus get-up. They told us all about it."

"The Kaufmans," Old Red said wistfully.

I nodded. "The Kaufmans"

They'd died in the same flood that had swept away the last of our family.

"So that's a costume," Ammon said, his voice suddenly firmer, his back straighter.

"Yup," said Old Red. "And I reckon it's time to see who's in it."

He reached out for the scowling black mask.

"Don't look," I told Ammon and Sariah.

Rather than turning away, they came a step closer.

My brother pushed the mask back. Beneath it was the pale, gaunt face of a young man around my own age. He had a light, peach fuzz beard and short-cropped blonde hair and piercing blue eyes that gazed up at us vacantly.

My brother glanced over his shoulder to see if the kids were still staring at the man. They were.

"Recognize him?" he said.

They shook their heads.

"You know most of the folks hereabouts?" my brother asked.

The kids nodded.

"So you'd say this here's a stranger," Old Red said. "Not from these parts."

The kids kept nodding.

"What's going on?" Gideon hollered from over the ridge.

"Nothing!" Ammon and Sariah shouted together.

My brother turned back to the body. He put a hand to the man's cheek for a moment, then took hold of his Krampus get-up —sort of a fur-covered union suit, with the mask attached at the top—and gave it a tug.

"What are you doing?" Sariah asked.

"Tryin' to figure how long he's been down here," Old Red said without looking back. "Body's still warm-ish, costume ain't that stiff. And then there's that trail in the snow that ain't completely covered over yet. The poor fella ain't been here that long. Y'all see anyone else out thisaway?"

Ammon and Sariah went back to shaking their heads.

"How about wagon or horse tracks?"

The kids shook their heads again.

"There's only one way to figure it, then," my brother said. He began brushing snow from the front of the man's outfit. "Only this here costume don't make a lick of…hel-lo!"

He pinched something between thumb and forefinger and held it up. It was so small I had to step closer and squint to see what it was: a stubby little sliver of green.

"Is that a pine needle?" I said.

"Yup," said Old Red. "And what *ain't* we got around here?"

I looked at the trees the body was jammed up against. Aspens. Scattered around them on the hillside were more aspens as well as some cottonwoods and boxelders. If there'd ever been any evergreens around there, they'd already been cut down and hauled off.

My brother went back to dusting snow off the man's chest.

"There's more needles here," he said. He began working on the man's left shoulder and side. "And a *lot* more here."

Old Red pulled the body forward and began slapping at the back. He didn't have to tell me there were even more pine needles there. I could see them mixed in with the snow.

When my brother had cleared off about half the man's back, he came to a sudden stop.

"Well, there it is," he said sadly.

He went back to brushing away snow, but he worked at it more slowly and gently now.

Some of what came away from the body looked icy and red.

"Is that blood?" Sariah asked.

"Yup," said Old Red. "Our friend here was shot in the back."

"You mean he was…he was…m-murdered?" Ammon said.

He swung his gaze to the right, to the left, to the bank across the river, clearly leaping to the logical conclusion.

Where there's a murder, there's a murderer.

I scanned all around us, too, though I tried to look calm and casual about it.

"Just because the man was shot don't mean he was murdered," I said. "Could've been an accident."

"An accident?" Sariah scoffed.

I pointed at the body. "Look at what he's wearin'. We thought he was a bear. Maybe someone else did, too. Someone with a rifle."

"I guess that's possible," the girl said. "But why was he out here in that crazy outfit in the first place?"

I shrugged. "Looks warm. Maybe he didn't have a union suit handy."

My brother whipped around to gape at me.

"You might be onto somethin' there," he said.

"Uhh…I was jokin', brother."

"Oh." Old Red shook his head in disgust. "Shoulda known."

He turned back to the dead man and began fiddling with the front of his costume. Beneath the black fur were buttons that Old Red began undoing. Once he had four or five unfastened, he was able to pull the fur aside wide enough to reveal what the man was wearing underneath: a brown sack coat over a frayed and stained hickory shirt.

"A workin' man, judgin' by the spots on his clothes," my brother said. "Looks like some kinda oil or grease. Whatever the job, it didn't pay much. His coat ain't no thicker than a maple leaf."

He undid the top two buttons on the man's shirt.

"And no," he said. "He ain't got no union suit on."

"Hey, there's a lady present," Ammon protested in a whispery, warbly voice. "Well…my sister, anyway."

"Oh, hush," Sariah snapped at him. "He's just trying to figure out who the man is and how he got here."

Old Red glanced back at the girl and tugged the brim of his Stetson.

"Thank you, Miss," he said.

"Well, it seems disrespectful to me," Ammon grumbled.

"What is going on down there?" Gideon called out from the top of the ridge.

"Nothing!" Sariah and Ammon shouted back again.

My brother had already gone back to work, unbuttoning the Krampus outfit enough to reach in and search the man's pockets. He pulled out four things and lined them up on the snow: a tin soldier, a harmonica, and an ornate four-pronged hairpin, all of them shiny new, along with a wadded-up length of rough twine. A fifth and final discovery he turned and tossed to me.

It was a book. Even if Old Red could read, he would've had a tough time with this one. It was *Im fernen Westen* von Karl May. *In the Far West* by Karl May. In German. I opened it up and found an inscription in German, too.

"'Fur Mutter, mit Liebe—Ernst,'" I read out. I offered up a translation for the kids. "'For mother, with love.'"

"So he stole that book from some lady?" Ammon asked.

Old Red shot the boy an infuriated glare. Hearing the inscription seemed to light a fire inside him, and he pushed himself to his feet and started stomping off up the hill.

"No. And he didn't steal any of that other stuff, neither," he said.

Sariah nodded at the body.

"He's Ernst, isn't he?" she said.

Old Red stopped and turned toward her, his expression softening a bit.

"Yes, he is," he said. "And now we know why he was in that outfit, where he was going and what he was doing when he was killed."

Ammon blinked at him.

"We do?" he said.

"Yeah," said Sariah. "We do?"

My brother nodded. "Just look at what he was wearing under that suit, what he had in his pockets, what he *didn't* have in his pockets and the slant and size of his trail from the top of the ridge by the tracks down to here. It tells the whole story."

"Including who shot him?" I asked.

Old Red's scowl returned, fiercer than ever. "Yes. That, too." He turned to Ammon and Sariah again. "Y'all look after Ernst and his things. We'll send someone along for 'em when we can."

He went back to galumphing up the hill. I quickly slipped the book back into the dead man's costume, then turned and hurried after my brother.

"Where are you two going?" Sariah said.

"To get our hands on the fella who left Ernst there," Old Red replied without stopping. "If we ain't missed our chance already."

When we reached the top of the slope, we found little Gideon still holding our horses on the other side of the railroad tracks.

"It's a man, isn't it?" he said.

"Yup," Old Red said.

He took the reins of his horse and swung up into his saddle. I thanked Gideon, then did the same.

"What happened to him?" the boy asked.

"Christmas," my brother said, and he gave his mount a "Heeyah!" and galloped off.

"Umm…there was a bit of what we professionals call 'foul play,'" I told Gideon. "But don't worry: The man responsible is miles away, and we're gonna go see that he pays for it."

I rode off after Old Red hoping I wasn't a liar.

We headed north, backtracking along the same white-frosted

fields and distant mountain peaks we'd passed when all we had on our minds was a little tree for our landlady. I'd have had to bellow like old Miss Derringer herself to be heard above the crunch of hoof-crushed snow and the panting of the horses, so I didn't ask my brother where we were going. I figured I'd soaked in enough Holmesifying to know anyhow.

I was right, too. We never strayed from the tracks, following them all the way into town to Union Station, hub of rail travel for half the West. There the tracks split and curved and merged again into a great steel jumble beside the big, brick station building. Usually just the sight of all that rail would be enough to give my locomotive-hating brother the collywobbles. But Old Red was so grimly intent upon the task at hand he didn't blanch, flinch, or tarry. There was a Union Pacific train parked behind the depot— five passenger cars and one freight car—and he pointed at it and simply said, "There."

We left our mounts at the hitching posts out front and hurried in, bound for the platform out back. I swung my head this way and that as we rushed through the cavernous station building, searching for a high-peaked blue bowler and matching coat and trousers—the uniform of the Ogden City Police Department. I could have darted up to any ticket window and asked for the railroad police, of course, but I didn't bother. We needed a lawman, not some bull with a tin badge.

I saw passengers, porters, and clerks, but no law. We'd have to proceed without it.

We burst back out into the snowy cold and found the train right before us. The passenger cars were mostly empty, with but a smattering of stragglers still making their way from the platform. That made it easy to spot the little group gathered by the boxcar attached to the back of the train.

Four men stood there: the conductor, two gentlemen in dark suits and overcoats, and a little way off, a younger fellow in a flat cap and scarf fiddling with a camera on a tripod. The door on the freight car was open just wide enough to reveal a burly, bearded man peeking out of the shadows. The photographer seemed to be pointing the camera at him.

The conductor turned to eye us as we hurried up, but the other men didn't notice.

"So we'll have the door open all the way, with Mr. Turner in the center," said the photographer, lifting up a flash pan in his left hand. "Mr. Holm, Mr. Eichelberger, you'll be looking up at him."

"I think I should be shaking Mr. Holm's hand," said the slimmer of the suited gents—Eichelberger, presumably. "Like so."

He turned to the other businessman-type, took his right hand in his own, and smiled stiffly.

"Sure. The ol' grip and grin," the photographer said. "It's a classic."

The conductor, meanwhile, had peeled away to intercept me and my brother.

"Can I help you?" he said quietly.

"You on this when it came to town?" Old Red said, jerking his thumb at the train.

"I was," the conductor replied, voice still low. He glanced back nervously to see if the other men were watching. They weren't.

"A railroad detective aboard with you?" my brother asked.

That finally got the other fellows' attention. They all looked our way. Even the big, bearded man in the boxcar leaned out to peer at us, and I noticed for the first time that he was wearing a scarlet cloak and stocking cap.

"Yes," said the conductor, still speaking whisper-soft. He nodded back toward the fellow in red. "Mr. Turner. Is there a problem?"

"I'm afraid so," said Old Red, making no effort to quiet himself at all. "Some kids and us, we found a man's body a couple miles outside town. He'd been shot in the back...and I believe the deed was done on this train."

The conductor jerked up so straight it was a wonder his little flat-topped hat didn't fly off like a blackbird taking wing.

"What?" he blurted out.

The men in suits, however, weren't having any of it.

"They're drunk," said Holm, the tubbier of the two, sneering at our rough cowboy clothes.

Eichelberger turned to the photographer.

"Sorry about this, Bellinger," he said. "Just carry on."

The young man behind the camera nodded but immediately went back to watching me and my brother with a little smirk on his face.

"Don't be ridiculous," the conductor was telling us. "I think I'd know if a passenger on my train had been shot."

"If they was in a passenger car, sure," Old Red said. "But this one wasn't."

"It's just a prank," Holm assured the other gentleman. "The rougher elements of the West find it amusing to guy respectable people."

The conductor took a small step to the side, placing himself even more directly between us and the train.

"If you really found a body outside city limits, that's a county matter," he said, lowering his voice again. "Go tell your story at the sheriff's office."

Old Red shook his head. "Any evidence'll be gone by then. Now if you'd just let me take a look in that there car...."

He started to step around the conductor.

"This has gone on long enough!" Holm barked at the man standing in the freight car. "Remove them!"

The railroad dick looked stricken, yet he nodded and hopped down onto the platform. The photographer and conductor had called him "Mr. Turner," but any passing child would've had a different name for him: Santa Claus. The man was done up like St. Nick all the way from his black buckled boots to the tip of his red stocking cap. He was a bit too young for his beard to have gone snowy white, but he already had the belly that would shake like jelly when he laughed. Only he wasn't laughing.

"Alright, Tex," he snarled as he lumbered toward us. "Move along."

And move Old Red did. Not skedaddling, but stepping to his

left to better see through the freight car doorway the man was no longer blocking.

"Hel-lo!" he said. "And there we are!"

I stepped to the left, too. Inside the boxcar, I now saw, were bound green-and-brown shapes stacked nearly to the ceiling.

Pine trees. Dozens of them.

The "Christmas Special" we'd heard about at breakfast had arrived.

"There were pine needles on that man we found—and not a pine *tree* for miles," Old Red said. "The body had been dumped down an embankment by the railroad tracks, but it didn't roll straight downhill. Its trail through the snow shows it came down at a slant. 'Cuz it had whatchamacallit."

"Momentum?" I said.

"Momentum," my brother repeated firmly without looking over at me. He had the full attention of the businessmen and the photographer now, and he kept his eyes on them so as not to lose it. "It was already moving, fast, when it hit the top of the hill. And that snow trail makes the direction plain. South to north. Toward Ogden."

The big, seething Santa had stopped, stunned, when Old Red started in about the pine needles. But now he recovered his wits and began stalking toward us again.

"That's enough," he snapped. "Joke's over."

My brother began walking backward without looking away from his audience.

"He had toys and a book inscribed for his mother on him," he said quickly. "But no ticket. He was going home for Christmas the hard way. Freight-hopping."

I was walking backward now, as well, for if I hadn't, Turner would've already overtaken me. I was hoping the men in suits would call him off, but instead Eichelberger just turned to his stout friend and said, "Uhh...shall we try a shot *without* Santa Claus?"

"If there's proof, brother," Old Red said, "it'll be in that boxcar."

"Right," I sighed, knowing what he was *really* saying.

I stopped backing away.

Santa Claus kept coming. Another four steps, in fact, and he'd be treading on my toes.

"Did you get my letter?" I asked him.

He'd been aiming his glower at my brother, but now he shifted it my way with a "Huh?"

I stepped forward and delivered a right to Santa's gut, followed by a left to his bearded chin. The first blow started to double him up, and the second jerked him straight again.

"Sorry," I said as he went stutter-stepping backward, stunned. "Ain't no way you're bringin' me a pony after this, is there?"

My brother had already darted off, headed for Holm and Eichelberger. They both shrank back and put their hands up and spluttered out things along the lines of "Now, wait just a minute!"

Old Red shot between them, leaped up into the boxcar, and disappeared.

Turner/Claus blinked his eyes twice and cleared his head with a shake.

"You naughty, naughty boy," he said to me.

(Actually, he gave me a label quite unfit for a Christmas story or indeed, any publication remaining on the right side of our nation's obscenity laws.)

He brought up his right hand and pressed it against his left breast as if reaching for something there. His fingers just clutched at the fabric of his suit, and he looked down in surprise.

In the heat of the moment, he'd forgotten he was dressed as Santa.

"Shoot," he spat.

(That's not quite what he really said either.)

He bunched up his fists and started toward me—then seemed to notice for the first time that I was now alone. He whipped around, saw the businessmen and the conductor and the cameraman looking back and forth between us and the boxcar door, and realized where Old Red had gone.

"Get him outta there!" he roared.

Before anyone could move (not that anyone seemed inclined to), two syllables echoed out of the darkness of the car.

"Hel-lo!"

I turned to Bellinger, the photographer. "You might want to get that camera ready."

Holm jabbed a finger at the man.

"Don't you dare," he said.

My brother reappeared at the boxcar door, a gray flannel blanket in his hand.

"This was over the blood," he said. "Wasn't no way to mop it up 'cuz the car's so cold. It's froze solid to the floorboards. You'd have to hope no one noticed before you could get rid of it with hot water...right, Turner?"

"Codswallop," said Holm.

"Balderdash," said Eichelberger.

But the conductor turned to Turner looking aghast.

"What have you done?" he said.

Turner's mouth fell open, but no words emerged, so Old Red answered for him.

"Shot a man in the back. The poor feller chose the wrong car to hide in. So cold he had to put on a costume he was takin' home with him just to keep from freezin'. Is that what got him killed, Turner? The fur suit he had on?"

"Fur suit?" said Eichelberger.

Holm put one hand to his head while stretching out the other as if searching for something solid to prop himself up with.

"He was dressed like a bear!" Turner blurted at them. "I came back to check on the trees, and this big hairy thing attacked me. So I defended myself. It's not my fault!"

Old Red shook his head sadly.

"Shot a man *in the back*, I said. He wasn't attackin' you. He was hidin' or tryin' to get away. But you panicked and shot him anyway. Which is why you decided, once you realized what you'd done, to toss the body. Maybe that's what you were plannin' for one of these here trees the U.P. was bringin' in. Wasn't no need to 'check on 'em.' You knew a good spot to leave one behind for yourself—a place where the tracks run up so close to a ridge you could dump something big unnoticed. But that's guesswork. Stickin' to the facts, you killed an unarmed man, and even with you bein' a railroad dick and him ridin' the rails, you'd have to answer to the law. On top of which you'd be spoilin' your employer's Christmas stunt. Your job was on the line, maybe even your freedom...so you threw that poor young man out like trash and carried on like nothin' happened. And if some kids out lookin' for a tree of their own hadn't come along at just the wrong time, you'd have gotten away with it, too."

Turner, Holm, Eichelberger, the conductor, the photographer —all of them just stood there gawping at my brother. They weren't alone by this time, either. The commotion by the boxcar had been noticed by the stray passengers and porters still out on the platform. More than a dozen people had heard my brother's speech. And now they were glaring at Turner and the railroad men, all of them obviously wondering the same thing.

You gonna let him get away with that?

Eichelberger cleared his throat.

"Umm...well...these are serious accusations, sir. Very serious," he said. "I think it would be best if this conversation took place in private."

Then *foom*. There was a whoosh and a burst of harsh, white light, and a little cloud of gray smoke went billowing up over the platform.

Bellinger had finally set off his flash powder and taken his photograph.

Now, there's a reason you never saw that picture in any papers, though the fact that it existed surely worked in our favor. Bellinger was from *The Ogden Examiner*, the Union Pacific's primary mouthpiece in these parts. They were planning a cute little item about the U.P. playing Santa for the town by bringing in Christmas trees. The fact that this could now be replaced by a new, not-so-cute item—with photo (and witnesses)—no doubt made Eichelberger and Holm all the more receptive to what Old Red and I had to say.

Which is why, once Turner had been sent off to the sheriff's office to turn himself in (after changing out of the red suit, of course), we were able to get down to brass tacks. The dead man's family was to be located and compensated. (And you can bet I double-checked on that later. I don't believe in Santa Claus *or* a railroad doing the right thing out of the goodness of its heart. So I can confirm that the Müller clan of Willard, Utah, has received both an apology and a sizable check from the Union Pacific.) As for me and Old Red, we didn't ask for much: We each rode away from the station with a little pine tree strapped down behind us. One we left with Ammon, Sariah, and Gideon when we went back out to make sure the sheriff's deputies were doing their jobs. The other returned with us to Miss Derringer's boarding house.

"DELIGHTFUL!" our landlady declared as Annie and Claypool set it up in the parlor. She then squinted and leaned so far forward I worried she was about to topple over like a felled tree herself. "A BIT ON THE SCRAWNY SIDE, THOUGH, ISN'T IT?"

"THAT'S WHY MY BROTHER PICKED IT OUT TO BRING HOME," I replied, slapping a hand on Old Red's slight shoulder. "REMINDED HIM OF HIMSELF!"

My brother shrugged away my hand and stalked off to avail himself of the eggnog Annie had made for the occasion.

If you're wondering about that photograph young Bellinger took, recall that Ogden is a company town and *The Examiner* a town paper. The next day Holm and Eichelberger were indeed featured on page one, but it was in a different picture: one that showed a new Santa Claus presenting the Union Pacific men with a freight car full of much-needed trees. This Santa didn't fill out his suit nearly so well as the first, and behind his fake white beard I spied the unhappy face of a man who wished to be off checking his watch and shouting "All aboard!"

Of course, New York City is a long way from Ogden, and Smythe & Associates Publishing, Ltd., isn't beholden to any railroad. Old Red and I didn't make any promises about keeping the story to ourselves, so if you want it for that Christmas special, Mr.

Smythe, it's yours. I would only ask that you split payment three ways, sending the proceeds to the addresses below. I know the money won't reach everyone until well into the new year, but, for some, a little late Christmas cheer will be far better than none.

Ingrid Müller
57 Tams Road
Willard, Utah

Ammon, Sariah and Gideon Oaks
Riverdale Road
Weber County, Utah

And yours truly,
O.A. Amlingmeyer
2955 Adams Avenue, Room #4
Ogden, Utah
December 21, 1893

CURIOUS INCIDENTS

Urias Smythe
Smythe & Associates Publishing, Ltd.
175 Fifth Avenue
New York, New York

Dear Mr. Smythe:

As you might have surmised from the relatively puny size of this missive, this is *not* the new book I have promised you. I don't try to compete with *War and Peace* or *Crime and Punishment* for sheer forest-clearing volume of pages, but I am well aware that the novel you await—*Murder and Mayhem*, let's call it—shouldn't fit into a standard four-by-eight envelope. (By the way, I'm actually calling my novel-in-progress *The Double-A Western Detective Agency*. This will, I hope, both intrigue readers and advertise the new business my brother and I have launched to potential—and desperately needed—clients. Of course, what it's called when printed is for you to decide. I can only entreat you to give my suggestion some consideration before defaulting to "Cowboy Brothers Battle the New Mexico Death Baron!" or some other title of the type Smythe & Associates usually favors.)

Title aside, fear not! Though not yet finished, the new novel already weighs as much as a small dog. I assure that it will reach full-grown Great Dane dimensions in plenty of time to fill some summertime edition of *Smythe's Frontier Detective*.

What you hold in your hands now is what you might call the appetizer before the full-on gorge of the main course. And it's one you yourself ordered. I'm sure you'll recall the letter you forwarded to me in Ogden at the start of the new year, as well as your suggestion that my brother and I do as it requested "as a kindness to an admirer" (which I took to mean "as a kindness to your publisher...who needs all the publicity he can get"). But just in case 1894 has proved such a whirlwind you've already forgotten even so memorable a correspondence, allow me to jog your memory by reproducing it here.

———

Mr. Gustav "Old Red" Amlingmeyer (and "Big Red")
Care of Smythe & Associates Publishing, Ltd.
175 Fifth Avenue
New York, New York

Dear Mr. Amlingmeyer,

I have read of your adventures in *Smythe's Frontier Detective* with great delight. That our West is blessed with as keen a crime-solving mind as can be found in old Europe should have the breast of every true American swelling with pride. Never did I imagine, however, that I would have need of that remarkable intellect myself until this week, when I found myself entangled in as bewildering and grotesque a series of circumstances as was ever faced by your idol, Sherlock Holmes.

I could say it began when my father, a gentleman farmer still reeling from the death of his beloved wife, my mother, decided to move us from our native Virginia and take up ranching in Idaho's rugged Bannock Range. Yet the stage had been set for tragedy and mystery long before that by the dusky residents of the dark and desolate realm we would eventually journey to as heavy-hearted pilgrims. The former masters of that land, the Shoshone Indians, called it "arimo inkom malad"—the lair of the Phantom Puma. For on the rocky ridges around Elkhorn Peak there prowled, they said, a beast that not just fed by night but was in some otherworldly fashion the night itself, black and formless and utterly unstoppable.

At first, the Idahoan rustics we encountered upon taking up residence on our new lands informed us of this legend with smirking, simpering sarcasm. As you know so well, the West and indeed the whole world are filled with malicious simpletons who look upon those turning to learning and books for solace and stimulation—as do you, as do I—with distrust and even disgust. Such boorish louts we found in abundance in Idaho, and they made plain their antipathy for me and my quiet, studious, erudite ways by turning every conversation to the ghostly beast that supposedly stalked nearby. But soon these transparent attempts to tease and terrify a newcomer were flavored with an unexpected zest: sincerity. Something began to prey on both our livestock and that of our neighbors—something that killed in the night and left behind no trace of itself save for shredded carcasses and scarlet-splattered snow. The talk thereafter still centered on the Phantom Puma, but without the air of enmity and schoolboy snickering.

We had through these dark days one stanch ally: our foreman, Jesse Ibarolla. A well-formed, virile and fearless man, Jesse hunted the spectral cat just as it hunted our stock, though with considerably less success. Night after night, he lurked and skulked upon the snowy slopes, risking his life for the chance to strike at the killer who haunted the hills. For weeks I would awake at some midnight howl or growl, perhaps real, perhaps dreamt, and lie in darkness till dawn praying for dear Jesse's safety and the creature's defeat.

Onto this already ominous scene came a stranger. With our losses mounting, my father let it be known in the area that into our home, Wendellbreeze, we would accept lodgers. While still rude and rough compared to the plantation house we left behind in Virginia, Wendellbreeze is at least roomy, and with only myself and my father in residence, and Jesse and a few other underlings in the servants' quarters, it would be easy enough to accommodate paying guests if any of sufficient funds and character presented themselves. And one seemed to five days ago. Mr. Norton Huggins came to us in a hired cart from the nearest town, having arrived via railroad and ascertained that Wendellbreeze was accepting boarders. Despite an off-putting appearance—tall and gaunt and sunken-eyed, with a bushy gray beard and a peg leg that clapped upon the floorboards like gunshots—Huggins was respectably dressed and comported himself like a gentleman. He had means to pay for a month's stay in advance, so my father welcomed him into our home. I tried to make him welcome, as well, but Huggins was a surly and secretive man, in the habit of hobbling off for long walks he refused to discuss. He would only say that he was an engineer and that he was awaiting word on an opportunity with a local mining concern.

The second day of Huggins's stay, Jesse took me aside on the veranda to ask what I made of the man.

"He is disagreeable, but no more so than most of our neighbors in this unwelcoming place," said I. "At least he, like them, keeps his distance most of the time. What is your assessment?"

Jesse looked this way and that before leaning his manly frame closer.

"This morning I chanced upon Huggins in the north pasture," he said, his husky voice hushed. "He was consulting a large and well-worn map, which he hurriedly folded and stuffed into his greatcoat upon espying me. At first he scowled at me in his usual inimical way. But then, much to my surprise, he gestured for me to join him. When I did so, he made some strained and dissembling comments on the beauty of the Bannock Range before veering into a suggestive line of inquiry. Had I ever observed, he wanted to know, any caverns in the surrounding foothills that seemed to have been, in his words, 'expanded and exploited'? 'You mean mined? No, not near here. But there are gold, silver, and copper mines throughout the county,' I informed him. 'Did I ask about *mines*?' the man ejaculated, and he bade me good day—in that way that makes plain he wished me no good whatsoever—and stormed off toward Wendellbreeze."

"Our guest is indeed contrary," I said. "I'm not sure I see what is so 'suggestive' about the encounter, however."

"It is this, Miss Wendell," said Jesse. "It reminded me of another Shoshone legend—the one that says the Phantom Puma guards 'pocatello chubbuck tyhee.'"

Our foreman glanced over his shoulder again before going on in no more than a whisper.

"The underground city of gold."

For a moment I was disappointed that our most loyal friend thereabouts should subject me to more impertinent "ribbing" in the manner of our uncouth neighbors. But the grave and troubled look on his handsome face quickly told me this wasn't some new line of mockery. The legend was real. As was, perhaps, Huggins's interest in it.

"I hope you will do me the service of keeping an eye on Mr. Huggins," I said. "My father may trust that he comes to us without ulterior motive, but I do not."

"Nor do I," Jesse replied. "Fear not, Miss Wendell. I shall watch over you and your father as a shepherd guards his flock."

That night I again awoke to the sound of an animal yowl in the distance. I had almost convinced myself it was but the moan of the winter wind through the hills when a nearer noise caught my ear: a steady drip of liquid. I might have dismissed it as the melting of icicles upon the eaves had it not so clearly come from somewhere inside the house. The incessant, metronomic click-click-click of it chipped away at my nerves like little raps of a miner's pickax. At last I could stand it no more, and I wrapped myself in my dressing gown, lit a candle, and crept into the hall to seek out the source of the sound.

The first door I passed yielded another noise—the gruff, irregular grinding of snores—that told me my father still slept. But at the next door I lingered, for the drip plainly came from just beyond it.

It was the door to Mr. Huggins's room.

"Mr. Huggins?" I said.

I gave the door a gentle knock. There was no response.

My heart flooded with a dreadful foreboding, yet somehow I found the fortitude to reach out and grasp the doorknob. As I turned it, the dribbling seemed to intensify, changing from a mere drip to a pounding thump—one I didn't just hear but felt within my quivering breast.

I was perceiving the beating of my own heart. It grew louder and faster as I pushed open the door and stepped into the room.

The small, flickering flame of my candle revealed little at first but the shadowy shapes of the wardrobe, washstand and chiffonier. When I moved toward the center of the room, however, I could make out the bed—and the dark, lumpy, sodden thing upon it.

It was a body wrapped in black robes such as nuns or priests wear. The cloth glistened with moisture, a trickle of which seeped over the side to splatter upon the floor.

I froze for a moment, but then forced myself to inch forward. A piece of ragged paper was laid atop the body, and I could only make out the words scrawled upon it if I stepped closer.

"BEWARE THE COUGAR WHO WALKS AS MAN!" the note read.

Just above it, staring at the ceiling with wide and unblinking eyes, was the waxy gray face of Mr. Norton Huggins.

It was then, at last, that I screamed.

My father came running. Jesse did not—and not because he couldn't hear me from the servants' quarters. He was nowhere to be found. The next morning, tracks in the mud and snow told us part of the story: Jesse had ridden out on his favorite horse, Darcy, presumably to stalk the beast that made a nightly feast of our animals. His trail tapered off in the rocky hills, however, and to this day no fresh ones have been found. Jesse and Darcy have disappeared.

Missing, too, is the map that Jesse told me he saw Huggins consulting. Before burying our unfortunate lodger—who seemed to have died by drowning despite the fact that the nearest body of water is a sliver of a stream a hundred yards from the house—I made a search of his things, hoping to find some correspondence that would allow me to send word of his passing to his family. Yet I found no letters, no postcards, no papers of any kind. I could not even be sure that the single word scrawled upon the man's makeshift pinewood headstone—HUGGINS—had any truth to it.

Who was he really? What brought him to Wendellbreeze? How did he die? Where is his map? What is the meaning of the menacing message left upon his corpse? And, most importantly, what has become of our dear, devoted Jesse?

I bring these questions to you, Mr. Amlingmeyer, because in reading of your adventures, I presume to have found more than a kindred spirit who shares my deep esteem for the late Sherlock Holmes. I feel—or at least hope—that I've found a champion willing to journey to Wendellbreeze armed with Mr. Holmes's methods and girded by his tremendous courage. Although I cannot offer you any payment should you come to my aid, I implore you to take up the cause of justice, as you have so often and so bravely in the past, and demonstrate again why you have won renown the world over as our heroic "Holmes of the Range."

Your ardent admirer,
  Ann Wendell
  McCammon, Idaho
  January 8, 1894

———————

That last paragraph didn't just lay it on thick: It dumped it on by the bucketful. But I don't hold a little flattery against anyone. I've been known to do some pretty generous buttering up myself, as you, with your fine eye for detail and profound perspicacity, have no doubt noted.

Nor did the letter's more uncanny elements put me off my feed. A strange tale it was, but hardly the strangest my brother and

I have heard (or lived through) since he got it in his head to follow in Mr. Holmes's footsteps. "The Phantom Puma of Elkhorn Peak" might sound fantastic, but when you've already run up against the Water Indian of Utah, the Black Dove of San Francisco and the Giant Muskrat of Folderol Falls, as we have, it seems almost humdrum. (All right, we haven't *actually* run up against the Giant Muskrat of Folderol Falls. Yet. The way things have been going for us I keep expecting it, though.)

So it was decided. As soon as Old Red and I wrapped up the first paying case for our new detective agency, we would sally forth to Idaho for a gratis rescue of yon damsel in distress. (Patience! How that paying case turned out you will learn when my new book is done.) When we were at last free to don our shining armor, I wrote Miss Wendell to inform her that her knights-errant were on the way.

Usually my brother would have insisted that we make our way there on horseback, McCammon being just a hundred miles north of Ogden and him viewing trains as torture chambers on tracks. But with the dead of winter upon us, even he had to admit that half a day of nausea on the rails beat half a week of freezing on the trails. So when we first set foot in McCammon, it was at a Union Pacific station.

It wasn't much, as stations go: just a white wooden building the size of a line-camp shack plopped beside the tracks without even the added extravagance of a platform. The town around it matched it for plainness, and if any of the three dozen or so buildings within city limits was any bigger or fancier than a barn, I didn't see it.

Which made our welcoming committee easy to spot. She was perched upon the driver's seat of a faded green farm wagon, the reins of a swayback draft horse in her hands. Her threadbare, oversized coat and limp-brimmed hat looked like hand-me-downs from an older brother or perhaps a great-great-great-grandfather, and her fingerless gloves were so frayed she seemed to be wearing a pair of gray doilies.

She also looked to be all of sixteen years old.

"Big Red? Old Red?" she said with a smile as we stepped off the train. "Is it you?"

"I'm not sure. We find train trips a bit discombobulating," I said. I looked over at my brother. "*Is* it us?"

"It's us," Old Red told the girl. (Me he was ignoring.) "And you are…?"

"Your ride to the house," the girl said. She jerked a thumb at the bed of her wagon. "Climb in!"

"I was afraid she was gonna say that," I grumbled under my breath—which I could see, by the way. It was going to be a long, cold ride out to our client.

We walked over and tossed our carpetbags into the wagon bed, avoiding the little dirty-white puffs lodged in each corner. (It wasn't snowing at the moment, but the sky was one solid gray cloud that seemed ready to dump on us whenever it would make us most miserable.) Then we hoisted ourselves up and made ourselves comfortable—or as comfortable as one can get in a conveyance intended for sacks of feed and barrels of flour rather than people's posteriors.

"Let's go, Heathcliff," the girl said, giving the reins a gentle snap.

The old gelding shook his head and snorted before setting off at a plodding pace. The girl steered him around to a trail by the tracks that stretched off to snow-dusted bluffs on the horizon.

"So what do we call you, Miss?" I asked.

"Josephine, if you like," the girl said. "Or Jo. That's what my friends call me."

She swiveled to smile at us. I had no worries about her taking her eyes off the road, as we were in no danger of careening out of control. We would've picked up considerable speed, in fact, if Heathcliff and I had changed places.

"You look just like I pictured you," she said.

"Like *you* pictured us?" I said.

Jo nodded. "Writing to you was my idea. I've been reading about you since you first started showing up in *Smythe's Frontier Detective*, so I knew you'd come." She looked at us like she was sizing up bulls at auction. "You're nothing like the illustrations in the magazine, but I always figured those were all wrong. The way they make you two look so fancy and heroic and clean…"

"Oh?" Old Red said. He'd been slumped down beside me in the wagon bed, but now he sat up straight and frowned.

Jo laughed. "Even that expression on your face—it's just like your brother describes it in his stories. And your clothes. You look like you could be on a cattle drive, Old Red."

"A man oughta dress practical," my brother mumbled. He threw a look over at my clothes, and his frown twisted into a little smirk. "And fittin' the circumstances."

Though I was bookended as he was with a Stetson up top and boots down below, otherwise I was attired for respectable business in a three-piece suit and topcoat. Already I'd acquired a few splinters in the seat of my fine woolen trousers.

"Depends on what the circumstances are," I said. "And at the very least no one could accuse me of looking *unclean*."

"I'm sorry. I didn't mean to say anyone seems dirty," Jo said. "It's just…I know what cowboys really look like."

I straightened my black necktie. "Devilishly handsome, you mean?"

Jo cut loose with another laugh.

"You're just like in your stories, too, Big Red," she said.

"Why, thank you."

"I wouldn't assume that was a compliment," said Old Red. "So…Jo. Still no sign of that foreman fella?"

The girl's grin dimmed, and she finally turned away to watch where Heathcliff was (oh so slowly) going.

"No," she said. "Jesse is still missing."

"How about Huggins?" Old Red asked. "Y'all learn anything more about the man?"

"I should let Miss Wendell talk to you about that. I'm just a servant," Jo said. She gave Heathcliff another snap of the reins, but his ponderous trudge didn't speed up in the slightest. "So what did you think of 'The Adventure of the Final Problem'? I knew Sherlock Holmes was dead, of course, but it was still a shock to finally read the details in *McClure's* last month. Was it that way for you?"

My brother just narrowed his eyes and muttered, "I'm still chewin' on it."

"You know what I wonder? If they had a memorial service for Sherlock," Jo said. "The story doesn't say. Obviously they didn't have a body, but still—wouldn't they do something? What denomination do you think Sherlock was? Or John Watson? Would they have to be Anglicans? Is that how it works over there? Is everyone automatically in the Church of England?"

The girl wasn't looking back at us as she babbled, so my brother felt free to give her the kind of sour glower he usually reserves for me.

"I don't rightly know," he said.

"I didn't get the feelin' ol' Holmes was the church-goin' sort," I said.

"Big Red!" Jo cried, whipping around so quick any other horse might have spooked and bolted. (Fortunately, Heathcliff appeared to be deaf as a post in addition to slow as molasses.) "Really!"

"'Really' what?" I said. I've inadvertently given offense on many an occasion, so I've had practice working my foot out of my mouth. How it got there this time, though, I couldn't see.

Jo shook her head and harrumphed at me.

"'The Adventure of the Naval Treaty,'" she said. "Right, Old Red?"

My brother stared back at her blankly, and the girl's expression shifted from incensed to suspicious.

Then Old Red's eyes widened, and another smirk crinkled a corner of his bushy mustache.

"Ohhhh…I get you," he said. "The rose."

The look on Jo's face changed again. Suddenly, she was beaming.

"'Our highest assurance of the goodness of Providence seems to me to rest in the flowers,'" she said. "'All other things, our powers, our desires, our food, are all really necessary for our existence in the first instance.'"

"'But this rose is an extra,'" my brother said, picking up the passage where she'd left off. "'Its smell and its color are an embellishment of life, not a condition of it. It is only goodness which gives extras, and so I say again——'"

The girl jumped back in to say the last words in unison with him.

"'…that we have much to hope from the flowers.'"

"Amen," I said.

I must've read "The Adventure of the Naval Treaty" forty times for my brother, him being unable to read it (or anything else) even the once. Yet somehow the full meaning of Holmes's literally flowery speech hadn't got through to me before.

"Hardly the words of a man without faith," Jo said to me.

Before turning away again, she flashed Old Red a grin, and I got the feeling he'd just passed a test the girl had been giving him.

"So who would have organized the service for Sherlock?" she said. "John? Mycroft? Some other member of the Holmes family? And who do you think would come? Sherlock helped so many people, but a lot of them probably wouldn't acknowledge it in public. You know—'discretion' and all that. Still, I bet Helen would have been there, don't you?"

"'Helen'?" I said.

Jo groaned, and from the way she swiveled her head, I could tell she was rolling her eyes.

"Stoner, of course!"

"'The Adventure of the Speckled Band,'" Old Red reminded me.

"Oh. Right. Her."

"And Mary would be there," Jo went on. "That goes without saying."

"Indeed," I agreed.

I threw Old Red a puzzled look.

"Marston," he whispered. "Mrs. Watson."

Jo continued to fill the pews with imagined mourners. Jabez (Wilson, "The Red-Headed League") would have paid his respects, as would Violet (Hunter, "The Adventure of the Copper

Beeches") and James (Turner, "A Case of Identity"). Irene (Adler, "A Scandal in Bohemia") would slip into the back row in disguise, keeping her out of sight of the small regiment of Scotland Yard inspectors up front (Barton, Forbes, Forrester, Gregson, Jones, Lanner, Patterson). A select group of Yardsmen (Bradstreet, Brown, Gregson, Lestrade) would assist John and Stamford (the medical man who introduced Holmes and Watson in "A Study in Scarlet") with the pallbearing, while revenge-minded lackeys of the late Professor Moriarty, done up as gravediggers, lurked nearby, watched for signs of trickery.

It was thoroughly thought out, that's for sure. I got the feeling Jo had been daydreaming about it for weeks, and she certainly painted a picture far more interesting than the one around us: the ragged outskirts of town giving way to mile upon frosty mile of rolling hills splotched gray with slushy, muddy old snow. But after a time even Old Red began to weary of it, and I could tell from the way he fidgeted that he was anxious to get to the matter at hand.

Eventually, though, the matter at hand came to us. Part of it, anyway.

Three riders appeared on the trail ahead. From their wide-brimmed hats and heavy work coats and the ropes coiled near their saddle horns, it was clear they were cowhands. Jo stiffened as they trotted closer. She stopped chattering about the scene in London post-Holmes, too, concluding with "That's how I imagine it, anyway." She scanned the ground around us as if she might steer old Heathcliff off the road to avoid the men approaching us. But the sloping hillside we were slowly rolling across was slushy and pocked with rocks. If she took the wagon off the road, there was no guarantee she'd get it back on before the spring thaw.

"Don't bother talking to me," she told the cowboys when they were within speaking distance. "I have no time for your insults today."

"Aww...little Miss Priss don't wanna visit with us," one of the cowhands said.

"Must be deep in conversation with those other little misses she's haulin'," said another.

"Baaaaa!" bleated the third.

All three men had big grins on their unshaven faces.

They gave their horses their heels and began galloping around the wagon.

"All we wanted to do was wish you a fine day, Miss Priss!" said the first, tugging on his hat brim.

"And to you, too, ladies!" said the second, doffing his hat to me and Old Red.

"Baaaaaaaaa!" said the third.

Now cowboys have a reputation for rough "fun"—one I know from experience to be well-earned—and the best way to ensure that they'll get *really* rowdy is to ask them to stop. But I didn't like the nasty leers these three were giving the young lady or the way they seemed to be competing to see who could crowd Heathcliff the closest as they circled past.

"And a good day to you, fellers!" I said. "Fine display of ridin' there. I'd sure appreciate it if you didn't nettle our horse so, though. If he gets to runnin', I'll probably roll out the back and break my dang neck."

I said all this with a smile to show that I appreciated a good lark and wouldn't dream of being bossy and was merely making a good-natured request, one working man to another.

It didn't work.

"Sounds like something I'd like to see, fancy pants!" the first cowboy called out, and as he rode around in front of us this time he swiped at Heathcliff's muzzle with his hat.

The old horse was still snorting and shaking his head as the second hand galloped past and gave him yet another swat. This time, Heathcliff reared up in response. Yes, he was only able to get his front hooves half a foot off the ground, but still—if he bolted he could break a leg, Jo could bounce off the driver's seat, or my brother and I really could fly out and snap our necks.

Old Red muttered an obscenity and reached for his carpetbag. Coiled up within it, same as in mine, was a gun belt holding a forty-five. (We don't make it a habit to heel ourselves for a simple train trip—though given our luck the last couple years I'm starting to think we shouldn't even take our irons off for a bath.)

"Baaaaaaa!" said the third cowboy—quite the conversationalist, he was—and as he rode past the front of the wagon again he leaned out and slapped Heathcliff's muzzle with the flat of his hand.

The horse whinnied and reared up once more, higher this time, then charged forward. One would've expected Jo to pull back on the reins and cut loose with a "Whoa there, Heathcliff!" Instead she stuffed her right hand under her shabby old coat and jerked out a hogleg as long as a hatchet even as she fought to keep her balance on her seat.

"Goodbye, Little Miss Priss! Hello, Little Miss Sure Shot!" the first cowboy laughed.

He and his friends peeled away and took off down the trail.

Jo tried to point her gun at them, but it was too heavy for one hand, and the barrel drooped down toward the wagon bed—which, by some miracle, still had me and my brother in it.

Old Red had finally managed to get to his holstered Colt, but he immediately stuffed it back in with his spare clothes and started waving his hands at Jo.

"Put that thing away!" he blurted out.

"It's over! They're leaving!" I added as the muzzle of the girl's gun weaved this way and that. "For god's sake, keep both hands on the reins!"

Two of the cowboys were yipping as they galloped off. The third, predictably, shouted back a last, extra long "Baaaaaaaaaaaaaaaaaa!"

"Expurgated!" Jo shouted at them.

(What she actually shouted I know you couldn't commit to print. I leave it to you whether to replace it with "Dirty rotten varmints!" or "Dad-blasted sidewinders!")

Jo turned away and plopped the gun onto the seat beside her, and my brother and I heaved sighs of relief as she got her right hand on the reins again. Not that Heathcliff needed much slowing. For him running wild meant speeding up from a trot to a canter for a few seconds.

"I'm sorry about that," Jo said as the horse eased back to his old clomping walk. "Some of our neighbors are…well…"

"We heard your wording a moment ago," I said. "And I can't say I disagree with it."

"Who were them three, anyhow?" Old Red asked.

Jo shrugged without looking back at us. "Nobody important."

"You sure about that?" my brother pressed. "Seemed to me like that wasn't just foolin' around. They got some special beef with you? Or your father? Or with Jesse the foreman, maybe?"

The girl snorted as if he'd made a joke. "No. There's no special beef. They're just…you know…what I shouldn't have said. You two always seem to meet a bunch in your stories. John and Sherlock, too, of course. Who would you say was worse: Dr. Grimesby Roylott from 'The Adventure of the Speckled Band' or Jim Browner from 'The Adventure of the Cardboard Box'? I think we're supposed to hate Roylott more, but Browner's just as bad if you look past his excuses. Of course, neither of them can hold a candle to Professor Moriarty. You know, I wish I could've shoved him off that cliff myself. I'm sure John feels the same way. What do you think would've happened if he hadn't fallen for Moriarty's trick and gone back to the hotel without Sherlock?"

And off she went again, describing the scenario as she saw it —our two heroes overpowering the vile Napoleon of Crime together, then returning to England to continue their crusade against the various Grants, Lees, and Custers of Crime—as more low, snow-speckled hills slid slowly past us. Old Red slumped in the back of the wagon like a half-filled sack of beans, a curiously dejected expression upon his face. (Not that his face was any stranger to dejection. It's just that the one thing usually guaranteed to brighten it up is talk of Mr. Holmes.)

The girl kept at it as we turned off the main road and followed a thinner one toward a cluster of dark structures in the distance. I didn't see anything that looked like the rough but roomy Wendellbreeze of the letter, so I assumed it was tucked around the next hillside.

My brother leaned over the side of the wagon to peer down at the ground, then sighed and sagged again. I took a look myself but didn't see anything more than ruts in the mud and a patchy path through the frozen grass, but Old Red's always had a sharper eye for trail sign than me.

"What is it?" I whispered to him.

"Baaaaa," he replied softly.

And I suddenly understood why Old Red's "They got some special beef with you?" might have seemed like a jest to the girl.

I picked at the nearest tuft of gray-white in the wagon bed—what I'd taken earlier for snow. It was soft and spongy, and I knew that if I lifted it to my nose, I could inhale a pungent lungful redolent of musk and piss.

"Oh, no," I groaned, flicking the little white ball away. "Do you reckon—?"

My brother silenced me with a quick shake of the head.

"Jo," he said. "I hate to interrupt your thoughts on Mr. Holmes. You're touchin' upon much I've wondered myself. But seein' the stable and barns up ahead there puts me in mind of a question. Percy—he likely to come home on his own if given the chance?"

"Percy?" the girl said. "Oh. Um. I'm not sure."

"Well, you know how some horses are," Old Red said. "Somethin' happens to the man in the saddle, they'll come on back to the corral if they can. Be good to know if Jesse's horse was thataway. Could be 'instructive,' as you-know-who would say."

Jo glanced back at us, then looked ahead again quickly. She gave the reins a listless little snap that Heathcliff didn't even notice.

"I see what you mean," she said. "But I never heard of Percy doing anything like that."

Old Red gave his head a weary shake.

"I don't suppose you would, Miss Wendell," he said. "Seein' as he don't exist."

The girl flinched, then drooped, then slowly turned to peer back at us warily.

"What did I call him in the letter?" she asked.

"You said Jesse's horse was named 'Darcy,'" Old Red told her.

She clenched her fists and stamped her foot.

"Stupid! Stupid dumb dumb stupid! Why did I even mention the horse at all?"

"I reckon you got carried away. I know how that can go when spinning a yarn," I said. "And yours was a real corker, I grant you. Heck, if I wasn't so vexed I'd suggest you finish it and send it off to *Smythe's Frontier Detective*. 'The girl turned the wagon around and drove the detectives straight back to the station' isn't much of an ending, though. Guess you'd have to make that up, too."

The girl's eyes popped wide.

"No! Please! You've got to understand! I *do* need your help! Jesse really is missing! But we can't pay you anything, and I know how cowboys feel about…people like us."

"Sheepmen, you mean," Old Red said.

"And sheepgirls," I added.

"Yes," said "Jo"—henceforth "Ann." "My father and I came to Idaho after my mother died two years ago. From New Jersey, not…Virginia?"

I nodded. That part of her letter she'd remembered correctly.

"The West is where sheep are booming," she went on. "But you know how it is. Cattlemen despise us. Claim sheep ruin the range. The ranchers and their hands around here—they've been hateful to us from the moment we arrived. Malicious, spiteful. Like on the road from town just now. That's why I think they did something to Jesse."

Old Red looked off into the distance. Not at anything in particular. He was just studying nothing the way he does whenever it suits him. In the meantime, old Heathcliff kept plodding along toward the stable and sheds and barn up ahead.

There was a house in among the outbuildings, I now saw. "Wendellbreeze." It wasn't much bigger than the little sodbuster hovel Old Red and I grew up in.

"So he really does that?" Ann said to me after a minute passed without a word.

She nodded at my brother. In my stories, I'd described many times his habit of eyeing the horizon in silence when lost in thought.

"Of course, he does," I replied. "What *I* write is true."

Ann winced.

"So," Old Red said, turning to face her again, "there's no 'Phantom Puma'?"

"No," the girl told him.

"No Huggins drowned in his bed?"

"No."

"No lost map?"

"No. I made all that up. I figured the only way to get your attention was with lots of…"

Ann struggled to find a word other than the obvious one (which describes both hogwash and what he-cows leave so plentifully upon the plains). When the right alternative came to her, she dared a small, shy smile.

"Curious incidents," she said.

Old Red frowned at the familiar phrase—coined by Mr. Holmes himself to describe a particularly puzzling clue in "The Adventure of Silver Blaze." Then he barked out a gruff chuckle, obviously awestruck (as was I) by the girl's considerable gall.

He conceded defeat by throwing up his hands and shaking his head.

"Well, it worked. We're here," he said. "May as well make ourselves useful, I suppose."

The girl's tentative smile turned into a full-on grin.

"I knew you'd see it that way," she said.

She turned around and gave the reins another jaunty snap that did absolutely nothing to speed our journey.

I, meanwhile, gave my brother a long, steady stare.

"What's that look supposed to mean?" he snapped at me.

"Oh, it means a lot of things," I said. "But mostly it means

I'm not going to let you forget this the next time you want to drag me along on a quest."

Old Red scowled and spat out his preferred all-purpose rejoinder.

"*Feh.*"

I nodded placidly.

"That's what *I'm* gonna say," I said.

I looked away from my brother as we rolled slowly into the barnyard, but I couldn't stay quiet long. A wave of raucous laughter burst from me out of nowhere.

Both Old Red and Ann turned to peer at me in puzzlement.

"'Beware the cougar who walks as man'!" I said, wiping tears from my eyes. "Oh, Miss Wendell…you are a natural!"

My guffaws drew us an audience. A bearded man stepped from one of the weathered, unpainted outbuildings. He was wearing a patch-elbowed coat and worn trousers and a look of profound puzzlement. Cradled in his arms was a spindly little lamb with huge, droopy ears that jutted from its white face like wings.

"Ann," the man said as the wagon came to a stop before him, "what's going on?"

"Dad, this is Gustav and Otto Amlingmeyer," the girl said. "You know—from *Smythe's Frontier Detective*? They've come to help us find Jesse."

Ann's father gave us a skeptical up-and-down once-over. The lamb just stared at us with eyes as black and blank as currants.

"No," the man said in disbelief.

"Oh, yes," I said. It took effort not to sigh it.

"You're real?"

"I know it's hard to believe, sir, us being so amazing and all," I said. "Why, at times I even have doubts about us myself. But then I look in the mirror and I am reassured. Yes—the world is lucky enough to have us."

Old Red groaned and rolled his eyes.

"See?" Ann said. "Just like in the stories!"

"So you really wrote to them?" Mr. Wendell asked her.

"Yes, Dad. Obviously."

The man looked at me and my brother again, his incredulity giving way to astonishment.

"And you came all this way?" he said.

I started nodding.

"To look for a dog?" he went on.

I stopped nodding.

Old Red buried his face in his hands.

"A dog," he said.

"A *dog*?" I said.

"Of course, Jessie's a dog," said Mr. Wendell. "What else would she be?"

"Your foreman," my brother said into his palms.

I leaned toward him.

"Curiouser and curiouser, this case of yours," I said. "And dumber. The next time you want to do some charity work, do me a favor and pick up a bell for the Salvation Army."

"*Ann*," Mr. Wendell said sharply, "you didn't lie to get these men here, did you?"

The girl slumped in the driver's seat. "Not exactly. I just... tried to put things in an enticing light."

"And you succeeded, miss," I said. "*By lying.*"

Ann looked thoroughly abashed and repentant...for about two seconds. Then she straightened her back and raised her chin.

"It'll still make a great story for the magazine, Big Red. Everybody loves dogs," she said. "And Jessie's amazing. The best sheepdog in the county. That's why they took her, I'm sure of it."

My brother peeped out through spread fingers.

"'They'?" he said.

Ann nodded, her expression souring.

"Cowboys," she spat. "Hands from the Turkey Foot Ranch. Like those bas—" She glanced over at her father and did some quick editing. "...ruffians we met on the road."

"What happened?" Mr. Wendell asked. The lamb in his arms noticed the way he stiffened and bleated weakly. "Were Huggins's men bothering you again?"

Old Red spread his fingers even wider. "So there *is* a Huggins?"

Ann nodded again. "Oh, yes. He's a cattleman. His land surrounds ours on three sides. And he and his men hate us." She turned to her father. "Three of them rode up on us on our way here. They tried to spook Heathcliff."

"Actually, they succeeded," I said. "It's just that with Heathcliff it's hard to tell the difference between unspooked and spooked."

My brother finally lowered his hands.

"Do *you* think these Turkey Foot fellas did something to your dog?" he asked Mr. Wendell.

The man shrugged. "I don't know. Maybe. It did seem a mite suspicious the way she just disappeared."

"'A mite suspicious'?" Ann blurted out with an exasperated roll of the eyes. "It's flagrant skulduggery is what it is!"

I had to cock an eyebrow at "flagrant skulduggery," it being a phrase I never would've expected to encounter spoken aloud—especially not by a teenage girl dressed like a Louisiana sharecropper.

Her father just spoke over her.

"Jessie's not our dog, though," he told my brother. "She belongs to Josu Ibarolla. Our sheepherder. It's him you should talk to. If you're really curious, I mean."

Old Red replied with a grunt, his gaze going glassy.

He *was* getting curious.

Me, I was just getting cold. There didn't seem to be much I could do about it, though. The Wendells didn't strike me as the types who'd be serving hot toddies in the drawing room.

I sighed resignedly and jumped off the wagon.

"Well, come on," I said. "Let's go talk to this Josu before one of us freezes to death."

I tried to warm myself by hopping in place and brushing the newly acquired splinters from the seat of my trousers.

"So you're taking the case?" Ann asked.

"I don't know about that," Old Red grumbled as he climbed

out beside me. "But as long as we're here, I suppose I may as well go see a man about a dog."

The man to see about the dog was off in the hills seeing to the Wendell's sheep. So after we stowed this and that—Heathcliff in the corral, our bags in the shabby little ranch house, the fluffy white bundle in Mr. Wendell's arms back in what sheepmen call "the lambing barn"—the four of us trudged off to look for him.

"A bit early in the year for that little runt you was holdin'," Old Red said to Mr. Wendell as we went.

"A bit," the man replied. "First bummer of the season."

Ann noticed the puzzled looks Old Red and I gave him.

"Bummers are motherless lambs. Rejected or orphaned," she explained. "If we don't take care of them, they die."

"Ahh. Happens with calves, too, of course. Only we'd call 'em 'dogies,'" I said. "Nursemaided quite a few over the years, haven't we, brother? Sometimes feels like we can't get out of the habit, in fact."

I gave Old Red a waggle of the eyebrows and a nod at the shabby-dressed "sheepgirl" trudging along beside us.

He ignored me.

"Tell me about Jessie," he said to the Wendells.

Ann was happy to oblige.

Jessie was a two-year-old border collie. Josu brought her with him when the Wendells had hired the man—a Basque, famous for their gift for sheepherding—to help with their flock. She'd been little more than a yappy little black-and-white puppy at the time. But she was bright and eager to please, and it didn't take long for Josu to train all the pup rambunctiousness out of her and turn her into a calm, confident, quiet work dog. She herded the flock with nothing but steely stares and firm stances, sniffed out strays far and wide, and held off coyotes and wolves and even the occasional puma (though never yet the Phantom kind) until Josu could make use of his rifle. To hear Ann tell it, Jessie was smarter and braver than any dog in the county—and most of the men thereabouts, as well.

"She have any enemies?" I asked.

Old Red shook his head and muttered something that sounded suspiciously like "Idjit."

"It's what we'd ask if a person went missing," I pointed out.

Ann took the question seriously.

"Sure. The same enemies me and Dad and Josu have," she said. "Consarned cowboys."

"Ann!" Mr. Wendell chided.

(A word a good deal stronger than "consarned" had actually slipped from his daughter's lips.)

"Sorry, Dad," the girl muttered. "And no offense, Old Red, Big Red. You're different. It's just that the rest of them are so... disagreeable. And stupid. And obnoxious. And filthy. And—"

"You thinking of any of these disagreeable, stupid, obnoxious, filthy cowboys in particular?" I cut in. "Or is it just them as a race with the two notable exceptions?"

"Well, they're all against us," Ann replied. "But Hoot Piney— he'd have special reason to hate Jessie. She bit him on the hand once when he and his pals harassed Josu in town. It was a miracle he didn't shoot her then and there."

I turned to my brother and folded my arms across my chest.

"The dog had an enemy," I said.

Old Red cleared his throat and kept his eyes on Ann.

"And where would we usually find this Hoot Piney?" he asked.

"Why, you've already met him," Ann said. "He was one of the Turkey Foot men we passed on the road." The girl's already sour expression positively curdled. "The one who wouldn't stop baa-ing."

"Oh. Him," I said. "A real raconteur, that one."

Old Red just narrowed his eyes and rubbed his mustache.

"Almost there," Mr. Wendell said. He raised a pointed finger. "There's Josu."

I looked ahead, but all I saw at first was yet another rocky slope dotted with pockets of snow. After some squinting, though, I noticed that some of those pockets were moving, and thin wisps of smoke tapered off from the largest mound of white among the bunch.

It was the Wendells' flock spread across a hillside around a wagon with a humped cover like an overflowing loaf of rising dough. A little iron chimney poked up out of the canvas—the source of the smoke. As we drew closer, a man emerged from the wagon with something long and black in his hands.

We were still a good three hundred yards away, yet he'd sensed us coming…and had gone to fetch his Winchester.

Ann gave Josu a wave, but he didn't wave back. He just stood there watching us work our way up the grade, rifle at the ready. Ann waved again when we were close enough to smell his woolly friends.

"Ky-sho!" she called out. (This, I later learned, is Basque for "Hello!" No one could tell me how to spell it, so—as with so many things—I've just had to wing it and hope folks will indulge me.)

Josu lifted his chin in greeting this time but still said nothing. Though he sported a thick beard he was a youngish man, I could see now, with a slender frame draped with a faded pullover and threadbare woolen cardigan. He was eyeing Old Red and me warily, as if he feared we'd somehow made the Wendells our prisoners (even though we'd left our gun belts in our grips back at the house). The dozens of sheep we began threading through, meanwhile, paid us no mind at all, concentrating instead on their methodical munching of the tor's stiff, yellowed grass.

"Ky-sho, Josu!" Ann said again, looking very pleased with herself to be greeting the sheepherder in his native tongue. She lifted mittened hands toward Old Red, then me. "Look—they came!"

Not a jot of suspicion left Josu's face. Nor did the Winchester leave his grip. He wasn't pointing it at us, but all it would take was one quick pivot to do so.

"Who came?" Josu asked Ann. He had an accent that sounded a bit Mexican, a bit Italian, and a bit Kansan.

"Gustav and Otto Amlingmeyer!" the girl told him.

I gave the man my friendliest grin and resisted the urge to offer him an autograph.

"Who?" he said.

"Old Red and Big Red!" Ann said.

Josu's brow beetled under the droopy brim of his battered brown fedora.

"*Who?*"

My grin faded.

"This is starting to hurt my feelings," I said.

"You know—the detectives I told you about," Ann said to Josu. "From the magazine!"

The man finally nodded in understanding.

"Ohhh. Them," he said. He looked me and my brother up and down and furrowed his brow even further. "*Really?*"

Old Red scowled and opened his mouth to shoot something back. But he caught himself and took a deep breath instead.

"Son," he said (though the sheepherder was five years his junior at most), "we've come a long way to see if we could help. So why don't you just show me where you last saw your dog, hmm?"

Josu regarded him coolly a moment, then pointed toward another rise about a quarter mile off.

"I had the flock bedded over there that night," he said. "Jessie was gone in the morning."

"The stock was on the same side of the hill as now?" Old Red asked. "To keep 'em out of the wind?"

"That's right. In the winter it's the wind that's the killer."

My brother nodded. "Same with sheep as cattle thataway." He marched off toward the other hill. "All right…let's go have a look."

Josu turned uncertainly to Ann and her father.

Mr. Wendell shrugged. Ann darted away after Old Red.

I bent at the waist and stretched out my arm like a maître d' welcoming a couple tuxedoed customers into a posh restaurant.

"Shall we join them?" I said. "Or do you gentlemen have other social engagements today?"

"Come on, Josu," Mr. Wendell said, starting after his daughter. "The flock'll be fine."

The sheepherder shot me another wary glare before following.

I brought up the rear, trying not to wince as I set down my freshly polished boots in one warm, squishy mound after another. (One thing cattle and sheep *don't* have in common is the size of their scat—and, correspondingly, the ease with which one can see and avoid it.)

As we neared the slope Josu had pointed at, my brother began walking hunched over, gaze on the ground, as he does when cutting for sign.

"Jessie disappeared how many days ago, exactly?" he said.

"Uhh…eight, maybe," said Josu.

"Nine," Ann corrected.

"A lot either way," Old Red grumbled. "Looks like you've had freezes and thaws and snows and melts since then, too. Not to mention a few hundred sheep trompin' over everything. Don't leave doodly for me to see."

"I beg to differ, brother," I said as yet another little mound was smooshed underfoot. "There's no shortage of doodly around here."

Old Red threw a glare over his shoulder. "I'm talkin' about footprints, not what you keep between your ears."

"See, Miss Wendell?" I said. "He is every bit as charming as my stories make him out to be."

"Feh," my brother spat. He pointed down at a set of ruts in the ground so deep even all those tromping sheep couldn't grind them away. "So you had your wagon up there at the time, huh, Josu?"

"That's right," the sheepherder said.

"Dad and I come out and help move it every week or so," Ann explained. "So Josu can always sleep near the flock as he takes them around to new places to graze."

"And how about Jessie?" Old Red asked. "What would she be doin' when Josu's asleep? Nighthawkin'?"

The sheep people looked at each other in confusion.

"That means watching over the animals until dawn," I told them. "It's cowboy parlance. My brother likes to sprinkle in a little of the old bunkhouse patois from time to time so no one mistakes him for Nick Carter."

Old Red shook his head and muttered something I'm sure we couldn't put in print even if I'd heard it.

"Yes, to answer the question," Josu said. "Jessie was always out all night with the woolies."

"And what would she do if she spotted trouble?" my brother asked. "Coyotes, let's say. Or a stranger sneakin' up. Start barkin', I assume?"

Josu shook his head. "Oh, no. She knew better than that."

"Your *guard dog* knew better than to bark when there was danger?" I said.

"Absolutely," Josu told me. "She was smart."

"And well trained," Ann added.

"So what was she supposed to do if somebody started making off with sheep?" I asked. "Send you a telegram?"

"She would stop them," Josu said. "Quietly. Without making a lot of noise that would spook the flock."

Old Red stopped walking and straightened up. "Ahh…just the way a drover nighthawk would do so as to not send every head runnin' off into the dark. Very smart indeed." He glanced back at me. "Sure does help when you got a pard who appreciates the value of silence."

"I'd prefer one who appreciates the value of an occasional bath," I replied.

This was what the sportsmen would call a "cheap shot." Despite his rough look my brother bathes more than occasionally. Why, it's almost regularly, even! (My cheap shots continue.) But when reaching for a quick rejoinder sometimes you have to grab whatever's nearest at hand.

Old Red's only rejoinder was a growl—something that's always close at hand for him. After that he doubled up and set to hunting for sign again. For the next few minutes, we all gifted him with the silence he claimed to prize. He broke it himself at a spot by some rocks where the hill tapered off into a long gully.

"Hel-lo," he said, taking a knee beside the biggest boulder of the bunch.

He pulled his hands from his coat pockets and ran his fingers over something on the ground. I couldn't see what it was till he lifted up a little lump the size and color of a penny. When Old Red rubbed it betwixt his fingertips, it dissolved into copper crumbs.

"What the heck is that?" Mr. Wendell asked.

"Looks like fried cornmeal. Over-fried, actually. Burnt to a crisp," my brother said. He lifted up another clump. "You ever fix yourself corn dodgers, Josu?"

"No," the shepherd said. "I don't care for them."

Old Red looked over at Ann. "So you never bring him any."

The girl shook her head. "No. Like he said—he doesn't like 'em."

"Me neither," Mr. Wendell threw in.

"It's a clue, isn't it?" Ann asked with a grin. "What does it mean?"

My brother slipped the little brown-gold clod into a pocket, then straightened up.

"'It is a capital mistake to theorize before you have all the evidence,'" he said, dusting off his hands.

Ann and I finished the Holmes quote for him in unison (I with a roll of the eyes).

"'It biases the judgment.'"

Old Red just turned and walked away.

"So he really does do that when you ask what he's thinking," Ann marveled, watching him go.

I shrugged. "I keep telling you I don't write fiction."

My brother, meanwhile, was moving slowly down the gully, eyes again on the ground.

"No footprints?" Mr. Wendell asked.

He was asking Old Red, but it was Josu who answered.

"There are too many, like the man said before. I looked myself the morning I realized Jessie was gone. All I saw were some of her tracks and lots from sheep, of course. Nothing bigger, except my own."

My brother stopped.

"How about this here wash I'm walkin' along?" he said without looking back. "You looked down here?"

"Sure. I looked all over. I missed that…whatever it is you just found. But like I said—I didn't see any tracks other than Jessie's and the sheep's and footprints I could've made myself."

"Oh ho," Old Red said softly. He stood there rubbing his mustache a moment, obviously theorizing furiously. The hypocrite. But I knew better than to ask what conclusions he might be creeping up on.

A sudden, sharp noise jerked him out of his reverie. It echoed up the vale from the east, and we all turned toward it.

Bolting across a distant ridge, its low and lunging shape silhouetted against the blue-gray sky, was a dog.

"Jessie?" said Old Red, sounding surprised and perhaps even disappointed that the mystery he was stewing on had apparently solved itself.

"Idiot," growled Josu.

He wasn't talking to my brother. He was talking about the dog.

It zigzagged awkwardly across the hillside, barking frantically. Not angrily, though. Joyfully.

The dog—more lumbering and clumsy than the graceful, poised border collie I'd pictured—was chasing a rabbit. Badly. As we watched, the rabbit drew further and further ahead until it could have stopped for a cup of coffee and a doughnut while waiting for the dog to catch up. Instead it just darted over the top of the knoll and disappeared, leaving its pursuer to plod hopelessly after it, now howling forlornly.

"So that isn't Jessie and it isn't the Phantom Puma of Elkhorn Peak and if I don't miss my guess it isn't Grover Cleveland either," I said. "So who is it?"

"Champion," Josu said with disgust.

"He's a champion, all right," Ann added. "Dumbest dog in the world."

"I see," I said. "And this 'Champion' just sort of roams the West in search of sheep to herd and rabbits to harass, is that it? Or does someone actually own him?"

Mr. Wendell jerked his stubble-covered chin at the rise the big dog was clumping over. "He belongs to the Pfeifers. Another sheep-ranching family. Their land abuts ours over that way."

"Champion's not very good at remembering where their property ends," said Ann.

"Or whose sheep are whose," said Josu.

I gave that a significant "Oh ho" of my own.

"He and Jessie ever tussle?" I asked. "He may be dumb but he looks big. And probably dangerous in a fight."

I almost added "It is a dog-eat-dog world, you know," but at the last second, I scraped up enough tact to shut my mouth after "fight."

Josu shook his head. "What you're thinking makes sense, but no. They never fought."

"Well, if they weren't enemies, were they..." I gave Josu a big wink. "...friends? Maybe the kind who'd wander off together for a time?"

Ann folded her arms and cocked her head. "I've helped raise sheep all my life, Big Red. You don't have to beat around the bush. Just ask if they were fornicating."

Josu's face flushed scarlet. Mr. Wendell turned away and pretended to admire some particularly puffy clouds. Old Red had drifted off to a spot about twenty yards ahead of us, so I couldn't see his expression. But the way his head jerked up made me think he was flinching. I *knew* I was.

"What? You don't like 'fornicating'?" Ann asked. "Please. It's in the Bible!"

"I would never allow Jessie to mate with a *norbera* like Champion," Josu told me. (I never did get an exact translation of "norbera," but I assume it's something you can shout the next time you get in an argument with a Basque.) "And if he'd come around the night she disappeared—for any reason—I would have known."

A final far-off howl echoed out from somewhere over the ridge.

"He's not quiet," Josu said.

Old Red turned toward the sound and scratched his chin for a moment. Then he crouched down to stare at another dark spot in the gully chewed up by footprints and hoofprints and sprinkled with snow and dung.

"Champion's people. The Pfeifers. They badgered by the cowboy crowd same as y'all?" he said.

"Of course," Ann replied. "They're sheepmen, like us. That's enough to get those sons of..." The girl cleared her throat and peeped over at her father, who'd ended (for the moment) his careful study of the clouds. "Those *brutes* on your back."

Old Red leaned to the side to look at something in the mud from a different angle. "And these Pfeifers got grit? Backbone?"

"I suppose so," Mr. Wendell answered slowly.

"I know so," Ann threw in. "Mrs. Pfeifer's got almost as much grit as *me*."

Old Red finally stood up. "So if y'all was to ask 'em for help handlin' Hoot Piney and the Turkey Foot boys, they'd give it?"

Mr. Wendell shrugged. "They probably wouldn't be thrilled about it, but I imagine they'd help us if we really needed them to."

"What are you thinking?" Josu asked my brother.

"That if any sheepman was gonna go onto a big cattle ranch —one with plenty of hands spoilin' for a scrap—he'd best have him some friends along," Old Red said. "Especially if he was gonna accuse them hands of sneakin' onto his land and messin' with his property."

"I knew it! Those censored abridged unprintables!" Ann exploded, unable to contain herself this time. "All right! Let's go get the Pfeifers and make those heavily edited expletives answer for what they've done!"

For just a fraction of a second—far too here-and-gone for anyone but me to notice—a little admiring smile puckered one corner of my brother's bristle-brush mustache.

"Sir," Old Red said to a wincing Mr. Wendell, "I'm gonna let you explain to the young lady that this is a matter for men and somebody needs to keep watch on your flock while we go collect the Pfeifers for a call on that cattle ranch."

"What? Old Red! No!" Ann protested, betrayed. "You can't make me miss the ending!"

"What I want you to miss," my brother told the girl, "is a bullet."

And with that he swept past her, striding swiftly back toward the Wendells' barnyard. Josu and I made a quick escape in his wake, leaving it to Mr. Wendell to placate Ann (or attempt to, anyhow).

An hour later, the four men of the matter—me and Old Red and Josu and Mr. Wendell—were rolling up to the Pfeifers' ranch house behind a trudging Heathcliff. I hopped out of the wagon bed before Mr. Wendell even pulled back on the reins out of fear each step hauling so much man-flesh was bringing the old horse closer to a heart attack. Old Red joined me as a bony little woman with frizzy white-streaked hair stepped out of the house wiping her hands on a rag.

"Will! Philip!" she called out. "Anthony Wendell and his Basque man are here! With…"

The woman eyed me and my brother suspiciously—squinting in particular at the gun belts we'd strapped on before setting out from the Wendells' place.

I smiled and tipped my hat to her.

She didn't smile back.

"…a couple strangers!" she finished.

"Mrs. Pfeifer," Mr. Wendell said to her. He nodded at me and Old Red. "These are—"

Two tall, thin men hurried out from around one of the barns. It was plainly father and son, for one looked like a gaunt, grizzled, gray version of the other. They were both dressed for winter ranch work, with heavy boots and splatter-covered coats, and thick, stained gloves.

"Mr. Pfeifer. Philip," Mr. Wendell said to them. "I was just telling Mrs. Pfeifer. These are the Amlingmeyer brothers. Gustav and Otto. They've come to help us with something, and we're hoping you can help, too."

Unlike his wife, Mr. Pfeifer greeted us with a big grin.

"Well, sure! Anything to help a neighbor," he said. "But why discuss it out here in the cold? Let's go inside and you can tell me all about it over coffee. Philip'll take care of your horse."

"That's mighty nice of you, sir," Old Red said. "But I think Josu here should keep ol' Heathcliff at the ready. After we explain the lay of things, we'll wanna be gettin' along quick before we lose the light."

Mr. Pfeifer nodded. "All right. Philip—you keep Josu company while I hear what this is all about."

"Sure, Pa," the man's younger reflection said as the rest of us headed for the house.

The interior was what you'd expect: a little roomier and fresher and tidier than the Wendells', but still the home of a hard-working, borderline poor ranching family. There were a few rough-hewn furnishings, faded and frayed pictures clearly clipped from magazines and calendars, and, propped in a corner, a long rifle that looked like it had passed through the hands of a dozen previous owners, the first serving under George Washington.

Mrs. Pfeifer headed to the kitchen at the back while us men stopped in the little parlor/dining room beyond the front door. The woman returned with two cups of steaming coffee just as Mr. Wendell finished explaining about Jessie's disappearance and the plan to confront Hoot Piney at the Turkey Foot ranch.

"Seems like a lot of fuss over a dog," Mrs. Pfeifer said as she handed one cup to Mr. Wendell, then the other to Old Red.

They thanked her as she turned and whisked back into the kitchen.

"Jessie's not just any dog," I said.

Mrs. Pfeifer just gave that a grunt.

"Mr. Wendell tells me you got two sons," Old Red said to Mr. Pfeifer. "I assume the other's out with *your* dog? Mindin' your flock?"

"That's right," said Mr. Pfeifer, who'd claimed a rocking chair in the corner when we came in. "But Philip and I can go with you over to the Turkey Foot, if you really think that's wise."

Mrs. Pfeifer returned with two more cups of coffee as the man spoke. She gave one to me—guests first, of course—then turned to pass the last to her husband. He leaned forward and started to reach his glove-covered hands for it, then changed his mind and waved the woman off with a muttered, "You have it, Laura."

"I'm inclined to agree with the missus, though," he went on to the men again. "It could get ugly. Is it really worth it? And what makes you so sure someone from the Turkey Foot messed with the dog anyway?"

"Well…" Mr. Wendell said uncertainly.

He turned to Old Red.

My brother tossed off another Holmes quote from "The Adventure of Silver Blaze."

"'I follow my own methods, and tell as much or as little as I choose. That is the advantage of being unofficial.'"

Mr. and Mrs. Pfeifer exchanged a puzzled look.

"Uhh…all right. If that's good enough for Mr. Wendell…" Mr. Pfeifer said.

"It is," Mr. Wendell said.

Mr. Pfeifer nodded, then lifted himself up out of the rocking chair with a groan, careful to keep his dirty gloves off the unvarnished oak arms.

"We'd best get to it, then," he said. "Before dusk sets in, like you said."

"Now this is what a feller likes to see," my brother said with a smile. "Neighbor standin' up for neighbor. Sir—thank you."

He stepped toward Mr. Pfeifer and offered the man his hand.

"Oh. No need to make a fuss about it," Mr. Pfeifer said. "Just trying to do the right thing."

He reached out to take my brother's offered hand.

Instead of clasping for a shake, Old Red grabbed Mr. Pfeifer by the wrist.

"What are you doing?" the man demanded.

"Followin' my own methods," my brother replied.

Mr. Pfeifer tried to jerk his hand back. But Old Red still had the steel grip of a drover. For years, he'd flanked calves and bull-dogged steers. He had more than enough strength to hold Mr. Pfeifer's arm in place with one hand while he stripped the man's glove off with the other.

"Well, well," Old Red said. "Will you look at that."

He let Mr. Pfeifer go, and the man stumbled back a couple steps—enough for me to see the scabby, raggedly round wound on his right hand.

Bite marks.

"I figured there was a reason you didn't take them filthy things off even when you brought us inside 'for coffee,'" my brother said.

He turned and stalked toward the front door.

"How dare you!" Mrs. Pfeifer hollered at him. "Get out of my house! Get off our land!"

"It...it was...it was Champion," her husband stammered. "He...he's...I was trying to...he killed a lamb, and..."

Mr. Wendell shook his head sadly. "Mr. Pfeifer, if that dog of yours had killed a lamb and bitten your hand, he wouldn't be alive now to chase rabbits, would he?"

Mr. Pfeifer had no reply to that. He just stared down at the scuffed floorboards, shoulders slumping.

"That's right! Go on!" Mrs. Pfeifer yelled at my brother as he opened the door and stepped outside. "Get out of here! All of you!"

"Stop it, Laura," Mr. Pfeifer said without looking up. "It's done."

It wasn't, though. Not quite.

"Josu," Old Red said to the young man waiting in the wagon, reins in hand. "Call her."

Josu wasn't confused or surprised by it. On the way to the Pfeifers' spread my brother had explained his real suspicions—as well as his wish to keep Ann away in case the Pfeifers made trouble if those suspicions proved true.

Yet young, gangly Philip Pfeifer made no move to stop Josu as the sheepherder lifted his right hand to his mouth, spread his lips with his thumb and forefinger, and cut loose with a series of shrill whistles. It sounded like a couple finches fussing at each other over a handful of seed.

The sound that came in response was no bird, though. It was muffled whimpering and scratching.

But no barking. Jessie was too well trained for that.

Mr. Wendell turned toward the sound as he and I joined my brother outside.

"She's in the lambing barn. Of course," Mr. Wendell said

"There'd be a nice, warm, private stall in there for her?" I asked him. "And her pups, when they come?"

The sheepman nodded.

"We were gonna let her go once we'd weaned the litter," Philip Pfeifer said.

Old Red and I shot skeptical looks his way.

"Really we were!" he insisted. "We just needed better dogs so bad, and we knew Josu would never let us breed her with Champion."

There was more whining and crying from the lambing barn.

"No. I wouldn't have," Josu said, seething. "She wasn't even in heat anyway. You were going to keep her in there for months?"

Philip looked down at the nearest rock as if he wanted to slither underneath it.

Old Red walked out to the wagon and took hold of Heath-cliff's bridle.

"Go and get your dog, Josu," he said.

Josu dropped the reins and hopped down, Philip falling into step beside him as he headed for the lambing barn.

"I'll help untie her," Philip said.

"Best leave that to her master," said Old Red. "Wouldn't want you gettin' bit like your pa." He swiveled to look back into the house. "When'd she get ya', Mr. Pfeifer? Not when you first grabbed her, I assume. Jessie may be trained to stay quiet, but I bet you hollered good and loud when she sunk her teeth in."

"It was the next morning. When I went to check on her in the barn," Mr. Pfeifer said. He heaved a resigned sigh. "I tried to pet her."

Old Red nodded. "And for that, you got a wound you had to keep hidden when we showed up. Couldn't take those dirty gloves of yours off when you came inside or to take coffee or to shake hands. That was when I—"

"Oh, just shut your mouth and get off our land!" Mrs. Pfeifer snapped.

Old Red shrugged. "All right, then."

He turned away to face the lambing barn.

I had a better sense of storytelling, though. Naturally.

"Ma'am," I said. "That is *not* how it works. You say, 'But how did you know we took the dog?' And my brother there says, 'Well, the first thing I noticed was the footprints—and how there didn't seem to be any.'"

"Shut up," said Mrs. Pfeifer.

"Josu told us he couldn't find any that didn't look like his own," I went on. "If cowhands had been out there, that wouldn't be the case. You know how cowboy boots are. Narrow toe and high heel. For fittin' through and stayin' snug against a stirrup."

"Shut up," said Mrs. Pfeifer.

"Speakin' of which, you know how cowboys feel about walkin' anywhere…and not just 'cuz them boots ain't made for it," I continued. "It's beneath their dignity. They wanna go somewhere —like way out into a sheepman's pastures—they do it in a saddle. Yet there were no hoof prints. Not big enough for horses, anyway. Plenty for sheep. And another thing—"

"*Shut up*," said Mrs. Pfeifer.

I held up a finger.

"Almost done," I said. "Dang…I lost my place."

"Shut up!" yelled Mrs. Pfeifer.

I snapped my fingers.

"Oh, yeah. The hands from the Turkey Foot," I said. "Them fellows wouldn't come all the way out there for a dognappin'. Not when they had a chance to poison Jessie with old corn dodgers. Nah. They would've just killed her. So that food was to lure her away from Josu. Get her guard down long enough to get a rope on her. Which probably wouldn't have worked at all if she hadn't already met the men with the food and seen that they weren't a threat...because they were the Wendells' trusted neighbors."

"Dammit, Henry—if you won't make him shut his mouth, I will!" Mrs. Pfeifer raged, stomping out of sight.

Her husband hurried off to intercept her.

"Laura!" he cried. "You leave that be!"

I started backing toward the wagon, remembering the long rifle in the corner.

"Tell me, Philip—your mother the type to do anything foolish?" I said.

"Well, 'borrowing' the Wendells' dog was her idea," the young man grumbled. "And she'll take potshots at any salesmen or tinkers or preachers who come by."

We could hear his parents scuffling and grunting and cursing now.

"I see," I said. "Mr. Wendell...?"

"Right."

He was already scurrying to the wagon.

"Josu!" he called as he hauled himself into the driver's seat. "Time to go!"

Once Mr. Wendell had the reins in hand, Old Red let go of Heathcliff's bridle and headed for the back of the wagon.

"I knew your damn mouth would be the death of me eventually," he said to me.

"I was just doing what you usually do!" I protested.

My brother gave that a "Feh."

As Old Red and I climbed into the wagon, Josu came jogging around the barn with a shaggy black-and-white shape at his heels. He pointed and said something in Basque, and his hairy companion—Jessie the sheepdog, of course—charged ahead and did a long, graceful leap that landed her in the bed beside us.

Once Josu joined him up front, Mr. Wendell snapped the reins, and we made our escape...at about one mile an hour. We could still hear Mr. and Mrs. Pfeifer arguing, and all of us in the wagon except Jessie watched their house grow smaller behind us with agonizing slowness.

"Maybe you should just get out and run," Philip suggested helpfully.

We all stayed put behind Heathcliff, though, and after what seemed like an hour or two, he managed to haul us out of range of the Pfeifers' rifle.

"Well, I hope you feel good about yourself," I said to Jessie. "All that fuss was over you, you know."

I reached out to pet her.

She bared her teeth and growled.

"That's gratitude for you," I sighed.

"Good dog," said Old Red.

Ann was about as grateful as Jessie at first. Though thrilled to see Josu's dog back safe and sound, she was furious at us for excluding her from the rescue party.

"I can't believe you lied to me!" she howled at us.

Old Red slouched like he was Jessie getting a "Bad dog!" (or whatever the equivalent in Basque would be) from Josu.

I reached into my coat pocket and pulled out an overstuffed envelope.

"'A piece of ragged paper was laid atop the body,'" I read out when I found just the right passage, "'and I could only make out the words scrawled upon it if I stepped closer.'"

"All right," Ann said. "Fair enough."

I went on anyway.

"'Beware the cougar who walks as man!'" I said.

"I said all right!" Ann fumed. "You made your point."

I suspect the girl might still be plotting her revenge, however. That evening, over the mutton and dumplings she prepared for our supper, she remarked upon the many curious and dramatic incidents of the day.

"It would make a fine story for John Watson," she said.

"It's going to make a fine story for *me*," I replied.

Ann smiled slyly.

"Or for whoever writes it up and sends it to a publisher first..." she said.

Which is why you've likely noted that my penmanship is sloppier even than normal. I had to write this fast, you see.

I respectfully suggest that you purchase and publish it with equal alacrity.

Your humble (and, I hope, exclusive) chronicler of matters Sherlockian out West,

O.A. Amlingmeyer

Ogden, Utah

January 29, 1894

BAD NEWS

Urias Smythe
Smythe & Associates Publishing, Ltd.
175 Fifth Avenue
New York, New York

Dear Mr. Smythe:

I am delighted to hear that my latest literary effort meets with your approval and look forward to seeing it printed with the usual Smythe & Associates panache. Admittedly, I would have preferred it had you kept the title I supplied, "The Double-A Western Detective Agency"—free advertising for our fledgling enterprise here in Ogden. But I will bow once again to your instincts as to the fickle tastes of the reading public. I won't dwell on the fact that I offered up the alternative you've chosen to use ("Cowboy Brothers Battle the New Mexico Death Baron!") as a joke to illustrate exactly the kind of title I *didn't* want. No, I shall not dwell on that at all—though I will perhaps take more care with the jokes I make in the future. (This would no doubt make my brother a happy man. Or a slightly less unhappy one, anyway.)

I wasn't idle while awaiting word on the new book. In fact, I had but a few days to work the cramps out of my writing hand before fate—with a little assistance from the United States Postal Service—offered fodder for a whole new adventure. The A.A. Western Detective Agency is still very much in need of clients, and a potential one had contacted our partner Colonel Crowe with a case that seemed right in my brother's line: A Colorado newspaperman had been stopped by a menacing, cloak-clad bandit who relieved him not of his valuables but of that morning's edition.

Old Red wasn't thrilled about the where of it: in Littleton, just below Denver and a long day of rail travel south of Ogden. The who, what, why, and how were enticing enough to coax him to the depot, though, despite his hatred of trains. When we stepped off in Littleton, he looked peaked and grumpy, but only slightly more so than usual, and I complimented him on how he'd weathered the preceding hours of shimmying and shaking.

"I suppose practice really does make perfect," I said. "Why, another dozen or so trips on trains and maybe you'll be able to ride one without looking like you're gonna upchuck."

I waited with bated breath to see which response this would get: icy silence or "Feh." I am not a gambling man, but I'd have staked my life savings ($345.23, thank you very much) on it being one or the other.

"Yeah…maybe," Old Red muttered, and he went striding off past the little snow-dusted depot building, carpetbag in hand.

I guess it's a good thing I'm not a gambling man.

I'd say I know my brother like the back of my hand even though it's another kind of backside he more often brings to mind. (The kind attached to a horse.) But as you'll no doubt recall from "Cowboy Brothers Battle the New Mexico Death Baron!" (née "The Double-A Western Detective Agency"), there's been a change in him of late on account of distressing news from abroad.

Not that the passing of my brother's hero, Sherlock Holmes, was news exactly. We've known Holmes is dead for almost a year now. But the recent publication of "The Adventure of the Final Problem" in *McClure's* stirred up all the old sadness and disappointment in Old Red. He used to hint that he had doubts about

Holmes's demise, his unshakable faith making it inconceivable that the great detective should be defeated by so mundane a thing as death. Dr. Watson's description of events in Switzerland, however, seemed to dash these last, pitiable hopes. I wouldn't have thought it possible, but Old Red's been even Old Reddier—yet at the same time less predictable—ever since.

When he reached the streets of Littleton, he headed for the first local in sight: a fortyish fellow in a beaten bowler and a ratty beaver coat staring down forlornly at the shoe that had been sucked off his foot by the deep muck of the thoroughfare. The man was standing on one foot while he held the other, shoeless one aloft. He seemed to be contemplating how to retrieve his buried brogan without plunging his stockinged foot into the cold brown mire. When he noticed our approach he gave us a smile as wobbly as his stance.

"Quite a predicament," he said. He had one of those accents that made it clear that wherever he hailed from it was well below the Mason-Dixon.

"Need a hand?" Old Red asked him.

"I am a firm believer in the necessity—the moral imperative, in fact—for every man to stand on his own two feet," he replied. "On the other hand, it's damn cold today." He lifted his shoeless foot a wee bit higher. "And this is my best sock."

"So that's a yes?" I said.

He nodded, though with a hint of wistful regret. "Indeed it is."

Old Red and I looked at each other.

"You're the one who volunteered," I said. "And you're dressed for it."

As usual, my brother was outfitted like the cowpuncher he used to be—Levi's, boots, sheepskin coat, Stetson. I, on the other hand, had attired myself town style, in a suit and topcoat and patent leather shoes, all of which I hoped to keep as filth-free as possible.

"Well…least you can do is hold the gent steady while I get to it," Old Red grumbled.

"It would be a pleasure."

I stepped close to the man and bent a bit at the knee—my frame being considerably larger than his (and most others)—so he could wrap an arm around me.

"Here you go, sir," I said. "A shoulder to lean upon."

"Thank you," he said as he got a grip on me. "Your kindness to a stranger warms one's heart on this frosty February day."

My brother squatted and eyed the hole in the mud. It looked to be at least half a foot deep, and the sides were slowly collapsing in on themselves, as if the street was literally swallowing the man's shoe.

Old Red sighed, reached in and started rooting around for leather.

"You gentlemen are brothers?" the man said as dark sludge slathered Old Red's hands and sleeves.

"Indeed we are," I said. "Whatever gave it away?"

I gave the man a smile, and he smiled back.

My brother and I look about as much alike as a weasel and a grizzly, but the flaming red hair we both sport (Old Red on his thick mustache to make sure no one misses it) is a dead giveaway we fell from the same family tree.

Old Red began tugging, but the muck refused to give up the shoe.

"Here on business?" the man asked.

"Correct again," I said.

"With whom, may I ask?"

"You already have asked," I could have pointed out. Such open inquisitiveness is considered impolite out here in the West, where a man's past is often something he'd rather leave in the East. Being in the detecting business, Old Red and I often have to push past such proprieties, but most folks prefer to respect them. Saves them a lot of pokes to the nose (or worse).

"We're…here…to see…Harvey…Beeler," my brother grunted as he wrestled with the street for possession of the shoe. "Of… *The*…*Littleton*…*Repub*—"

With a wet *shlorp*, the brogan popped free—and Old Red

plopped back into the mud. He sat there looking thoroughly disgusted for a moment, then heaved a sigh and held the shoe up over his head.

"*The Littleton Republican*. I see," the man said as he took the shoe. He peered at the brown glop inside it and seemed to stifle a sigh of his own. "Thank you."

Grimacing, he took his right arm from my shoulder and slipped his foot back into the shoe, plunging his "best sock" into slime after all.

Old Red pushed himself up and began wiping handfuls of sludge off the back of his pants.

"I was about to ask you for directions to the newspaper when we got sidetracked here," he said.

"Ah. Well. I wouldn't have told you…and I believe I still won't," the man said. He tipped his weather-beaten bowler. "With regrets. Might I inquire as to your names?"

Old Red and I gaped at him in surprise.

"I believe *I* won't tell you *that*," my brother said.

"Fair enough," the man replied, unoffended. "I shall describe you as 'mysterious, scarlet-maned strangers with gracious natures but poor taste in business associates.'"

He tipped his hat again and went teetering off, careful now not to set foot where it wouldn't hold his weight. It was a slow, laborious journey—and one intended to take him, it was clear, to the nearest saloon.

"Curious fella," Old Red said.

I nodded. "In more ways than one." I stepped back to make a full assessment of my brother's Levi's. They weren't a pretty sight. "Looks like we'll need to check into the hotel before we carry on with business. I can't imagine you want to set about deducifyin' lookin' like a mud pie."

"No, I reckon not," Old Red said. "At least the clerk'll tell us how to find the *Republican*."

And that he did, after my brother cleaned up. Littleton isn't what you'd call a metropolis—a hundred-ish buildings and six or seven times as many people—so it didn't take us long to find 2592

Main Street now that someone deigned to point us in the right direction. Inside the squat, rather shabby building were the offices, composing room and print shop of *The Littleton Republican*, all of them clustered around a pot-bellied stove at the center of one cluttered room. Three people were clustered there, as well: a balding, bespectacled fellow at a desk, a much younger man—little more than a boy really—leaned over a case of type, and a young lady closer to my own twenty-one years sitting primly before a composing table.

"May I help you?" the older gent asked as we walked in.

"We're here to help *you*, I believe," I said. "Would you be Mr. Beeler?"

"I am. And would you be the gentlemen from the A.A. Western Detective Agency?"

"We are," I said. "I'm Otto Amlingmeyer, and this is my brother Gustav."

Beeler regarded us guardedly. Though Old Red didn't look like he'd been dipped in chocolate anymore, he didn't look much like the average person's picture of a detective either, having merely traded one set of work duds for another. We've started to encounter folks who know of us thanks to our appearances in *Smythe's Frontier Detective*, but Beeler clearly wasn't an *S.F.D.* reader. Neither were his employees, who were appraising us with their own curious yet unimpressed gazes.

"Well…how do you propose to begin your work?" Beeler said.

"I'd like to hear the whole story, Mr. Beeler," said Old Red. "Your letter gave us the general idea, but if I'm gonna do you any good, I need to know the particulars. Every last one."

The young folks stole a quick glance at each other that suggested barely suppressed eye rolls. They'd already heard every last particular a hundred times, I gathered.

Beeler got up and walked to a stack of papers by the clunky-looking hand-operated printing press.

"It just so happens you'll find the whole story right here," Beeler said, patting the papers. "In this week's edition of the *Republican*."

He peeled off the top sheet and started toward us with it.

"I'd prefer to hear it direct from you, sir," Old Red said hurriedly. "So's I can pursue whatever questions I have as they arise, you understand."

Beeler stopped, looking like he *didn't* particularly understand. But I did—and felt foolish for not understanding sooner.

Old Red's got as good a mind as there is for making deductions. What that mind can't do, however, is read. And a case revolving around the doings of a newspaperman would be sure to rub his nose in it.

"My brother is quite the one for questions," I said. I held out a hand. "But I'll still take that paper, if you don't mind. It'll save me a lot of note-takin'."

Beeler started toward us again, still looking dubious. As he handed me the newspaper, I noticed that there was only printing on one side.

"Slow news day?" I said, nodding down at the blank side of the paper.

"We've only finished the front and back pages," Beeler explained. "We're working on the inside spread—pages two and three—now. They'll be printed on the blank side tonight, the sheet will be folded, and there you have it. A new edition of *The Littleton Republican*."

"We're learning things already," I said as I rolled up the paper and slipped it into the pocket of my overcoat.

"But I understand it's the *last* edition of the *Republican* we should be talkin' about," said Old Red.

Beeler nodded, then tapped a finger against his chin. "Where to begin, where to begin?"

"When you got near the bridge?" the boy suggested. He was still waiting for his voice to change, apparently, for his words came out so high-pitched and warbly he could've passed for a goldfinch.

Beeler frowned and shook his head. "Oh, no no no. That's too much in the thick of the things, Lawrence."

"You always say a story needs to grab people from the very beginning," said the girl.

"Yes, but these gentlemen don't need *grabbing*, Lucy. They need information. Context. The full picture."

"So begin when you started for the bridge?" said Lawrence.

Beeler threw the boy a scowl meant to discourage further suggestions. Which it did. When Beeler turned back to me and Old Red, he puffed out his chest and took hold of the lapels of his coat in the manner of a politician on the stump.

"*The Littleton Republican* was founded in 1891," he said.

Here came the context. Perhaps too much. I was just relieved the man hadn't started with "I was born in the log cabin my father built…"

"It was, at the time, Littleton's only newspaper, *The Littleton Independent* having failed during the panic of 1890," Beeler went on. "I came here with my Ramage press and my type and my extensive experience in journalism and printing from Ogallala, Nebraska, which had the opposite problem as Littleton. Namely, too many newspapers—none of which were doing me the courtesy of failing."

Beeler gave us a little smile.

I smiled back. Old Red didn't seem to, but who can truly say what goes on behind that walrus mustache of his?

"The *Republican* was quickly embraced by the community, and our subscription rolls swelled," Beeler said. "At our height, we had nearly five hundred local subscribers, two hundred more on our mailing list, and advertisers from far and wide."

Beeler beetled his brow, and when he continued his tone turned ominous.

"Then, inevitably, it came," he intoned. "*Competition.*"

"*The Littleton Democrat?*" I guessed.

"Precisely," Beeler said.

I threw Old Red a gloating grin and a waggle of the eyebrows. Like Mr. Holmes, he considers guessing the eighth deadly sin, yet every so often, I imperil my soul and cut loose with one anyway. Sometimes they're even right, which always calls for a hearty celebratory gloat.

My brother ignored it.

"When did this '*Democrat*' start up?" he asked Beeler.

"About a year ago. The editor just appeared in town one day, secured a storefront practically across the street from me, and began putting out papers. We release each new edition on Wednesday morning, so he picked Thursday morning for his. That way he could fill half of each issue copying—or denigrating—the stories I'd worked so hard to gather. Well, it had its effect. Local subscriptions started falling off, and before long advertising did, as well. Then things got even worse. More competition."

"*The Littleton…Progressive?*" I guessed.

"*The Littleton Populist*," Beeler said.

I snapped my fingers. "Shoulda known."

My brother resisted the urge for a celebratory gloat of his own.

"When did that paper get goin'?" he asked.

"About six months ago," Beeler said. "And what's worse, it was started by a local. A popular one. Littleton's postmistress, in fact. Subscriptions slid even further, and ad sales have been decimated. We still have a few local advertisers, thank goodness, but every single one from outside town disappeared. Our inside spread used to be awash in ads, and now I find myself filling it with poetry and dime novel balderdash so the pages don't go out empty!"

That did get me a little sidelong look from Old Red, but I maintained my dignity and didn't let on to Beeler that I'm a purveyor of dime novel balderdash myself.

"Which brings us to last week," I prompted Beeler to keep things moving along (past the balderdash).

"Yes. I suppose it does," Beeler said. "Exactly one week ago, I spent the entirety of the night tossing and turning about the dire straits I find myself in. The *Democrat* and the *Populist* have been draining me of readers, of advertising, of revenue. What to do? How to fight back? And fighting—taking up arms against my sea of troubles. That's what provided the key. As dawn arose over a new day, a new hope came to me. A dim one, but at least one I could act upon in the moment. I got up and dressed myself and came back here to set my plan in motion. Fort Logan is only thirteen miles off, on the outskirts of Denver. Well—soldiers read, don't they? That's a thousand could-be subscribers mere miles away! So I would head to the fort and distribute free copies of the *Republican*. Assuming the post commandant would permit such a thing. But I have it on good authority that Colonel Henderson is a loyal member of the Grand Old Party. If I showed him my paper —and its stanch defense of the War Department against the assaults of that corrupt and incompetent scoundrel Grover Cleveland—how could he refuse me?"

Beeler leaned back, looking pleased with his little speech. But then a sudden look of horror wiped away his satisfaction.

"You're not...*Democrats*, are you?" he said.

"We are not," I replied.

"Nor Populists?"

I shook my head.

Beeler grinned. "Ahh. So you are Republicans."

"We come from a family of Republicans, yes," I said. "But my brother and I prefer to remain unaffiliated."

Again, Beeler looked aghast—this time, apparently, at the notion that remaining unaffiliated was an option.

"Who we do or don't vote for ain't gonna change the data," Old Red said. "Facts is facts."

Now Beeler looked aghast and puzzled.

"Please continue, Mr. Beeler," I said, figuring it'd be a mercy to all of us to scoot around politics. "You came here figurin' you were headed to Fort Logan. And...?"

"And I grabbed some papers and headed to the livery to rent a buggy and horse for the day. The rest was in the letter. About half a mile outside town, I was—"

Old Red held up a hand. "What time was this? When you got you them papers?"

Beeler looked affronted—not that my brother should interrupt, I think, but that he should do so with such poor grammar.

"Around seven," he said.

"Usual for you to be up and about at that time on a Wednesday morning?"

Beeler looked even more affronted. "Of course! I'm not some layabout!"

The smirks Lawrence and Lucy shot at each other told a different story. I was sure Old Red caught it, yet he pressed on with his questions.

"And who'd you run across when you was bustlin' about in your usual industrious way?"

"Well, Lucy and Lawrence, of course. And——"

Old Red held up his hand again.

"What *now*?" Beeler snapped. For a newspaperman, he sure didn't seem to like questions.

"The young lady and the boy always in here that early?" my brother asked.

Lucy did the answering.

"Only on Wednesdays," she said. "My brother and I finish whatever printing remains to be done and then take copies out for delivery. Since the edition has been 'put to bed' at that point—finalized—there's no need for Mr. Beeler to be here that early."

She spoke in a calm, collected, confident way, with a coolness that bordered on coldness. I have to admit to being a bit stung that a lady my own age would be so obviously undazzled by the sight of me in my thirty-dollar suit.

"I see," Old Red said to her. "So Mr. Beeler can usually... catch up on his sleep that day?"

"Yes, yes—I suppose perhaps I do," Beeler cut in before Lucy could reply. "My apprentices are quite reliable. Indispensable, in fact."

He threw a patronizing smile at the young lady and her brother. Lawrence smiled back. Lucy didn't acknowledge the compliment at all.

"Who else did you see?" Old Red asked.

"A few townspeople going about their business, but that hardly matters," Beeler said. "The important thing is who could have seen *me*. As I mentioned already, the offices of the *Democrat* are right over there." He wagged a finger at the street behind us. "And I passed Agnes Johansson's place—that's the postmistress I told you about, the one who runs the *Populist*—on my way out of town. Either one could have spotted me heading north with a stack of newspapers."

My brother gave that an unhappy sort of "Hmm." Something about the "data" he was getting didn't sit right.

"What was the weather like?" he asked.

"The weather?" Beeler said. "Freezing cold. Gray. It snowed that afternoon. What difference does it make?"

Old Red shrugged. "Maybe none. So you get a half mile outside town, and…?"

"Oh. Right."

It took Beeler a few blinks to find his place in his story again. When he had it, he straightened up and put his hands back on his lapels.

"That is when the ruffian waylaid me. A ghastly apparition he was, clad in a flowing robe and a gunnysack mask. In his hand was a revolver…pointed straight at my heart! 'Stop or die, Beeler!' he thundered, his words sweetened with the syrup of the South yet bitter with hatred and resolve. I had no choice but to—"

Old Red held up his hand yet again.

"'Sweetened with the syrup of the South?'" he said.

Lucy did the translating.

"The man had a Southern accent," she explained.

"Oh," my brother said.

He looked over and give *me* a disdainful roll of the eyes, obviously thinking "Writers…"

"Well, when I heard that deep, gruff, *Southern* voice and saw him standing there in his dreadful shroud, I knew what was happening," Beeler continued. "The Ku Klux Klan had come for me!"

It's not often I see my brother shocked. You might recall that we've encountered men smothered in cheese, heads bouncing from trains and squirrels attired in tuxedos without him being what you'd call "thunderstruck." But the words "Ku Klux Klan" sure struck him hard.

"The KKK?" he said. "Your letter didn't say nothin' about *them*."

"I didn't think it needed saying," Beeler replied. "A man in a white robe threatening a Republican crusader. It's obvious, isn't it?"

"Well...no," I said. "Most folks would tell you the Klan was busted up twenty years ago. And I don't think they ever got seen much outside the old CSA. Certainly not sportin' them white robes some of 'em favored. Now, I know there've been rumors a few of 'em carried on, but—"

"Anyone send you any seeds?" Old Red cut in.

To him reports that the KKK wasn't altogether dead amounted to far more than "rumors," as they'd come from the pen of a writer he'd never roll his eyes at: Dr. John Watson.

"I beg your pardon?" Beeler said.

"Orange pips, to be specific. It used to be a sort of warning the Klan sent folks it meant to come after," I explained.

Beeler beetled his brow. "Really? I've never heard of such a thing. Why orange pips?"

Old Red and I looked at each other. It was a good question. One we had no answer for.

"Who can understand the ways of men who run around wrapped in bedsheets?" I said to Beeler.

"Yes, I suppose. But where'd you learn of this pip business? Have you had dealings with the Klan yourselves?"

Old Red and I looked at each other again. Fond as he is of Doc Watson's stories, my brother knew that citing "The Five Orange Pips" from *The Adventures of Sherlock Holmes* would *not* fill our client with confidence.

"No, we ain't run up against any Klansmen," he said. "But...a friend did once. A few years ago. Over to England. So they do get around still."

Beeler's eyes lit up. "I knew it! I *knew* it! There are people who've told me to my face they don't believe me. Who say what you did." He jabbed a pointed finger at me. "That the Klan's been gone these twenty-odd years and isn't coming back, and I must be making the whole thing up!"

"I didn't say you made anything up," I started to say.

Old Red cut me off somewhere around "didn't."

"We ain't disputin' you. Just askin' questions," he told Beeler. "Now if you could tell us the rest…? What happened after this fella stopped you…?"

"Yes. Of course. He climbed into the seat behind me—it was a surrey, you see—and ordered me to drive on. Well, I was terrified, of course. I assumed he wanted to be further from town when he shot me. But what could I do with his gun pointed at my back?"

"What kind of gun was it?" Old Red asked. "Anything special?"

"I don't know. He was too clever to let me get a look at it. Kept it under the sleeve of his robe."

I'm not sure if my brother gave that a skeptical look, but I know I sure did.

"It wasn't a stick or a pointed finger!" Beeler snapped at us. "I'm not a fool! It was a gun! He didn't hide it until he came up close!"

"Like I said, we ain't disputin' nothin'," Old Red said soothingly. "Anything else you can tell us about the man? Large? Small? In boots? Brogans?"

Beeler looked thoroughly disgusted, though with himself now rather than us.

"I don't know. He shocked me with his sudden appearance, then once he was behind me, I didn't dare turn around for another look. He was a man of average height and build with a Southern accent. That's all I can say. But it should be enough."

"Alright," said Old Red. "So there you were with this fella, gettin' farther and farther from town and expectin' a bullet in the back any second. And then…?"

"Then he told me to stop and get out. Which was when I was *really* expecting that bullet. But instead of shooting me, he climbed into the front seat and picked up the reins. 'You can go on spreading your Republican lies in Littleton, Beeler,' he said to me. 'But stay there…or else.' And he turned the surrey around and drove off."

"Back toward town," Old Red said.

Beeler nodded. "He left the buggy somewhere along the road. The horse eventually wandered home on its own. Naturally, Pickett, the liveryman, was concerned, so he came looking for me. We met on the road not far from where I'd been stopped. There was no sign of the Klansman."

"Howzabout them papers he took? Any sign of them?" my brother asked.

"No."

Old Red's gaze went glassy. "Interestin'," he muttered. "How many copies you have with you?"

Beeler shrugged, obviously oblivious (as was I) to whatever it was that made the newspapers' disappearance so "interestin'." "I didn't make an exact count. I'd just grabbed…oh, maybe fifty to take to Fort Logan."

Old Red held his left hand up before his face, the thumb and forefinger about an inch apart.

"Fifty newspapers," he mused, squinting at the space between his fingers. "Ain't a lot…but ain't a little."

Beeler squinted at *him*. So did Lucy and Lawrence.

"Umm…yes, I suppose," Beeler said.

My brother lowered his hand. "No one seen hurryin' in or out of town around this time?"

"No," said Beeler. "As I told you earlier, it was a cold, cold day. Freezing, in fact. People were staying indoors as much as possible. So—"

"No witnesses," I said.

Beeler nodded again—ruefully this time. "No witnesses."

"Which makes it easy for folks to be skeptical," said Old Red.

"Exactly. Are you familiar with the phrase 'publicity stunt'?"

"Sure," I said.

I almost added that we've been accused of them on occasion

ourselves, as not everyone believes what they read in *Smythe's Frontier Detective*. I kept that to myself, though.

"That's what some people say this is," Beeler said. "Pure fabrication designed to promote the *Republican*. Which is why I wrote Colonel Crowe. I covered some of his activities when he worked for the Southern Pacific Railroad Police. He's a good man—and a stanch Republican, I might add. He promised me two of his best operatives…and vindication."

Old Red scowled at the description of us as Colonel Crowe's "operatives." We're supposed to be his partners, yet he's taken to giving orders and we (after some bucking from my brother) always end up following them. But that was an argument for another day.

"Well, I ain't makin' no promises except that we'll see where the data takes us," Old Red said. "I reckon we'll start with the liveryman. Pickett."

Beeler's eyes went wide, and Lucy and Lawrence shot what looked like smirks at each other.

"Pickett?" Beeler said. "Why him?"

"'Cuz he knew you were takin' a buggy out of town with a bunch of newspapers. He a Republican, too? Or more inclined to the other side?"

"Oh, he's a Republican all right. A loyal subscriber," Beeler said with a strangely smug nod. "You'll find his livery on Low Street. Head left, then turn left again in two blocks. It's right by the corner. I don't think you'll be there long, though. The man you really want to see is Julius Horatio Riggs."

"Of *The Littleton Democrat*?" I guessed.

"Precisely," said Beeler.

I was two for three for guesses—not bad, I thought. But of course I got no credit from Old Red.

"Well, let's get to it," he grumbled, and back out to the gloppy, sloppy street we went.

It was so gloppy and sloppy out there, actually, a dray hauling beer barrels had become mired hub-deep. Several concerned citizens—moved to action, no doubt, by the horrifying prospect of undelivered beer—had waded into the mud to help free it. They were quickly filthier than my brother had been before his change of clothes, but all seemed to find the sacrifice worthwhile.

"A community pulling together toward a common goal," I said. "Uplifts the spirit."

Old Red just grunted. He was more interested in the young man who'd stepped outside on the opposite side of the street. He looked a bit older than Lawrence and was dressed, like him, in the manner of junior clerks: white shirt, black vest, bow tie. It might have been the fun with the beer wagon he'd come out to see, but he ended up staring—and quickly glaring—at *us*. Above him, painted across the false front of the building he'd come from, were these words:

THE LITTLETON DEMOCRAT
NEWS OFFICE • JOB PRINTING • STATIONERY
VITAM IMPENDERE VERO

"That fella across the street look like a 'Julius Horatio Riggs' to you?" I asked Old Red.

"Nope. Don't look ready to shave neither." He nodded up at the sign. "That say what I think it says?"

"More or less."

I read it out for him, including the "vitam impendere vero" part even though I had no idea how to pronounce it.

"What the hell's 'vee-tame impy-in-deer vee-row'?" Old Red said.

I shrugged. "Looks to be Latin. Probably one of them old Roman mottoes the high and mighty trot out to sound profound. Like 'Truth and beauty know no earthly master' or some such bunk. But for all I know, it means 'Toilet paper available at reasonable rates.' Shall I ask the whippersnapper?"

The young man was heading back in out of the cold—though he threw us one more glower over his shoulder as he stepped inside.

"He don't look especially inclined to answer," said Old Red.

"Probably saw us coming and going from the *Republican*.

Beeler was right about them having a front-row seat for whatever goes on in his office."

My brother gave that a neutral "Mmm" and carried on up the street.

"If the KKK really is up to its old tricks here, we'd best watch ourselves," I said.

Old Red just Mmm-ed again.

"Somebody hands you a buncha orange pips, you let me know," I said.

This finally got a real response.

"Shut up. I'm thinkin'."

"Mmm," I said.

Sidewalks thereabouts were a sporadic affair—in some places little more than rotting boards laid across muddy puddles, in others absent entirely. So it took us a few messy minutes to tramp our way left and then left again onto Low Street. As Beeler had promised, it was obvious after that second turn that we had reached our destination, for before us was a barn-like building that —unlike the office of *The Littleton Democrat*—put on no airs. There was but one word across the front.

LIVERY

We walked up and knocked—and soon learned why Beeler thought it so obvious that the proprietor was a Republican. The man who opened the wide door was fairly wide himself, being so squat and pot-bellied he was as close to a perfect sphere as a human being could get. He was also black.

"Pardon me," I said. "Would you be Mr. Pickett?"

"That's right. Can I help you?"

He had a deep, rumbling voice that was entirely unseasoned, I noted, by "the syrup of the South." And a sheet, should he choose for some perverse reason to cover himself in one, would hardly provide ample disguise for the man. It'd be like trying to hide a haystack under a handkerchief.

As usual, Old Red let me handle the preamble—introductions

and explanations as to our purpose—before cutting loose with questions.

"Beeler tell you why he was rentin' a rig that mornin'?"

Pickett nodded. "Sure. He was full of talk about all the new subscribers he was gonna get. Seemed to think it meant I should start paying for advertising in his paper."

The liveryman snorted and shook his head.

"You don't pay for it now?" Old Red asked.

"I don't have to. I've gotten free advertising the last four months. Well…'free' in that I don't give Mr. Beeler any cash for it. It's how he pays for taking out a horse and carriage from time to time."

"Ahh. Beeler said the *Republican* ain't doin' the business it used to. Guess he's havin' to get by on swaps and credit and such…?"

"Oh, I wouldn't want to speculate…but if you look at his paper these days, you might notice the only ads are for local businesses. A couple restaurants and the sundries store. And my livery, of course." Pickett gave us a significant look. "And the Eagle Saloon."

For a man who didn't want to speculate he was sure helping us do some.

"Beeler a regular at the Eagle?" Old Red asked.

"Well…it's probably not my place to say," Pickett replied. "But yes. He's there till closing every night."

"How about his whereabouts come mornin'? He just as predictable?"

"Far be it for me to note or judge another man's time of rising," Pickett said. "All I know is a liveryman has to be up and at 'em mighty early. A newspaperman, apparently, not so much."

"That also go for Mr. Julius Horatio Riggs of *The Littleton Democrat*?"

I was expecting a scowl at the mention of the name. Instead Pickett gave us a shrug.

"Mr. Riggs's comings and goings are none of my concern," he said. "I can only tell you those comings and goings never begin until noon and conclude nightly at a different saloon. The Fife and Drum. Beyond that I mind my own business."

Old Red and I gave each other a look. We'd already seen the Fife and Drum that day. And Mr. Julius Horatio Riggs, too, perhaps.

There was movement in the dim light of the barn beyond Pickett, and though it wasn't possible to see around the man—there being too much of him from side to side—I could get a look over top. A slender boy in a leather apron, perhaps fourteen years of age, was stepping out of one of the horse stalls with a shovel loaded with...well, what stable boys remove from horse stalls.

"You mention to anybody where Beeler was headed that morning?" Old Red asked Pickett.

The liveryman's expression turned wry, as if my brother had just offered him a pie made from the contents of the boy's shovel.

"Like my son Ben, you mean?" He jerked his head back at the lad, who was walking his load to a nearby wheelbarrow. "There was no need to tell *him*. He heard all of Mr. Beeler's big talk with his own ears. After that, he and I were too busy hauling out the surrey and hitching up the horse for idle chitchat with any townsfolk."

Ben dumped out the shovel and headed for another stall, watching my brother and me warily the whole time.

"And as soon as the buggy was ready, Beeler went straight on his way?" Old Red asked.

"That's right."

"Which direction?"

Pickett flapped a hand to the north. "Back to Main Street, then up the road toward Fort Logan."

Old Red nodded silently, pondering a moment. Such an awkwardly long moment, in fact, Pickett eventually turned to me with an expression on his face that said "This normal for him?" I shrugged in a way meant to say "Yes...unfortunately."

My brother finally returned to earth with no indication that he'd noted this back-and-forth at all.

"You ever see signs before this that you got the KKK around here?"

Pickett sighed in a way that suggested he'd have been happier if Old Red had stayed silent.

"No," he said, "though there are plenty of people who've made it plain they'd join up if they could."

"Readers of the *Democrat*?"

Pickett shrugged. "Readers of the *Democrat*, readers of the *Republican*, readers of the *Populist*, men who can't read at all." He coughed out a joyless laugh. "Hate is a great uniter."

"And Beeler rails against this hate in his paper, does he?"

"Not particularly. He rails more against the gold standard, free trade and women's suffrage. And Democrats in general." Pickett laughed again—this time with what seemed like real amusement. "And Julius Riggs in specific."

"You like Beeler?"

Pickett looked surprised by the question. I probably did, too. It didn't seem like the kind of "data" that would lead us to any Klansmen.

"That's the last thing I'll be asking, by the way," Old Red said. "Then we'll move along."

Answer me, and we'll leave, in other words. It proved an effective bribe.

"Beeler's all right," Pickett said. "Though he seems to think what the Republicans did thirty-something years ago means I owe him something now…and what the Democrats did thirty-something years ago means I owe him even more."

"And you don't agree?" I asked.

Both Pickett and my brother turned to glare at me.

"No one said *I* couldn't ask one more question," I pointed out.

Pickett put his hand on the door.

"I stay out of politics," he said.

He swung the door shut.

"I was doing fine till you opened your mouth," Old Red growled at me.

"You said you were done!"

My brother grunted.

"Good thing, too," he said.

He turned and stomped off. Or tried to. His usual stomp-off was hard to manage without solid ground to work with. He stopped stomping when it became obvious he'd just be splattering himself with extra mud.

"Let me guess," I said as I caught up to him with a few long, careful strides. "We are marching to the Fife and Drum."

His silence told me I was right.

After a few minutes of slipping, sliding, and sloshing, my brother was wiping the muck off his boots outside the Fife and Drum. I did the same for my brown Oxfords—while snaking a hand under my coat to check the shoulder holster holding my Webley Bulldog. By "check" it I really just mean "reassure myself fairies hadn't made off with it." It was a useless gesture but a comforting one, and I noticed that Old Red let his fingers brush the grip of the Peacemaker at his hip.

My brother can't read, but he knows the Confederate battle flag when he sees it. And the Fife and Drum featured one right over the bar where most saloons hang John Mulvany's "Custer's Last Rally," a mirror or a life-size painting of a naked lady. If the Ku Klux Klan really had had been born again in Littleton, this looked like its cradle.

The chatter of the bartender and his dozen or so customers faded away fast as we walked in. That made the one voice that continued ring out all the louder.

"And here they are at last! I told you they'd be along to see me eventually."

Seated at a corner table was the man whose shoe Old Red had rescued from being eaten by the street.

"Mr. Riggs?" I said to him. I leaned to the side to look down at his left foot. "We've come to check on your favorite sock."

He burst out laughing.

"It is muddy but unbowed, thank you. Much like myself," he said, voice drenched, as before, in Southern syrup.

Two men were seated at the table with him—one dressed in

formal but slightly shabby business attire, like Riggs, and the other a miner by the looks of him. Riggs glanced at each as he said, "Gentlemen, if you'll excuse us…? We'll continue our conversation later."

The men nodded grimly and shot us their best steely-eyed stares before picking up their beers and moving to another table.

Riggs held his hands out toward the seats they'd just vacated.

"Thank you, sir," I said as my brother and I approached.

"I would have no one accuse me of being inhospitable," Riggs said. He cocked an eyebrow. "In fact, I object to being *accused* of anything at all."

Old Red dragged one of the empty chairs a foot to the left before sitting. I did the same, only dragging mine to the right. That way we were nice and cozy on either side of Riggs—and didn't have our backs to the other customers.

"We ain't here to make accusations," Old Red said. "Just get information."

Riggs reached under his coat—prompting me to do likewise.

Riggs smiled and pulled out a notepad and pencil.

I smiled and pulled out nothing.

"I, too, desire information. It is, after all, my stock in trade as a newspaperman," Riggs said pleasantly. "Perhaps a little quid pro quo is in order…?"

Old Red might not be educated, but he knew what "quid pro quo" meant. It seemed to come up in our detectiving fairly regular. So he gave the right answer when one is proposed.

"Fine. I go first."

Riggs agreed with a nod and another smile.

"Where was you last Wednesday mornin' when Harvey Beeler was gettin' set to drive out of town?" Old Red asked him.

"In bed asleep—as my dear wife can confirm," Riggs replied. "What are your names and who do you work for and where did you come from and do you intend to persecute innocent Littleton citizens based on the outrageous claims of a known drunkard?"

Old Red snorted.

"That's a lot of quid for our little quo," I told Riggs. "Here's what I figure you're owed: I am Otto Amlingmeyer, and this is my brother Gustav, popularly known as 'Big Red' and 'Old Red.'"

Riggs began scribbling in his notepad.

"A-M-L-I-N-G-M-E-Y-E-R," I told him.

I turned to my brother and held out a hand, signaling him to go for another "quo."

"Anybody in your newspaper office when Beeler went by?" he said.

Riggs set down his pencil. "Yes, actually. My assistant, Robert Bell, was getting things set for the day's production. I didn't arrive until around eleven, when all the excitement was already over. Now...who do you work for and where are you from? Surely you can't object to those two 'quids' as one, entwined as they are."

"No objection at all," I replied before Old Red could. "We are partner-operatives of the A.A. Western Detective Agency of Ogden, Utah. Thorough investigations and guaranteed results. Send inquiries to the Ogden Chamber of Commerce Building, room 303."

I couldn't help noticing that though Riggs had picked up his pencil again, he stopped writing after "Utah."

"Y'all got the Klan around here?" Old Red asked him.

In an instant, all the smug amusement left Riggs's face. The other men in the saloon had been trying to cover their eavesdropping with low, listless conversation, but they stopped pretending now, and some turned to glare openly at us.

"General Nathan Bedford Forrest disbanded the Ku Klux Klan in 1869," Riggs said.

"And it carried on after that, only even more in secret than before," said Old Red.

Riggs picked up his pencil and pressed the lead to the paper so hard I was surprised it didn't snap.

"I ask again," he said. "Do you intend to persecute innocent men based on the ludicrous and offensive slanders of a drunken Republican?"

Old Red slowly shook his head.

"You still owe me a straight answer, Mr. Riggs," he said. "Are there any Klansmen here?"

"No. Not one," Riggs spat. "*Because the Ku Klux Klan no longer exists.*"

He eyed my brother angrily—as did everyone else in the place other than me.

Old Red met Riggs's gaze with steady, stubborn skepticism.

"Well, looks like we're back in your debt, Mr. Riggs," I said. "So to answer your question: no. We're not here to 'persecute' anybody. We follow the facts and stop when we get to the truth. It's never a straight line, but we don't make detours on purpose. And we certainly don't step off the trail to grind any axes."

Riggs started off ignoring me. But when he heard "We follow the facts and stop when we get to the truth" he jerked his head my way. As I went on he actually began to smile. By the time I was done he'd picked up his pencil and gone back to scribbling.

"You have an amusing way with words, Amlingmeyer. I only hope you mean them," he said. He set down his pencil and turned his full attention to me. "Do you know the phrase 'vitam impendere vero'?"

"Not intimately," I replied. "But I do believe it's the motto of your newspaper...?"

Riggs's little smile turned into a grin.

"Indeed! It's attributed to the Roman poet Juvenal. There are various ways to interpret it, but the most common is 'to devote one's life to the truth.' That is what I have always done. If there is deceit in this web you've come to untangle, it wasn't spun by me."

It was obvious who Riggs was accusing of spinning deceit. And rather like our client as he told his tale, Riggs did so in the pontifical tones of a politician addressing his constituents. Which Riggs was, to some degree. The other men in the saloon— Democrats all, I assumed—nodded and mumbled their agreement.

Yet Old Red looked unconvinced.

"Be that as it may," he said, "I got one more question for you."

The grin left Riggs's face.

"Well, I'm afraid you're out of luck," he said. "For *I* have no more questions for *you.*"

"Surely you can give us one answer on credit, Mr. Riggs," I said. "In the spirit of devoting one's life to truth?"

Riggs looked at me, searching for sarcasm. I stared back at him placidly and resisted the urge to bat my eyes.

At last he gave me an indulgent nod, a bit of his smile returning. Me he liked.

"What kinda gun you own?" Old Red asked him.

Riggs gestured down at his sides. "As you see, I don't carry a gun."

I gave him a gently chiding look.

That's not an answer, it said.

"But," he went on, "I am not without the means of self-defense. There is another way to interpret 'vitam impendere vero,' gentlemen. Not devoting one's life to the truth, but staking one's life upon it. And indeed a man in my line must be prepared for the outrages—even the murderous attacks—of ruffians and radicals. Which is why I keep a Colt's Dragoon revolver in my office. It was carried by my own father in the late unpleasantness between the states. He used it in the pursuit of his principles, as I use it now in the protection of mine...and myself."

Riggs picked up his half-empty glass of beer—ignored since Old Red and I walked in—and took a dainty sip.

"And now, if you'll excuse me, I find all this conversation has left me rather parched," he said.

He took another sip and said no more.

I rose and tipped my bowler to him. "We'll leave you to your hydration. Good day."

"Good evening," Riggs replied. For indeed the afternoon was waning, and the light outside had gone gray.

Old Red sat silently as Riggs took another little nip, pinky pointing out to the side in the style of a dignified lady at tea time. Then he stood and stalked out. I followed, offering a friendly nod to the barman, who was watching us leave with a distinctly *un*friendly scowl on his face. Maybe it was because we'd conducted business in his saloon without ordering so much as a sarsaparilla, but I doubted it. It wouldn't explain why every other man in the place was glaring at us, as well.

"Well, brother," I said once we were slogging through the muddy streets again, "I don't know for certain what *The Littleton Democrat* is going to say about us in its next edition, but I get the feeling it won't be a ringing endorsement."

"At least he'll spell our names right," Old Red muttered.

"Yes. I saw to that. Did my best to smooth down all the feathers you was rufflin', too. But you couldn't seem to stop your rufflin'."

"Some men you gotta ruffle if you want answers."

I let that suffice...for a few seconds. But the more I thought about it, the more I saw through it.

"Nah," I said. "You just didn't like him. What was it? He remind you too much of me?"

"He reminded me too much of Uncle Jürgen and Uncle Uwe and Uncle Hans. The whole damn place did."

That I let suffice and stay sufficed.

Our dear old Mutter never got over the loss of her brothers in the war to preserve the Union. Jürgen died at Chickamauga. Uwe was taken by cholera somewhere in Louisiana. And Hans starved to death at Andersonville. Old Red and I hadn't even come into the world before they'd all left it, yet our mother's stories kept them alive for us. Her hatred of Democrats she kept alive, too. But my brother and I didn't take on that particular family hand-me-down. How could we when half our friends on the cow trails had been Texas Democrats with rebel pappies?

Friends or not, though, even the proudest son of the South had known to watch his words around a couple Kansas boys like us, and the late unpleasantness was something drovers usually tiptoed around when jawing by the campfire. But that Confederate flag in the Fife and Drum had done no tiptoeing. It had marched up and spat in my brother's eye.

I looked back at the saloon. One of the customers—the rough-dressed fellow Riggs had been speaking to when we showed up—had stepped outside to either get a breath of fresh air or practice his menacing stares. On us. Which he was doing, breath of fresh air or not.

I saluted him. He returned the favor—though, unlike me, he limited himself to a single finger.

"How do you think he'd look in a sheet?" I asked my brother.

He glanced back at the man.

"Silly," he said. "But it might suit him."

"Seems like you could say the same for plenty of folks around here. Plenty of loyal readers of *The Littleton Democrat*, anyway. Gives us a lot of ground to cover. Speakin' of which…where the hell are we goin'?"

"Let's find out," Old Red said, and he veered off toward the nearest doorway.

It opened into a butcher's shop, and my brother asked the bloody-aproned man inside where one might go to post a letter. The butcher jabbed his cleaver to the right and told him to follow Main Street till there was no more Main Street to follow. The last house on the left belonged to the postmistress. But we'd best hurry. She was a real stickler about closing time.

The emphasis he put on *stickler* suggested he would have chosen another word around men he knew.

We thanked him and carried on to see the stickler.

Just as the butcher said, her house was the last in town, though Main Street didn't exactly end there. Instead it transformed itself from a muddy, chewed-up avenue into a muddy, chewed-up trail that swooped off into trees and hills to the northwest. It was certain to be a quiet neighborhood except of a Sunday morning, for the nearest buildings were two churches squared off against each other like gunfighters on the cover of a *Smythe's Frontier Detective*. Abutting each was a graveyard, one presumably well-sown with Presbyterians, the other with Methodists. It made for gloomy walking in the twilight hours, so I did as one is supposed to in such situations: I began whistling. Just in case someone from the Fife and Drum was following us it was "The Battle Hymn of the Republic." My brother shot me an "Oh, stop it" before I reached the first "Glory, glory, hallelujah."

We were walking up the path to the house by then. At first glance there seemed to be nothing unusual about the place—two stories, whitewashed wood, gabled roof, clean windows—except for the words "POST OFFICE" painted over the four-panel door. As we moved close, though, we noticed a peculiar decoration on the porch. A brick sat on the doormat, a lone envelope pinned beneath it. I pointed down at it.

"I do hope there's more to the post office than that," I said.

Old Red rolled his eyes. "We're just here after closing is all."

We stepped onto the porch, one of us to each side of the brick, and my brother jerked his chin at the door.

"Give 'er a knock," he said.

"Why don't you give 'er a knock?"

Old Red shrugged.

"You're better at openin' doors than me," he grumbled.

I wasn't going to argue with a compliment. I gave the door a knock.

"It's after five!" someone called out from inside. The voice was gruff and rumbly but definitely belonged to a woman.

"Sorry about that!" I called back to her. "But we need to speak to you, ma'am!"

"Post office opens at eight! This is just a house now!"

I could hear bustling footsteps on creaky floorboards, but they didn't approach the door.

"I do apologize," I said, "but we need a couple minutes of your time, if you please!"

"I *please* to fix myself supper and attend to post office business during post office hours!"

The footsteps continued. The conversation did not.

I looked over at my brother. He was glowering at me in a way that said he wanted to take his compliment back.

I held up a hand and turned back to the door.

"We aren't here to see the postmistress, ma'am!" I said. "We're here to see the publisher of *The Littleton Populist!*"

The footsteps stopped. When they started again a moment later, they grew steadily louder before stopping again on the other side of the door.

"News, advertising, or complaints?" the woman said.

"News," I replied.

"What kind of news?"

"About what happened to Harvey Beeler."

The woman's snort was so loud it was a wonder it didn't blow the door down like the Big Bad Wolf huffing away after a pig.

"Beeler's brought in a couple detectives to investigate," I went on.

"Oh, yeah?" the woman scoffed. "How do you know?"

"We're them."

The door swung open. Standing before us now was a stout, sixty-ish woman in a white frock dress so shapeless and plain it could've been knit from old flour sacks. She looked us up and down with obvious skepticism but didn't slam the door shut again.

"What do you want with *me*?"

"We just need to ask a few questions," I said, doffing my bowler. "I promise we won't keep you from your supper long."

As I spoke, my brother gave the lady a quick tip of his Stetson to show he wasn't raised in a barn despite dressing like he worked in one. A look of shocked wonderment came over the woman's face when she saw his red hair.

"I don't believe it," she said. "You're Big and Little, aren't you?"

"Umm...true," I said. "I suppose that can't be denied."

The lady pointed at our heads. "The detectives, I mean! With the red hair!"

It was our turn for shocked wonderment.

"Why, yes! That's us alright!" I said. "Big and Little Amling-meyer, at your service."

"Little" shot me a glare as the woman stepped back and swept an arm out toward the room beyond her.

"Well, get in out of the cold, you two!" she said.

When we started toward her, her already deep (for a woman) voice dropped an octave.

"But don't track any mud in here."

"Of course," I said. I gestured at the brick. "Seems you've got a late drop-off."

The woman looked down with an irritated frown. When she saw the envelope, she snatched it up and shoved the brick to the side.

"Well, come on," she said as she straightened up and stepped back inside. She jammed the envelope into a pocket of her dress without looking at it. "Let's not let in any more cold air."

"Yes, ma'am."

I quickly wiped off my feet, then Old Red did the same.

"How is it you know of us?" I asked as we came inside.

"A lot of magazines pass through here," the lady said. She shut the door and moved past us toward the hearth, which was putting out a cozy warm glow. "Sometimes they even fall open while they're being sorted."

"Ahh. So you've had a *Smythe's Frontier Detective* or two 'fall open' on you."

The woman shrugged. "Sorting is boring."

I gave that another "Ahh." What I could've said, though, was "So I see." Sorting was *so* boring, it seemed, Littleton's postmistress could barely make herself do it. Aside from a tall, broad bank of cubby holes blocking one wall, the place looked like a nice, normal home—except with every table, chair, and footstool covered with envelopes, magazines, and packages. They were even piled up precariously on the mantelpiece.

The lady could see what we were thinking as we took the place in.

"The Littleton post office burned down a year ago," she said. "That's part of the reason I got myself appointed postmistress. The man who used to have the job was as careless with our mail —particularly our money orders, if you follow—as he was with his kerosene heater. Things are run differently now, and at eight a.m. sharp all this"—she waved a hand at the clutter around us—"will be exactly where it's supposed to be, ready for pick-up. It's impossible to keep up during the day, that's all."

"I'm surprised you have time to do all that and put out a newspaper, Mrs....Johannson, I believe we were told?" Old Red said.

"You can call me Agnes," the woman said. She gave my brother a sidelong squint. "You're the smart one, aren't you?"

I tried not to look offended.

"I prefer to think of him as the better guesser," I said.

Old Red *did* look offended.

"Well, I'll let you in on a secret, Little," Agnes said to him. "I don't take newspapering very seriously. Not like I do postmistressing. I just started the *Populist* because the *Republican* and the *Democrat* were annoying me so much with all their feuding. They've done everything they can to divide this town, and I finally got sick of it. And you know what? I put out an issue every two weeks-ish and it's mostly recipes and gossip and gardening tips, and I *still* have more advertisers than Beeler and Riggs combined!"

She snorted out a laugh, then turned her attention to me.

"You get a cut of the ad money from that magazine you write for?"

"No, ma'am. Lump sum up front and that's it."

Agnes shook her head. "Too bad for you. Ads—that's where the money's at."

I made a mental note to ask my publisher about profit-sharing in some subtle yet hopefully persuasive way. Maybe I could even work it into a story somehow...

Agnes turned back to my brother.

"So—what do you think? Beeler make it all up or what?"

Old Red looked a bit taken aback. He was used to asking blunt questions, not answering them.

"I ain't got it figured one way or another yet," he said.

"But of course we believe Mr. Beeler," I threw in.

I shot my brother a warning look. The last thing the A.A. Western Detective Agency needed was its most famous operative casting doubt on our own client in a newspaper—even if the newspaper in question came out "every two weeks-ish" and was mostly recipes.

"You got some reason to doubt the man's story?" Old Red asked Agnes.

"No. I suppose not," she admitted reluctantly. "It could be true. Beeler's certainly got some folks around here mad enough at him."

"Democrats, you mean? Or Klansmen?"

The woman scoffed. "There you go!" she said, jabbing a finger at us. "There's a reason to doubt! There's no Ku Klux Klan around here."

"Begging your pardon, but how can you be so sure?" I said. "It is supposed to be a secret organization."

"So secret I'd never hear a thing about it? So secret the local postmistress wouldn't see a single sign?" Agnes shook her head. "No. That's hogwash."

"So let's say it wasn't a member of the KKK, strictly speaking," Old Red said. "It could be someone who used to be. Some fella who pulled his old Klan get-up out of mothballs when he saw a chance to put a scare in Beeler. *That* sound like anybody you know?"

"Maybe," Agnes said begrudgingly. "I don't know why someone like that would've waited to catch Beeler out on the road in his old robe, though. Not when Beeler's always stumbling home in the dark of night in no condition to defend himself, if you know what I mean. You want to put a scare in the man, why, he gives you plenty of opportunities to do it with no witnesses."

My brother looked chagrined in a way I recognized. I managed to make him look that way myself every once in a blue moon.

The lady had made a good point.

Old Red puckered his lips as if fighting to keep a sigh from escaping, then changed tack.

"All right...let's take the politics out of it. Anyone else around here with a grudge against Beeler?"

"Sure—enough to keep you here weeks if you want to talk to

them all. It's not just Republican versus Democrat anymore thanks to him and Riggs. Everything's a fight. You've got the rebuild-the-post-office-at-the-old-location faction against the build-a-new-one-on-Main-Street crowd. You've got the Welsh miners against the Irish miners, and both sides against the Mexicans. There's even been fistfights over whether Littleton should license dogs. And always Beeler and Riggs are egging on one side or the other. Why, when Beeler went and hired the Presbyterian minister's kids to be his assistants as a way to butter up the man's congregation, Riggs ran out and hired the Methodist minister's kid to be his. And what started as boasting and butt-kissing in the paper for one flock slowly turned into impugning and insulting the other, until now they can't even let Sunday services out at the same time for fear all those god-fearing Christians will start shouting obscenities at each other. And all that's leaving out the people Beeler owes money to now that his advertising's drying up. I think the only thing keeping him afloat are print jobs—and his most steady work comes from me for printing the *Populist*!"

As the woman spoke, my brother's expression changed. He didn't just look chagrined by the time she was done. He looked like he needed a fainting couch. In one conversation we'd gone from a handful of suspects to a townful, maybe a countyful. It would take forever to look into everyone who disliked our client— and even if we got lucky and caught the "Klansman," it was becoming painfully obvious Beeler couldn't pay us for it. We'd come to Littleton in pursuit of a highwayman and ended up chasing a wild goose. For free.

Old Red cleared his throat and made an effort (unsuccessfully) to look less depressed.

"Just two more questions for you, ma'am," he said. "Postmasters—and mistresses—are appointed by the federal government... which is mostly run by Democrats since Grover Cleveland got in again. So how is it the publisher of *The Littleton Populist* is picked for the job?"

Agnes smiled and narrowed her eyes. "That's a very good question. There *is* more to you than appearances would suggest."

"I try to make all my questions good," my brother grumbled.

"Unlike his appearance," I added.

Old Red cleared his throat again.

"And your answer to my 'very good question'?" he prompted the lady.

"Is that my late husband was the chairman of the Arapahoe County Democratic Party—and I was a loyal member, even though the state didn't give me the right to vote until last year. I turned Populist for various reasons...the biggest being that Littleton already had a Democratic paper."

Agnes leaned forward and dropped her voice as if confiding a secret.

"Plus Julius Riggs is a pompous ass," she added in a syrupy fake-Southern accent.

"We noticed," I whispered back with equal syrup.

"Alright...one more thing and we'll let you get to your supper," Old Red said (with no sweetening on his voice, of course). "As I understand it, Beeler went right by here on his way out of town the morning he was waylaid. You see him? Or anyone tryin' to get ahead of him?"

Agnes shook her head. "Wednesday mornings are busy for me. I mean—they're *all* busy, but Wednesdays and Thursdays in particular. First thing Wednesday I've got the Lawrence kids picking up the mail for the *Republican* and dropping off a couple hundred copies for their out-of-town subscribers. Then eight a.m. Thursday, it's Bobby Bell coming by to do the same for the *Democrat*. Plus you've got the first mail run coming in on the train from Denver every day at 7:25. I pay Ben Pickett—that's our local liveryman's boy—a nickel to bring it to me soon as it's dropped off. So between sorting the incoming and stamping the outgoing I can barely look up, let alone out the window, till lunchtime."

My brother took all this in with a hangdog expression that told me exactly how close to a solution we were: nowhere near. It was a good thing Littleton's one and only hotel was comfortable, because we were going to be there a while...if, that is, we even stayed to see the case through. Being stumped isn't much fun. Being stumped and stiffed is less.

"I see," Old Red said glumly. "Well...I guess that's that. Thank you for your time, ma'am."

He tipped his hat to Agnes, and I did the same.

"One more thing for you to chew on, Little," the lady said as she walked us to the door.

"Yeah?" my brother said hopefully.

"Before you leave town, come back so I can do an interview. A *Populist* exclusive. I'll make pie."

Old Red sighed.

"We'll see," he said. "Good night, ma'am."

The lady opened the door for us, and a frigid gust of wind told us of the cold, muddy slog that lay ahead.

"Remind me, brother," I said when we were about a dozen slip-sliding steps into it. "We ever hear about Sherlock Holmes having to so much as put on galoshes? Seems to me most of the time he could've cracked the case in his slippers and bathrobe. And did."

"What's your point?" Old Red growled.

My left foot disappeared into a sinkhole.

"Who says I gotta have a point?" I said. "I'm just jealous."

I'd just managed to extract my foot (and, thankfully, its attendant shoe with it) when Agnes's front door swung open again, sending a stripe of light stabbing into the night.

"Little! Big! Wait!" the lady called from the doorway.

"What is it?" my brother said as we turned to face her. "You remember something important?"

"No. I've got something for you. General delivery."

She held up her right hand. It was holding an envelope.

We fought our way back to her, and she handed the envelope to me. (Though the lady couldn't remember our real nicknames, she at least seemed to recall that Old Red can't read.)

At first glance, the envelope seemed like nothing special: plain white paper, standard five-by-seven size. Its sides bulged slightly, though, as if it held not a neatly folded letter but a few pebbles or dried peas. Written across the front was this:

O. and G. Amlinmeyer
Detectives

I read that out loud for my brother's benefit.

"Left out the 'g' in 'Amlingmeyer,'" I added.

"Good thing you two were just here or I would've had no idea what to do with it," Agnes said. "Would've ended up in our dead letter office…also known as my storm cellar."

"Where'd it come from?" Old Red asked.

"You saw yourselves. It was right here on the porch when you two showed up."

"That's what was under the brick?" I said.

"That's right."

Agnes looked down at the envelope expectantly, obviously eager for me to tear it open and give her another "exclusive" for the *Populist*.

I flipped the envelope over and started to dig a finger under the sealed flap.

Old Red grabbed me by the wrist.

"We've taken up enough of the lady's time," he said. "We can give that a look back at the hotel."

"Really, it's no bother!" Agnes blurted out. "You boys go ahead and open your letter!"

My brother plucked the envelope from my hand and gave the lady a little smile.

"Thank you, but I wouldn't dream of it," he said. "Just look at all the cold air we're lettin' into your house. You have a nice night, now, and we'll see if we can't pop by for that interview another time. Come on, 'Big.'"

And he turned and trooped back into the gloom.

"Well…good night again," I told Agnes.

She looked like she was about to cry. There'd been an "exclusive" literally on her doorstep, and now it was walking away. The lady might have dismissed the *Populist* as recipes and gossip, but she was truly a newspaperwoman at heart.

It was hard to tell in the dark (and with his mustache in the way), but when I caught up to my brother, it looked like he was still smiling.

"You and I both know what's in that envelope," I said.

"Yup."

"So why do you look like the cat that ate the canary and the Christmas goose to boot?"

"Do I?" He puckered his lips and gave me his usual beetle-browed glower. "This better?"

"Well, it ain't pretty to look at it, but it is more fittin'."

I scanned the nighttime town. We were walking between the two churches—and their cemeteries—while up ahead were darkened buildings offering plenty of corners to hide (and watch and wait) behind.

I reached under my coat and gave my Bulldog a pat.

"If we're right, we're bein' threatened," I said. "By someone or someones who know who we are and that we're on their trail. Heck, they got ahead of us on the trail. Enough to bushwhack us, maybe. And there you are smilin' again."

"I am?"

He was.

"Guess I can't help it. When we walked outta that house, I didn't have squat." Old Red lifted the envelope and gave it a flap. "And now we been handed our best clue yet—special delivery."

"'Our best clue yet'? How you figure that?"

My brother shrugged. "You know The Man's methods. Apply them."

So I did. But even when we got back to our hotel room and Old Red opened that envelope and shook out exactly what we expected to see—five little white-yellow seeds—I couldn't think like "The Man" (a.k.a. Sherlock Holmes) straight enough to steer me to any answers. Rather than point me in the right direction, my brother just stretched out on the bed and put his Stetson over his face.

"Guess that means I'm takin' first watch," I said.

"I got deducin' to do," said Old Red.

"Oh, is that what you're up to? Looks more like you got sleepin' to do…and with a band of Klansmen liable to bust down the door any second."

My brother tapped the crown of his hat. "Shhh. There's thinkin' goin' on down here."

"I'll remember that when the snorin' starts. Or the shootin'. I'll try not to let my dyin' distract you. You just go on deducin' right up to the second the Klan kills you, too."

"Feh," said Old Red. That meant "Good night." And "Shut up."

There was no snoring or shooting or dying that night, as it turned out. Not unless I did some log-sawing after I nudged Old Red and told him I was turning in somewhere round about 1. When I awoke I found him sitting beside me on the bed leafing through a magazine in the bright morning light. I lifted my head off the pillow to see which one.

It was the December *McClure's*—the issue with The Man's latest case, "The Final Problem." It was nothing new for my brother to revisit a Holmes story without me to read for him. He liked looking at the illustrations, too. "Gives me a better feel for him and Doc Watson," he said. "So's I know what to picture when I'm hearin' the words." I was a little surprised he'd chosen that particular tale to peruse, though. It wasn't just Holmes's latest case but his last—the one he could only close by going head over hills off a cliff in the arms of his archenemy. My brother had been down in the mouth about it for weeks now.

I let my head drop back onto my pillow.

"Don't go back to sleep," Old Red said.

"I won't. I'm wide…awaaa…"

At this point I *definitely* started snoring.

My brother gave me a shove.

"Ke!" I said.

Old Red leaned over to show me what he'd been looking at in the magazine. To my surprise, it wasn't H.C. Edwards's illustrations. It was a page of advertisements. Not the full- or half- or quarter-page ones with illustrations all their own. These were the teeny print-only ones, like classifieds—the ads they squeeze into boxes about two inches by two with letters so small you practically need Mr. Holmes's magnifying glass to read them.

"What's that say?" he asked, tapping one.

I squinted at it until the letters came into focus. (You try reading the fine print in a magazine ad before you've had your first cup of coffee.)

"'Easy to learn, easy to write, easy to read. McKee's shorthand taught by mail. Send for details: McKee Publishing Company, Ellicott Square, Buffalo, New York.'"

I turned from the magazine to my brother.

"If you're thinkin' of becomin' a secretary, I got some bad news for you," I said.

"And this one," he growled, tapping another ad.

"'Telegraphy. Unsurpassed opportunities. Six-month course. Proven methods, successful students. Write for particulars. Dodge's Institute, Valparaiso, Indiana.'"

Old Red nodded as if he'd heard exactly what he expected to hear.

"They're all like that, ain't they?" he said. "'Change your life. Write here.' And some address back east."

I scanned the rest of the ads. Old Red was right. You could master journalism, law, lip-reading, Latin, photography, music, acting—just about anything, all by sending for details to New York or Boston or Chicago or wherever. About the only thing I didn't see was a correspondence course for detectiving, which I very much could have used.

"So?" I said.

"*So* get up. There's somewhere we need to be come eight o'clock on the dot."

On our way out of the hotel, Old Red paused in the lobby to snatch up the latest *Littleton Republican*. Copies of that morning's edition had already been laid out here and there for the guests. My brother didn't even glance at his. He just handed it to me as he led us out to Main Street and from there to the north side of town.

We were going to the post office.

It didn't take us long to get there. The frigid cold of night had frozen the mud thereabouts into a solid sheet of brown. Though the streets were no prettier they were at least walkable, and for once in Littleton we arrived at our destination without looking like melted fudge from the ankles down.

A small sign was hanging from a nail in the front door. "OPEN," it said. So we went in without knocking.

Agnes was sliding an envelope into a slot in the wall of cubby holes. When she saw us step in she smiled.

"Well, well—morning, boys. You're my first customers of the day. Or did you come back to do that exclusive interview?"

"In a manner of speakin'," Old Red said.

He moved further into the house, signaling me to do the same with a jerk of the head. I closed the door and followed him into what was once the front sitting room before it became a makeshift mail warehouse. I had to take Agnes's word for it that she sorted everything before opening for the day. There were still piles of packages and letters here and there, but perhaps now they were at least organized piles.

"I didn't know you were coming, so I didn't bake that pie I promised," Agnes said. "Will you take an IOU?"

"Certainly, ma'am. I'm sure you're good for it," said Old Red. He pointed at a paisley-upholstered settee that was (unlike nearly every other surface in the place) relatively free of mail, having upon it only one large cardboard box. "Mind if we have a seat?"

"Of course not. Make yourselves comfortable...but do please take care with Mrs. Thompson's new sewing machine. Just arrived yesterday from Montgomery Ward."

"Yes'm."

My brother sat on one side of the box, I on the other. I looked across it to throw Old Red a raised eyebrow. "Did we come here for a reason or were you just angling for pie?" my expression said. He ignored me.

"I been wonderin' something," he said to Agnes. "Your paper. The *Populist*. It got out-of-town subscribers? Beeler said the *Republican* had a few hundred. Seems like a lot for a small-town newspaper."

"Oh, all sorts of people get papers from other towns." Agnes began pointing at slots on the wall before her. "The Suttons get *The Louisville Courier-Journal*. The Wiltrouts get *The Pittsburgh Press*. The Stanleys get *The San Francisco Chronicle*. Mr. DeCandido gets the Something-Something—I can't pronounce it—all the way from Milan, Italy. And I can't tell you how many people get *The New York World* and *The Chicago Tribune* and *The Washington Post*. I *can* tell you how many people outside Littleton I send the *Populist* to: one hundred and one. Just broke a hundred last week."

Old Red looked puzzled. Which probably made me look puzzled, since I'd assumed he knew what he was doing.

"A hundred and one?" my brother mused. "There really that many folks who want to keep up with doings here after movin' away?"

Agnes shook her head. "People who used to live here isn't even half the list. It's mostly other newspapers, libraries, businesses, advertisers, government offices in Denver and Washington. Things like that."

Old Red's head jerked up as the lady listed off her subscribers, but I couldn't tell what it was he found so interesting. (I rarely do until it's explained later…and sometimes not even then.)

Before he could ask for more fascinating details of the journalism business—requesting a step-by-step description of the manufacturing of paper, perhaps—the front door swung open. In walked Beeler's two apprentices, Lucy and Lawrence, bundled up in coats and scarves. Each had a canvas bag slung over the shoulder stuffed with rolled-up newspapers. The settee Old Red had seated us upon was off to their right, so they didn't even notice us as they headed straight to the dining table Agnes apparently used as a cashier's window.

"Good morning, Mrs. Johansson," said the young lady.

"Morning, Mrs. Johansson," said the boy.

They began piling their papers on the table. Each copy had been folded and rolled into a tidy little tube with its own plain brown band of gummed paper.

My brother got up and headed toward the table.

"Last delivery of the mornin', I believe?" he said.

Lucy and Lawrence whipped around to face him.

"Criminy!" the boy yelped.

His sister put a hand to her chest, fingers spread wide. "Oh! You startled us!"

"Sorry about that," said Old Red. He'd reached the table now, and he pointed down at the rolled papers covering it. "Those goin' to the *Republican*'s out-of-town subscribers?"

"Yes. Exactly," said Lucy. "It's as you said: We've made all our deliveries around town, and now we drop these off for mailing."

"Then we can finally go home for breakfast," Lawrence threw in.

My brother kept eyeing the newspapers even though the print and the addresses written on the wrappers would be but chicken scratch to him.

"And home's close by, I take it," he said. "Your father bein' the preacher for the...was it the Presbyterian church or the Methodist?"

"Presbyterian," Lawrence said, lip curling at the suggestion that he should be anything so low-down and indecent as a Methodist.

Lucy, on the other hand, put on what I think was supposed to be a coquettish smile. She had a dour, stern air about her that made it seem like a dollop of whipped cream atop a concrete block.

"And how go your efforts, Mr. Amlinmeyer?" she said. "Any progress?"

"Quite a bit actually," Old Red said.

He turned to give me a wide-eyed look. I doubt Holmes ever said to Watson "Even *you* couldn't have missed that!" But that's exactly what my brother was telling me now.

I nodded.

He snatched the nearest newspaper off the table and tossed it to me.

"Hey!" Lucy and Lawrence both blurted out at the same time.

"Open that up and tell me what you see on the inside pages," Old Red told me.

"Right."

I tore through the wrapper—noting as I did so that it was addressed to one J. Rekulak of the Philadelphia Correspondence School of Law—and unrolled the newspaper.

"You can't do that!" Lucy protested. "That's tampering with the mail!"

"Ain't mailed yet," Old Red said.

The young lady spun to face Agnes.

"You tell them!" she demanded. "They have to give that back!"

"Well...I don't know," the older woman said. "They work for Beeler, too, don't they?"

"Oh, you're useless!" Lucy spat.

She began marching toward me.

I stood and turned my back to her and fanned out the newspaper.

"Let's see," I said as I began scanning the pages. "We got news about a shipwreck in the Solomon Islands and an editorial about the Cripple Creek miners' strike and a weather bulletin with temperatures from all over and a *heck* of a lot of—"

Lucy reached around and ripped the paper from my hands. Literally. As she jerked the newspaper away, it tore, leaving me holding two little ragged, fluttering strips. But that was enough.

"—ads," I said. I looked at the paper in my left hand. "This one's for stove polish." I looked at my right hand. "And how nice. There *is* hope if you have a stammer. Or so says the Boston Institute of Elocution."

"Now look inside the copy we picked up at the hotel," Old Red said.

I stuffed the bits of paper into a coat pocket, then slid out the newspaper that had been there already.

"I do hope you'll let me read this one in peace," I said to Lucy.

I stretched up my arms to lift the newspaper out of her reach.

"Capitalist thug," she sneered. It was a new one to me as insults go—and, believe me, I've heard a few.

I cleared my throat and began telling my brother what I saw on pages two and three of that day's *Littleton Republican*.

"There's our shipwreck and our miners' strike and weather reports. But we also got poems by somebody called Charles Swain and chapter twenty of 'Ali Baba and the Forty Thieves.' And just four ads."

"All for local businesses?" Old Red asked.

I nodded. "A hardware store, a restaurant, a saloon and Pickett's Livery."

"Damn it, Lucy," Lawrence muttered. "I told you we should skip it this week."

"Shut up, Lawrence," his sister snarled at him.

"I don't understand," said Agnes. "What does this mean?"

I lowered the newspaper and turned toward her. "There's two versions of the *Republican*. The one delivered in town and the one you send out in the mail. That second one—it goes to all the advertisers Beeler thinks he doesn't have anymore."

My brother jumped in before I could go on. Usually he's the one who offers explanations, and he seemed anxious not to lose his job. Which was fine by me, as I couldn't have explained it any further anyway.

"Beeler's been leavin' more and more of his business to his 'apprentices' here," Old Red said. "Printin', deliveries, pickin' up his mail. So sooner or later one of 'em—I suspect Lucy here—figured out the opportunity that gave 'em: make Beeler think the out-of-town advertising's dried up and keep the money. 'Course, those advertisers want to see their ads in print for themselves. And they gotta get *some* business out of 'em, or the ads really *will* dry up fast. So there's the version of the paper that goes in the mail and the version for here in town. I don't know how long that's been goin' on, but I do know they almost got caught at it last week

—'cuz Beeler actually came into work at a decent time instead of stumblin' in around noon, as seems to be his way on Wednesdays. When he grabbed a bunch of copies to give away up at Fort Logan, he must've taken 'em off the out-of-town stack. The second he got a look inside one, it was all over. So they couldn't let him *get* a look inside."

"So…Lawrence…chased…him…down…in…a…Klan…getup?" Agnes asked slowly. And very, very skeptically.

I didn't blame her. The leap from the advertising scheme to a hooded highwayman seemed like a pretty huge one, and I was having trouble making it myself.

My brother shook his head.

"I don't think it was the plan to look like a Klansman at all," he said. "They just had to act fast. The snow hadn't come yet—nor melted yet, of course—so the streets were hard-packed dirt, not sop. Once they knew Beeler was gettin' himself a buggy for a ride north, they'd only have ten, fifteen minutes to get ahead of him. Now, you can just throw on an old flour sack or pillowcase with holes to hide your face. But what about the rest of you? Couldn't let Beeler see a suit of clothes he'd recognize. So why not cover yourself up from head to foot like you did your face? It'd be easy to do if you knew there was a church on the way out of town…and where they keep the choir robes." Old Red glanced over at Lucy. "Or was it the minister's robes? Or the ones for baptisms?"

Lucy snorted and looked away, so my brother turned to Lawrence.

"I don't know," the boy said with a sullen shrug.

Old Red squinted at him.

"Ah," he said. "He didn't tell you which it was?"

Lucy jerked her head around to glare at him again, and Lawrence widened his eyes.

"Hold on," said Agnes. "Who's 'he?'"

Old Red flapped a hand at Lawrence and Lucy. "Their partner. I didn't know for sure they had one till just now. But I was wonderin' why the 'Klansman' was so careful to keep his gun under his robe…and where that gun came from in the first place. Like the face and the clothes, the gun might be recognized—because it was the big old Colt's Dragoon revolver Julius Riggs keeps in his office, wasn't it? You been workin' with Riggs's apprentice, the Bell boy, to pull the same fast one on *him*. That's why the *Democrat*'s advertising's been drying up same as the *Republican*'s. I bet young Bell can do a pretty good imitation of his boss's accent, too, which would disguise his own voice while pointin' the finger elsewhere. Yup—it was Bell who did the runnin' up the road to get the papers…which were never found because he brought 'em back to Lucy and Lawrence, who lickety-split mailed 'em outta town from this very office."

The young lady was just staring at my brother with a silent scowl now. Her brother did the same with a pout.

"Lucky for you the *Populist* doesn't have any apprentices," I said to Agnes.

She was watching the conversation with an expression that was equal parts horror and glee. Old Red was giving her an exclusive, all right. "LOCAL MYSTERY SOLVED" right inside her parlor.

"When did you know it was them, Little?" she asked.

"It's 'Old Red' actually," I finally corrected her. I tapped my chest. "And 'Big Red.'"

Couldn't have our names wrong in print.

She dismissed me with a curt nod but kept her eyes on my brother.

"It was that message you handed us last night that broke it all open," he told her. "There were five seeds inside. An old KKK threat, accordin' to some, though it seems to be a mite…'obscure' I think is the word? We'd brought it up earlier that day—to Beeler, in the *Republican* office. With Lucy and Lawrence listenin' in. Now, it could've come from Julius Riggs, but my brother there seems to have developed a bit of a habit when it comes to newspaper folks."

"Oh, yeah," I said, just remembering it myself. "I spelled our names for him."

Old Red nodded, then squirmed before going on. "And… well…our names weren't spelt right on the envelope."

He didn't like admitting our biggest clue was one he could never have spotted himself.

I shifted attention from him quick.

"It's 'Amlin-*g*-meyer,'" I told Lucy. "With a 'g' in the middle."

"Well, you could hardly tell from the way you two talk," the young lady shot back. "That's the first time I've heard either of you use a g. Maybe *you* should take a course from the Boston Institute of Elocution so you don't sound like a couple hayseeds."

I barely kept in the "Ouch!" I felt.

Agnes shook her head and clucked her tongue.

"You and Bobby Bell stealing from Beeler and Riggs…your fathers are going to be shocked," she said. "Why did you do it?"

"Because the other newspapers around here are awful!" Lawrence said.

"Including yours," Lucy added. She gave Agnes a scornful, jeering smile it looked like she'd been holding back quite a while. "Nothing but politics, lies, distortions, hate and trivia. We were pooling our resources to start our own newspaper. One that would speak nothing but the truth."

Lawrence nodded and puffed out his chest.

"*The Littleton Communist!*" he declared.

Needless to say, Littleton, Colorado, is still muddling along without its own Communist newspaper. And *The Littleton Republican* and *The Littleton Democrat* are now muddling along without their apprentices—who were all fired but faced no charges. It's amazing how forgiving newspapermen can be when the perpetrators of outrageous crimes are the children of men leading half their readership. I suppose it helped that Pastor Gould of the Littleton Presbyterian Church and Reverend Bell of the Littleton Methodist Church made sure that most of the stolen advertising money was returned. Sadly, Beeler's portion was immediately claimed, he said, by local creditors.

In other words: We didn't get paid. The case wasn't without its rewards, though. The coverage in the *Populist*, the *Democrat* and the

Republican alike was rather flattering (although it amazed me that after all that talk about our names the *Populist* still managed to spell them wrong). And I worked out a deal with Beeler—which is why for the next year if you come across a copy of *The Littleton Republican* in a reading room or library or office or outhouse, you'll find this ad right below the weather reports.

The A.A. Western Detective Agency
The Unknown Revealed, the Missing Found, Problems Solved
Reasonable Rates
The Best in Detection with Dependable Discretion
Send Inquiries to Ogden Chamber of Commerce Building, Room 303,
Ogden, Utah
(Divorce and missing pet cases not accepted.)
We Never FAIL
As Featured in the Pages of Smythe's Frontier Detective*!!!*

Mr. Smythe—you're welcome.
O.A. Amlingmeyer
Ogden, Utah
February 13, 1894

CAN THE CAT CATCH THE RAT?

Urias Smythe
Smythe & Associates Publishing, Ltd.
175 Fifth Avenue
New York, New York

Dear Mr. Smythe:

While I like to think that my stories have brought throngs of new readers to *Smythe's Frontier Detective*, there is one new reader I am particularly happy—elated even—to claim credit for. He has not, so far, completed the reading of a single issue of your fine publication, however. Getting through one story, page or indeed paragraph remains beyond him. But he has, by sounding out the title on the cover, made substantial progress from his usual jaundiced perusal of the artwork and impatient waiting for *me* to divine all else.

I refer, of course, to my brother. Though blessed with a keen eye for clues and deducing, until now, he's lacked the schooling to read so much as the sign over a saloon door. He's also lacked the temperament for schooling—particularly if I'm the one trying to teach him. In our cowboying days, he was accustomed to showing *me* the ropes. (Literally, roping being one of the skills I lacked when we hit the cattle trails together.) But with our new status as professional sleuths putting the need for reading before him ever more, and the two of us finally settled permanent-like in comfortable digs as opposed to ever on the drift, the time finally arrived for Old Red to swallow his pride and pick up a primer.

McGuffey's Eclectic Primer, Revised Edition, to be exact. Our dear friend and colleague Diana Crowe secretly gifted me with a copy this Christmas. (I will admit that when she slipped me what was plainly a wrapped book and told me to open it in private, I dared dream it was a racy novel of romance or a collection of love sonnets or some such. When I saw that it was a textbook for the teaching of reading, my already sky-high esteem for the lady shot even further upward even as my poor pining heart sank.) When my brother told me he was tired of turning to others every time he needed reading done—and we know who he meant by *others*—I whipped out that *McGuffey's* and told him he was in luck. If he could stomach a few months of instruction, he'd find he needed me for nothing anymore save perhaps the fetching of hats from high shelves. (Though I'm confident Old Red could catch up to me in terms of reading, when it comes to height, I know I'll always be able to look down on him.)

With my brother's solemn promise not to shoot me when his studies (or I) became annoying, we opened the primer together and got started. The first pages, naturally enough, lay out the alphabet, first capitalized, then not. These we were able to move through fairly quickly, without *too* much worry on my part that Old Red would break his promise. Though his formal schooling hadn't lasted long—just one quick season as a boy back in Kansas —he did retain at least a passing familiarity with the ABCs. Once we'd reacquainted everyone ("Old Red, you remember H. H, you remember Old Red.") it was on to the first real lesson. And the first real challenge.

Words.

"A...suh...suh..." my brother said.

"C usually makes a hard sound, remember," I prompted.

"I remember," Old Red growled. "Cuh. A...cuh...a...tuh. A cuh-a-tuh?"

"Smoosh it all together...and don't forget the picture on the last page if you're looking for clues."

"Oh." My brother glared at me. "A cat." He jabbed a finger at the next words. "And I suppose that says 'A rat'?"

"Very good."

"Good, hell. The damn picture gives it away."

Across the top of the page was a drawing of a scampering rat.

"Not necessarily," I said. "That could've said 'A rodent.'"

"Feh. Not enough letters."

"Very good!" I said again.

Old Red shot me another glare. "Keep your voice down. And don't talk to me like I'm a four-year-old."

"Then don't act like one," I replied. Almost. I managed to stop myself just in time.

This was hard for my brother, and getting snippy with him wouldn't make it any easier. The only reason I could teach him was because, as the baby of the family, I'd been allowed to keep going to school instead of filling every day dawn to dusk with farm work like the other Amlingmeyer kids. Literacy had been a gift given to me by my brothers and sisters. The least I could do was pass it back to the last of them with some graciousness.

I tapped the page. "What's it say down here?"

My brother looked down. And kept glaring.

"Well, there's 'a cat' again," he said. "Then you got 'a...nuh... duh...' A-nuh-duh?"

"Smoosh 'em."

"Anuhduh. A-nn-duh. 'And.'"

"You got it."

Old Red started over again from the top.

"'A cat. A rat. A rat, a cat. A cat and a rat. A rat and a cat.'"

"Congratulations, brother—you have just read an entire page of fine literature. 'A rat and a cat.' My goodness—what could happen next?"

Old Red looked over at me, and for a second I thought he was going to snap at me again about talking down to him. Instead he did something almost as unheard of for Gustav "Old Red" Amlingmeyer than reading a book.

He smiled.

I turned the page. There again were our friends "cat" and "rat" along with a whole mess of new companions, all grouped and regrouped in various arrangements under another drawing: the aforementioned cat chasing the aforementioned rat. (Never let anyone tell you *McGuffey's* isn't exciting.)

Old Red's smile faded.

"Cuh-an. Can," he said. "Tee-huh-ee. Tee-huh-ee? Can tee-huh-ee? What the hell?"

Two words into his first actual sentence—"Can the cat catch the rat?"—and he was stumped. It was the "the" that threw him. Which meant I had to explain how "t" loses its "tuh" when there's an "h" crowding its backside. And if "the" was tough, "catch" was going to take us all day.

Already, things were getting complicated. In the primer, anyway. Things seemed unusually uncomplicated for us in all other respects just then. After quickly wrapping up our recent case in Colorado, we'd returned to Ogden to await new business. But the A.A. Western Detective Agency had nothing at the moment that required our particular skills—Sherlock Holmes-style deducifying in Old Red's case, smoothing down all the hackles he raises in mine. So we had a whole week of peace and quiet in our boarding house, which we mostly passed in my brother's room in the company of "McGuffey." We'd see our fellow boarders—all of them middlemen of one stripe or another for the various railroads with offices in Ogden—at breakfast and again at supper. But betweentimes it was just us in the house along with our elderly landlady, Miss Derringer, and her maid and manservant.

"What are you two up to these days, anyway?" one of the rail-road men asked us at dinner one night. Mortimer Gore, his name was—a scrawny, pop-eyed little fellow with a big bald spot and a perpetual smile. "Every time I go by your rooms I hear you muttering at each other."

"Eh? What's that about muttering?" Miss Derringer demanded from the head of the table.

If anyone was going to bring up muttering, it was usually her. She accused all her tenants of it. We were all mush-mouthed, she said. Never mind that the old lady was deaf as a post—that couldn't have anything to do with it.

"I was asking the Amlingmeyers what they've been up to lately!" Gore shouted back.

Shouting was one's only recourse with the lady, semaphore flags being unavailable. Smoke signals might've worked, but it'd be hell on the wallpaper.

"What's that?" Miss Derringer asked, leaning toward Gore with her ear trumpet up. "Stop whispering and *project*!"

"I WAS WONDERING WHAT THE AMLINGMEYERS HAVE BEEN UP TO!" Gore said.

"Well, how should I know?" Miss Derringer snapped back. "Ask *them*!"

She flapped a withered hand at me and my brother.

Gore never lost his smile.

Old Red, as you can imagine, didn't have one to begin with.

Prying into a person's private affairs simply isn't done where we come from. Not unless you're angling for a broken nose or a perforated liver. And the last thing my brother would want to admit in front of our landlady and seven railroad paper pushers was that he'd been holed up learning to read.

He turned to Gore.

"It is—" he began.

I didn't have a crystal ball or tea leaves on me, yet I saw what the future held plain enough: "—*none of your damn business*." I jumped in before it could arrive.

"WE'RE WRITING," I said. And it was even true-ish, for Old Red had indeed been tracing out the A-B-Cs as part of our studies.

"Oh?" said Gore. "One of your little detective stories?"

That Old Red and I are not only detectives but somewhat famous ones making regular appearances in a national magazine was known to all the other tenants. Because I'd told them. One has to say *something* at dinner other than "Please pass the rolls," and how are you supposed to go from "somewhat famous" to "famous" if you don't advertise?

"Speak up!" Miss Derringer snapped at Gore.

Still, he kept on smiling.

"ONE OF YOUR LITTLE DETECTIVE STORIES?" he repeated at three times the volume.

"THEY AIN'T LITTLE," Old Red replied. "AT LEAST NOT LITTLE ENOUGH TO SUIT ME."

"MY BROTHER FEELS MY WRITING IS OVERLY VERBOSE," I explained with a hearty (if not entirely heartfelt) laugh. "HE FORGETS THAT WE'RE PAID BY THE WORD."

I turned to the tenant to my left—a Southern Pacific accountant named Baker who'd been shoveling fried chicken and potatoes into himself like the fireman stoking up a locomotive.

"Please pass the rolls," I said.

This was meant to indicate that I was turning my attention back to the task at hand: eating. It was a task everyone should have been intent upon, in my opinion, as Miss Derringer's servant Annie had been baking up a storm of late, and the second you stepped through the front door the smell of fresh breads and cakes would set your mouth to watering.

"YOU'RE WRITING UP YOUR LATEST CASE?" Gore asked. "THE ONE THAT TOOK YOU TO COLORADO LAST WEEK?"

He wasn't taking the hint. I chalked this up to his being a newly arrived Easterner—he'd showed up two weeks before to scout out expansion and investment opportunities for the Pennsylvania Railroad Company—and forgave him his trespasses.

"INDEED," I said as I accepted the rolls Baker begrudgingly passed me (after helping himself to another couple). "JUST ABOUT GOT IT READY FOR OUR PUBLISHER. I WANT TO GIVE IT ONE MORE GO-THROUGH TO SEE HOW MANY ADJECTIVES AND ADVERBS I CAN ADD." I located the biggest roll remaining and dropped it onto my plate. "A MAN'S GOTTA EAT."

A couple of the other tenants gave that chuckle. I figured they were the only other people at the table who could recall what adjectives and adverbs were.

"GOT ANOTHER CASE LINED UP?" Gore asked.

"NOT JUST YET," I said. I favored Miss Derringer with a smile. "BUT DON'T WORRY, MA'AM. THAT DON'T MEAN THE RENT'LL BE LATE. WE GOT PLENTY STASHED IN THE BANK."

Miss Derringer frowned and lowered her ear trumpet, as if such jests weren't worth the trouble it took to hear them.

I turned back to Baker.

"SAY, CHARLIE...WHAT'S THE LATEST ON THE UTAH NORTHERN RAILROAD? STILL LOOKING LIKE THEY'RE HEADED INTO BANKRUPTCY?"

This was, I admit, a discourteous thing to ask an employee of the Utah Northern Railway as he tried to digest his chicken, potatoes, and rolls. But what can I say? I needed someone else to take over the talking while I got through some chicken, potatoes, and rolls myself.

"Umm...well...maybe," Baker said. "How about this cold snap we've been having, hmm? I for one can't wait for spring."

"Stop mumbling!" Miss Derringer snapped.

"I SAID I CAN'T WAIT FOR SPRING!"

And on the conversation went from there, with various tenants hollering at the top of their lungs about the weather until it was a wonder we weren't all as deaf as our landlady. Soon after, Old Red and I put down our forks and made our escapes.

The next morning it was off to the office for the railroaders and back to *McGuffey's* for me and my brother. We'd reached another exciting chapter in the primer.

"Sss...S-uh-e...Sue. Huh-aaa-ssss. Has. A nnnn-eee-wooo. New? Duh-o-llll. Doll. Sue has a new doll."

My brother scowled down at the page and repeated what he'd just read: "Sue has a new doll."

He looked disgusted by all the work it took him to decipher such a simple and childish thought.

"Perfect. You're making amazing progress," I told him. "Another week and we'll be reading 'War and Peace.'"

"I don't know what the hell that is, but if it's got more meat to it than 'Sue has a new doll' I'll be looking forward to it."

"Don't write off Sue's doll yet, brother. Things really heat up in the next sentence."

"Oh? It get stolen? Sue use it to beat somebody to death? What?"

"I'm afraid *McGuffey's* don't work like that. These ain't stories about Sherlock Holmes."

"Too bad," Old Red said glumly. Because, of course, there wouldn't *be* any new stories about our hero thanks to Professor Moriarty.

My brother stared hard at the next line.

"I-tuh. Ituh. Has. A. New. Buh-own-it. What? Who's Ituh and what the hell's a buh-own-it?"

"'*It* has a new *bonnet*,'" I said.

"Dammit! I shoulda got that."

"Don't worry. I'm sure you'll show the next sentence who's boss."

"Oh, don't mollycoddle me."

I turned the page. The first sentence there was the longest we'd encountered yet. It had a comma in it and everything.

Old Red sighed.

"Just take your time," I told him. "And don't forget what happens when you put an s in front of an h. You know—like in 'Shhhhhherlock.'"

But before my brother could take a crack at the first word on the new page—"she"—there were footsteps in the hallway. It was Wednesday, when the maid booted us from our rooms to change the linens and sweep the floor. That was over and done with as of half an hour before, though. And the footsteps sounded far too heavy for Annie, the maid, who was a little slip of a thing without the meat God gave a prairie chicken. It sounded more like another boarder—one of the burlier ones—had stomped home early in a bad mood.

Old Red went stiff as we paused to see which room the man would go to. I could see in his wide eyes the worry that we'd been overheard—and that one of the lodgers now knew he couldn't read. Most likely it was Mr. Gore or Mr. Baker, our neighbors at the end of the hall.

Yet the footsteps didn't move past to their rooms. Instead they stopped at my brother's door.

There was a knock—and not the tentative, quiet, polite kind. This was a *thump-thump-thump* of the *Get your ass out here* variety.

"Yeah?" Old Red said.

"Open up, Amlingmeyer."

It was Claypool, Miss Derringer's dogsbody. (I'd never heard of a "dogsbody" until our landlady used the word to describe the hulking, sulking, doughy-faced man who ran her errands, brought in the firewood and pushed her around the neighborhood in a wheeled chair for her daily "constitutional." I eventually figured out that "dogsbody" was just a fancy way of saying "fellow I pay to hang around for the dumb things I either can't do or don't feel like doing." He didn't chew her food for her, but I assumed he would if her dentures broke.)

Before going to the door, Old Red not only closed the *McGuffey's* but flipped it over so it was cover-down on the bed.

"What do you want?" he asked Claypool when face to face with him a moment later.

"Miss Derringer wants to talk to you." Claypool leaned to the side to shoot me a frown around my brother. "Both of you. In the sitting room."

"What for?" I asked.

"Do I look like Miss Derringer?"

I shrugged. "Not particularly. But then again, I ain't never seen you in a dress."

"You're very funny," Claypool said. Meaning, of course, that I'm about as funny as a bloody nose—which he'd be happy to provide if I wanted to ask for one again.

I'd never got the feeling the man liked me much. I'd never got the feeling he liked *anything* much. His face was perpetually set in an expression of surly disdain that suggested he was meant for bigger things than old lady's dogsbody but just hadn't got around to them yet.

He jerked a thumb toward the stairs.

"Come on."

"All right. Time I stretched my legs anyway," I said, sliding off the bed. "Mi-mi-mi-miiiiiiiiii! La-la-la-laaaaaaaaa!"

Claypool glowered at me.

"Warming up for the lady," I explained.

Claypool kept glowering.

Old Red did the same—at Claypool—as we headed down to the sitting room. If it came to a scowl-off between the two, I couldn't say who'd win. They were both champion glarers.

Miss Derringer was awaiting us in an overstuffed armchair that made her little wizened self look like a ragdoll perched on a throne. I knew then who'd win the household scowl-off. Her. She stared at me and my brother with such naked contempt I was tempted to say, "You don't know us well enough to look at us thataway. Give it another couple months, then you'll have earned it."

I opted for a smile and a "YES, MA'AM?" instead.

She raised one of her spindly arms. A watch on a gold fob dangled from her fingers.

"I suppose you know what this is?" she said.

"UHH…YES," I said.

"Oh ho! So you admit it!" the old lady cried.

"I ADMIT I KNOW A WATCH WHEN I SEE ONE."

"What's this all about?" Old Red said.

Miss Derringer lowered the watch and raised her ear trumpet.

"What are you whispering over there?" she said to him.

She looked past Old Red at Claypool, who'd taken up position behind us in the doorway as if blocking any attempt at escape. Which made sense in Old Red's case. He could barely tolerate five seconds of talk with the lady without looking like he wanted to run outside, knock the rider off the nearest horse and make for the hills.

"That one's always seemed sneaky, hasn't he?" Miss Derringer said to Claypool.

I assumed she was referring to Old Red. I'm about as sneaky as a herd of buffalo.

"MY BROTHER WAS JUST WONDERING WHY YOU'RE SHOWING US WATCHES," I said.

"Because it's more than just a watch, isn't it?" Miss Derringer shot back at me. "It's evidence!"

"OF WHAT?" Old Red asked.

Usually, he was happy to leave conversation with the lady to me. But talk of "evidence" changed things.

What came next changed things, too. In a big way.

"Of your lies and thievery!" Miss Derringer said.

"OUR WHAT?" I said.

"YOUR LIES AND THIEVERY!" the old lady repeated with such a shrill shout it was a miracle the windows didn't crack.

Of course, volume hadn't been the issue. It was the words themselves.

I glanced back at Claypool.

"She all right?" I said. "Ain't havin' some kind of spell, is she?"

Claypool just kept scowling at me.

"Two weeks ago, my boxing trophy disappeared," Miss Derringer continued.

"Ooo, she is havin' a spell," I whispered (and I mean truly whispered, not whispered as the lady would reckon it).

"YOUR *WHAT*?" said Old Red.

"My late nephew's 1872 College of William & Mary Amateur Cup Second Place Featherweight Boxing Trophy," Miss Derringer snapped. "Then last week I asked Annie to set out punch so we could toast Mr. Crowell's promotion to junior assistant vice president of administration and finance for the Denver & Rio Grande Western Railway. And she informed me that my silver-gilt punch bowl with matching ladle and tray were *also* missing. Then, yesterday Mr. Gore told Annie that he'd misplaced his favorite watch. A gift from the Pennsylvania Railroad Company. Another missing item in my household! And whose mattress did Annie find it under this morning?"

My brother may be the vaunted "Holmes of the Range," but let it not be said that I am incapable of deduction. Or at least reading the writing on the wall.

"Umm…mine?" I said.

"Speak up, Mr. Amlingmeyer…if that is your real name!"

"MY MATTRESS?"

"Oh ho! So you admit it!"

The conversation had come full circle. It was also starting to give me a headache.

I put my fingers to my temples.

"MISS DERRINGER, I ADMIT TO NOTHING BUT PUZZLEMENT," I said. "ARE YOU ACTUALLY ACCUSING ME OF STEALING FROM MR. GORE?"

"AND BEING SO DUMB AS TO KEEP WHAT HE STOLE UNDER HIS MATTRESS ON THE DAY ANNIE CHANGES THE SHEETS?" Old Red added.

"I am not making accusations!" the old lady blared back. "I am telling you that you have been caught, and you are no longer welcome in my home!"

"NOW NOW NOW, MISS DERRINGER," I said. "THIS IS SILLINESS. YOU KNOW MY BROTHER AND I ARE DETECTIVES."

"A lie!"

"YOU'VE SEEN OUR MAGAZINE."

"More lies!"

"WE'VE BEEN WRITTEN UP IN THE PAPERS."

"Even more lies!"

"MA'AM, I'M TELLING YOU I WOULD HAVE NO REASON TO STEAL A MAN'S TWELVE-DOLLAR WATCH!"

"Lying lies from a lying liar!"

Miss Derringer looked past me at Claypool.

"Watch these two as they gather their things. I won't have them helping themselves to my silver on their way out."

"Yes, ma'am."

"Speak up, man!"

"YES, MA'AM!"

Miss Derringer grunted and gave us one final glare. Then she lowered her ear trumpet, folded her arms over her chest, and swiveled to stare out the window at the gray February day. Which she was kicking us out into.

The conversation was over. As was our brief taste of hearth and home.

My brother and I looked at each other, but what was there to say?

I shrugged. Old Red spat out a "Feh." That was that.

"Go on—get your stuff," Claypool said. "And if you cause any more trouble, I'll bust your skulls then call the police."

I turned toward the man, fists clenched. If he aimed to bust skulls, he'd have to keep his own from getting cracked first.

"Claypool," I said.

And the fight just went out of me. Tussling with her dogsbody wouldn't change the old lady's mind about us.

"No need for threats," I said. "We're going."

That was indeed the end of the threats…of the spoken sort. There was lots of menacing hovering, with Claypool standing in doorways as we cleaned out our drawers and packed our carpet-bags. He followed us through the kitchen and down into the basement when we collected our things there, as well. The tenants were allowed to store their bulkier possessions under the house—a privilege one of the railroad man took advantage of to stow his collection of cracked vinegar bottles and spoiled milk, to judge by the sour, acrid smell of the place. There were trunks, valises, ice skates, roller skates, bowling balls, bicycles and a whole corner of bulky something-or-other under a tarp. But all we had down there were a couple boxes of second-rank detective magazines. (Our issues of *Harper's* and *McClure's* with Sherlock Holmes stories had the privilege of living upstairs in Old Red's room despite his inability, up to now, to read one word of them.) So it didn't take long for us to gather up our things and find ourselves on the wrong side of the front door—which Claypool not only closed firmly behind us but took the unnecessary, insulting step of locking, as well.

"I apologize, brother," I said.

Old Red threw me a wary glance. "What for?"

I sighed and shook my head. "If only I'd resisted temptation and left that boxing trophy alone. But I just had to have it. That little tin fella with his fists up—adorable! And then he looked so lonely under my mattress I just had to grab a few things to keep him company. Only thing I can't understand is why Annie only saw the watch. That punch bowl put a hell of a lump in the bed."

"Oh, shut up," Old Red said.

He trudged toward the street.

"I will momentarily," I said. I tried to suck in one last noseful of the smell of Annie's baking, but it was futile from outside. So I trotted off after Old Red. "One question first, though. Where are we going?"

"Where do you think?"

My brother reached the end of Miss Derringer's walk and turned left. It was the direction we most often turned upon reaching the street, for off that way lay downtown Ogden with its railroad station and restaurants. And its many office buildings— one of which was home to the A.A. Western Detective Agency. *Our* detective agency, though our partner Colonel Crowe tended to act as if it was all his and my brother and I were two not-entirely-competent underlings. Winning the man's respect has been be a long, hard-fought battle, and telling him we'd just been kicked out of our digs for supposed pilfering certainly wouldn't help us hold any ground we'd gained.

I didn't argue with Old Red on the direction he chose, though. It was a cold day, and I suddenly found myself walking through it carrying almost everything I owned in the world. If I was going to be humiliated in front of Colonel Crowe, at least I'd be doing it where I could set down my things and soak up some warmth.

We found both more humiliation and more warmth than we expected when we walked into the Double-A's office on the second floor of the Ogden Chamber of Commerce Building. Each came from the same source: Colonel Crowe's daughter, Diana. She'd been out of town on a case the colonel judged not fitting for our particular talents—one involving stealth, tact, and delicacy—and had apparently wrapped up early.

If we'd known she'd be there, Old Red probably would've steered us to the nearest hotel instead, for though he's loath to admit it he's sweet on our esteemed friend. I, on the other hand, lack my brother's reserve and make no bones about my feelings. To revert once more to all capitals: I AM SWEET ON DIANA CROWE! Which is another reason her father doesn't like to send us out of town with her.

The colonel looked up and shook his head as we plodded into the office with our meager possessions and hangdog expressions.

"Don't tell me," he said. "You've been kicked out."

He said it as if we truly didn't need to tell him. He'd been expecting it all along.

"Gustav, Otto—what happened?" said Diana.

She was sitting at one of the office's two desks—the one that's home to a typewriter and telephone and ledger books and such. The colonel's desk was bigger but had nothing upon it but some papers and an inkwell, giving it the appearance of a stage for him to hop upon if the mood struck. (Colonel Crowe's so short he'd have to look up when saluting Gen. Tom Thumb, so the scale would be about right.)

I put down the box and carpetbag I was carrying, and my brother did the same.

"The landlady thought we were stealin' things from around the house," I said.

"What in the world would give her that impression?" Colonel Crowe said in a skeptical way that actually asked a different question.

Were you stealing things from around the house?

"She got that impression because somebody wanted her to,"

Old Red grumbled. "Wanted it enough to steal a watch from one of the other tenants and blame it on my brother."

"And you have suspicions as to which somebody this might be?" Diana said.

"I do."

"You do?" I said. "Eight whole blocks we just walked, and you didn't say a thing about it."

"I didn't think it needed saying, it's so obvious."

Old Red looked over at me, head cocked, eyebrows raised. It was an expectant sort of look. The "It's so obvious even *you* could work it out" kind.

Sometimes you're the teacher, sometimes you're the pupil.

"Well, sure," I said. "Who else could it be? It's plain as day, ain't it? Plain as the nose on your face…which is particularly hard to miss in your case, Brother."

Diana cocked her head and raised her eyebrows, too. She knew stalling when she heard it.

"It was the maid. Annie," I told her.

I glanced over at my brother to see if his brows had pulled down into a scowl. They hadn't. So I went on.

"She has a master key for all the rooms. Goes in and out all the time doing her chores. So it'd be easy to pick up a watch in one room and leave it another."

"Or why bother with the leaving at all?" Old Red said. "All she'd have to do is bring Gore's watch to Miss Derringer and *say* she'd found it in your room."

"Precisely," I said as if I'd been thinking the same thing. Which I hadn't.

"This 'Annie,'" said the colonel. "She has something against you?"

I shook my head. "Not that I know of. I mean, sometimes I sneak crackers upstairs and eat 'em in bed, but I didn't think she'd take a few crumbs this hard."

"It ain't exactly us she don't like, I reckon," said Old Red. "Or the crumbs…though I can't imagine she loves those. It's something else about us."

He gave me that "Go on—work it out" look again.

"Yes, yes? And that something is?" Colonel Crowe snapped at him. "You can speak plainly, you know. You don't have to keep proving you're the 'Holmes of the Range' to us."

Old Red opened his mouth to reply. From the look in his eye I thought it best if said reply got headed off at the pass.

"It's our comings and goings, of course," I blurted out. "But mostly our stayings. That's what makes us different from the other boarders. They all head off to work at one office or another every morning. Us, though—if we ain't got a case out of town, we're mostly holed up upstairs. Been spendin' about all day up there lately working on…"

I threw a peep over at my brother. His glare told me what I suspected: Colonel Crowe knew about his lack of schooling, but reminders wouldn't be necessary (or appreciated). So "…teaching Old Red to read" was out.

"…my next story for *Smythe's Frontier Detective*," I said instead.

Old Red gave me a curt nod. "That's how I figure it. We been around too much, so we had to go."

I smiled. "Notch one up for the Watson of the West."

"And why would your presence be so unsettling that the maid should stoop to thievery herself to get you out?" said Colonel Crowe.

I was starting to wonder how offended I should be. When you're accused of a crime, your friends are supposed to say "How awful!" not "Convince me you didn't do it."

Old Red cleared his throat and threw a twitchy little glance over at Diana.

"'It is a capital mistake to theorize before you—'" he began.

The colonel thumped his desk with his little fist. "Don't go quoting Holmes to me! Just answer the question!"

"Canoodlin'!" Old Red hollered back.

Colonel Crowe snapped to attention in his chair.

"What now?" he said.

Diana looked like she was fighting back a grin.

"'Canoodling,' Father. It's a slang expression," she said. "It means—"

"I know what it means," the colonel grumbled. "What's your point, Amlingmeyer?"

"The point is the landlady has her a manservant. Claypool," Old Red said. It was hard to tell who looked more uncomfortable with all the canoodle talk in front of Diana: him or Colonel. Crowe. "Bein' that she's practically deaf, he and the maid coulda got used to…you know…without her noticin'. But then me and my brother moved in, and all of a sudden you got two folks with workin' ears hangin' around half the time. It'd take a big bite out of your…privacy."

My brother threw another unhappy glance at Diana before adding a muttered "Theorizin'. Feh."

"So you'd observed an intimate connection between the maid and the manservant?" she asked him.

"We didn't observe intimate anything!" he said. "Y'all wanted me to make guesses, so I'm makin' guesses."

Diana turned to me. I shook my head.

"I never noticed those two sneak off together or act flirty or even talk to each other particularly nice," I said. "I might not be the top deducifier around here, but I think I'm a fairly keen observer when it comes to women and men and the possibility of canoodlin'."

"We can all stop using that word now," Colonel Crowe said.

"And Annie and Claypool? Nah." I went on. "No spark. I think the only thing that would put a little light in Claypool's eyes would be the chance to pull the wings off a fly."

"Ain't no logic to you-know-what," Old Red said. I could tell his heart wasn't really in it, though. He hadn't seen any spark either.

"Well, whatever the motive, I don't like it," the colonel declared, giving his desk another little thump. "It reflects poorly on the agency."

"It certainly reflects poorly on me and my brother," Old Red snapped.

"Not to mention leavin' us with no place to live," I added.

"Oh, that's easily dealt with," Colonel Crowe said.

My hopes rose.

"Diana has today's *Standard* if you want to look through the room listings," the colonel continued. "She has the telephone directory, too, if you prefer to phone a hotel."

My hopes fell.

The Crowes have the cutest little home on the bluffs on the north side of town. It has the coziest little guest room, too. I thought maybe we'd get a chance to become better acquainted with it—and Diana—if we were to be under the Crowes' roof for a spell. But it was not to be.

"Thanks," I said anyway.

I picked up the box and carpetbag at my feet and walked them across the room. When I reached Diana's desk, I put them down again and looked back at Old Red. He knew what I was wondering.

"Hotel," he said firmly. So firmly it didn't just tell me what we'd be doing next but what we *wouldn't* be doing after that.

There'd be no hunt for a new boarding house. Not yet. We had something to prove to Miss Derringer first. Something to rub her nose in.

Diana opened a drawer and pulled out the Ogden directory. As she leaned forward to hand it to me, she wrinkled her own nose in a way that filled my heart with terror.

Something smelled. And not of lilac.

My cowboying days aren't far enough in the past for me to have forgotten the powerful musk a man can work up and teach his nose not to notice. So for a mortifying moment, I assumed I was wafting *eau de drover* about the premises. But after a surreptitious (I hoped) sniff I recognized the true culprit.

"My apologies for the odor," I said. "Miss Derringer's basement smells like a refinery, and the stink seems to have tagged along on our boxes."

Diana gave me a distracted, distant "Hmm."

"You said there were 'things,' plural, that had been stolen around the house," she said. "What else besides the watch?"

"A trophy and a punch bowl, ladle, and tray," said Old Red.

"And these weren't found in Otto's room?"

I resisted the urge to repeat my earlier joke about trying to sleep on a punch bowl.

"Nope. Just the watch," I said.

"You think it means something?" my brother asked Diana.

She gave him a little smile. "Really, Gustav…now you'd ask *me* to theorize?"

She pulled the phone to the edge of the desk so I could reach it.

"The Reed Hotel is close and always has rooms," she said.

"A bit pricey, though," her father added. "You might be more comfortable with one of the hotels near Union Station."

Old Red shot him a sour look.

"Or *they* might be more comfortable with *me*, you mean," he said.

I've taken to dressing city-style—suit, tie, and bowler—but Old Red doesn't seem to feel right in anything but a cow hand's working clothes. In a fancy place like the Reed he'd stand out like a mud pie on a plate of crumpets.

"Stay wherever you like," the colonel said with a dismissive flap of the hand. "It's no business of mine."

Old Red gave that a snort, then turned to me again.

"Call up one of them places by the station," he said. "I don't like fancy any more than it likes me."

"Right," I said.

Soon we were squared away with a room at the imaginatively monikered Ogden Hotel. The place itself was as no-frills as the name, catering to the sort of itinerant railroad workers who don't shuffle files in the same office every day. (You know—the ones who actually keep the trains going back and forth?) As the only frills we needed were a couple beds and a roof over our head, the Ogden would do.

When we were stretched out upon those beds that night I asked my brother if he wanted me to read him anything before we turned down the light. I suggested something from one of the detective magazines in our still-pungent cardboard boxes, since those had been stowed away and hadn't grown over-familiar like the Holmes tales that went everywhere with us. But Old Red had something else in mind—a story from "The Adventures of Sherlock Holmes."

"Let's hear 'The Adventure of the Beryl Coronet,'" he said.

"What put you in the mood for that one?"

It wasn't a particular favorite, though it had provided a line my brother quoted from time to time: "When you have excluded the impossible, whatever remains, however improbable, must be the truth."

"It's about a man accused of something he didn't do—and how Mr. Holmes sets it right," Old Red said. "This wasn't a good day for us, but that don't mean we can't get some learnin' out of it."

"Or some comfort, at least," I said as I pulled out the book and flipped through its fraying pages. When I got to "The Adventure of the Beryl Coronet," I began reading aloud.

"'Holmes,' said I as I stood one morning in our bow window looking down the street, 'here is a madman coming along. It seems rather sad that his relatives should allow him to come out alone...'"

If my brother found anything in the following passages particularly "instructive," he didn't say so. He just listened intently, then rolled over and said "Night" when I reached the end. I expected he'd wake me come sunup to announce some deduction or plan of action he'd thought up while I wasted my time dreaming of Diana, but that wasn't how the morning began at all. Instead it started with a knock.

"You didn't do something to get us kicked out already, did you?" Old Red asked as I pulled on my trousers and stumbled bleary-eyed toward the door.

"Not unless I did it while sleepwalking."

I opened the door to find a stack of boxes with legs outside.

"With the lady's compliments," the boxes said.

All I could manage in reply was "Huh?" (Please keep in mind that I'd been awake all of twenty seconds.)

The boxes came inside, revealing that the legs beneath them belonged to the Ogden's sole bellman.

"What lady you talkin' about?" Old Red asked him.

"The one waiting for you in the lobby. She said you'd be expecting her."

My brother and I looked at each other.

"We weren't, but we shoulda been," I said.

The bellman put the boxes on the bed where I'd been blissfully asleep so recently. Then he stood at attention and cleared his throat.

"Do you have a message for the lady?" he said.

He held out his right hand.

I got the message for *me*. I fished a coin from my pocket and took it over to him.

"Tell her we'll be down directly," I said.

I handed the coin—a shiny new dime—to the bellman.

He looked at it skeptically, then bit it. Apparently satisfied with its flavor, he stuffed it away and walked briskly from the room. As he closed the door behind him, I pulled out the calling card tucked under the string around the topmost box. There were five words printed on one side.

MISS DIANA CROWE
Ogden, Utah

I flipped the card over and found more handwritten on the other side. I read it out for Old Red.

If clothes make the man, they can <u>unmake</u> him, as well.
D.

"Any idea what that means?" Old Red said.

"I ain't doin' any theorizin' before my third cup of coffee."

I undid the string and opened the top box.

"I take it back," I said with a grin. "No coffee required."

I reached in and pulled out a brown bowler.

"I reckon this is for you," I said, handing it to my brother. "So you have something to keep your brain warm other than that old Stetson of yours."

My brother looked down at the hat and growled.

"Oh, come now," I chided him. "Just think of all the fancy get-ups we've known Mr. Holmes to throw on. Every day was Halloween to that fella. He did himself up as a sailor, a priest, a hophead, a drunk, an old man. Just about everything but a nun. And you're gonna turn your nose up 'cuz Diana wants you to stop dressin' like a saddle bum for once?"

Old Red sighed and put on the bowler. It did look a bit ridiculous on him, to be honest. It was slightly oversized as if he'd popped a cooking pot on his head Johnny Appleseed-style. The better to hide his red hair, I imagine.

I managed not to smirk. I think.

"Your first official disguise," I said. "Congratulations."

The rest of the disguises—intended to unmake Old Red and Big Red Amlingmeyer and leave more easy-to-ignore nobodies in their place—consisted of long top coats, new shoes, kid gloves, mufflers (perfect for wrapping around my brother's undisguisable cherry-red mustache) and (for me) a tweed flat cap.

"Well, we ain't a sailor and a priest, but I think this'll do the job," I said once we were dressed. "Shall we go thank Diana for the new wardrobe?"

"I don't think she's waitin' around just for the thanks," Old Red said.

He was right, of course. When we joined Diana in the lobby, she pretended not to recognize us for a moment—"Perfect! You are now utterly unremarkable!" she said after we "revealed" ourselves—then nodded toward the exit.

"To the scene of the supposed crime?" she said. "I assumed that's where you'd be headed this morning—back to your landlady's house to do some investigating—so I hope you don't mind that I've invited myself along."

"Mind? We are delighted!" I replied.

Old Red muttered some response of his own, but it didn't quite make it past his muffler. From the rumble of it, one could safely assume it conveyed no delight, however. As much as he likes Diana, my brother dislikes looking foolish in front of her.

He jammed his hands into the big pockets of his new coat and stomped toward the door.

"My presence should make your disguises all the more effective," Diana said as she and I caught up to him outside. "Your former landlady and her employees and boarders are accustomed to seeing the Amlingmeyer brothers together. Always a pair. A unit. Seeing two men, one tall, one…not so tall—that might be enough to make them think of you."

She reached over and twined an arm around Old Red's.

My brother's back instantly stiffened straight as a board.

"But a gentleman and his wife walking with some friend or relation offers an entirely different pattern," Diana went on. "One they'd have no reason to note."

I started to protest my casting as "some friend or relation" but held my tongue. Thanks to his big bowler up top and his thick muffler below, all that was showing of my brother's face was a three-inch strip running from one ear to the other. What I could see was blushing as hot pink as a slice of ham.

Old Red's painfully shy around women his own age, and Diana's one of the few he can converse with more than ten seconds without looking like he's going to jump out the nearest window. If he was going to learn to disguise himself—to take on the ways and appearances of others—getting over his fear of females would be another important lesson. So I figured I was helping him develop his detecting by leaving him yoked to our lady friend.

Plus it was pretty funny.

"Makes perfect sense," I said. "I shall be Cousin Cuthbert newly arrived from Omaha to visit Cousin Cornelius and his blushing bride Bedelia as they settle down to marital bliss in Ogden."

"Oh, shut up," my brother said.

"Shut up, *Cuthbert*," I chided him. "Do try to keep up."

"Actually, Otto's got the right idea," Diana told Old Red. "It's unlikely anyone will ask us who we are or why we're there, but just in case it's wise to have a response ready in advance. That way there's no hemming and hawing or contradicting one another. We're both wearing gloves, so no one would notice the absence of rings. So Cornelius and Bedelia we shall be. Freshly married and in search of our first home together."

My brother let out a little *Eep* that suggested he'd found a spider in his mustache.

Diana had just given his arm an affectionate squeeze of the sort newlywed might give newlywed.

"I have my heart set on a cottage with a garden and a trellised gate," she cooed to him.

I went back to resenting being the friend or relation.

"If ol' Cornelius lets you down, don't forget Cousin Cuthbert," I told "Bedelia." "Plenty of trellised gates to be had in Omaha."

Old Red let loose another mutter that was muffled by his muffler. Maybe he was expressing his appreciation for the stunning beauty of the crystal-clear Utah morning and the sun shimmering on the snow-dusted mountains ringing the town. Miracles do happen.

As we made our way to Miss Derringer's, Diana gave us another lesson in the fine art of surveillance. Before joining our little agency, she'd spent years as a spotter for the Southern Pacific Railroad Police keeping an eye out for thieves, swindlers and other undesirables, so surveilling was something she knew well indeed.

"You need to capture details in your mind's eye quickly. At a glance," she said. "You're watching, not gawking. That means spending a lot of time looking at what you're not really looking at. Let your gaze linger too long on someone, and you run the risk of making eye contact—and that changes everything."

We had time to practice our looking-without-looking soon enough, for we arrived at Miss Derringer's block just before seven thirty—the time when the other boarders began heading off to the various railroad offices sprinkled around Union Station.

"Here they come," Old Red said when Miss Derringer's door opened and railroad men began filing out like a big brood of suit-wearing ducklings.

We were strolling up the opposite side of the street, turning from time to time to remark upon the homes we were passing. Or to pretend we were remarking upon them, anyway.

"That sure is a house," I said as we swiveled to face one. I pointed at the roof. "Boards on top to keep the snow off you and everything."

Diana nodded and smiled as if a boards-on-top-to-keep-the-snow-off-you house was exactly the kind she was looking for.

"Do the boarders always leave in a bunch like that?" she asked.

"Yes and no," I replied.

My brother threw a casual glance over his shoulder. "Banks, Baker, Galloway, Crowell, Mead-Jones and Lassen. No Gore. He's lollygaggin'...as usual."

"This Mr. Gore is always the last to leave?" Diana said.

I nodded. "Like clockwork...if your clock's five minutes slow. The man's a talker. Always the last one sucking up coffee and gabbin' at the maid."

"Oh?" Diana said in that arch way that asks if an "Ooo la la" is in order.

I laughed at the idea. "Wait till you see him. He's no Romeo. About as easy on the eyes as a handful of sand."

"It was his watch that turned up under Otto's bed," Old Red added.

Diana gave that a long "Ahhhhh," then nodded to our right. "We'd better keep moving. This house-with-a-roof isn't *that* interesting."

We turned and headed back the way we'd come so as not to

put ourselves directly across from Miss Derringer's. Behind us, the six gentlemen all turned left to march away north up the street.

"What will be happening in the house after all the other boarders have gone for the day?" Diana asked.

"Annie'll start cleanin' up the breakfast mess while Claypool gets ready to take Miss Derringer out for her morning walk," I said. "Or her mornin' roll, more like, seein' as she gets pushed around like a pile of turds in a wheelbarrow."

Diana gave me a vaguely disapproving look, presumably for my choice of metaphors.

"I've had to clean out a lot of stables," I said. "And the old bitty did accuse me of bein' a thief."

"Fair enough," said Diana.

Old Red threw another glance over his shoulder.

"There he goes," he said.

Diana and I looked back, as well.

Skinny, bug-eyed little Mortimer Gore had left Miss Derringer's and was striding toward the street.

"You were right—he isn't exactly dashing, is he?" Diana said as we all faced forward again. "Which way will he go?"

"I ain't never paid attention," I said.

"North, like the others," said Old Red. "Away from us."

Diana nodded. "Good."

We took a few steps in silence, then Diana looked back again.

"Just as you say…"

My brother and I risked our own peeps back.

Gore had gone to his left, as predicted, and was heading away from us. As we watched him go, Miss Derringer's front door swung open yet again. Claypool was about to wheel the old lady out.

We all turned our attention back to where we were walking— which was fortunate, as we'd been about to flatten a pair of young boys coming toward us. They were on their way to school to judge by the leather-strapped books each carried in their mittened hands.

"'Scuse us, gents," I said as they scrambled around us.

"Which way will Miss Derringer's man Claypool take her?" Diana asked.

"No idea," I said.

"South," said Old Red. "Thisaway."

Diana gave that an "Ah."

There were two thumps against my back, and I heard guffaws and pounding feet behind us.

My broad shoulders had made me an easy target for snowballs.

"Turn and shake your head," Diana told me. "But don't do it long and don't say anything."

"Right."

I looked back and saw what I expected. The schoolboys were making their escape up the sidewalk—and Claypool was watching as he wheeled Miss Derringer away from her house. Miss Derringer wouldn't have heard the splatting of snow or the gleeful cackles of the splatterers, of course, so the assault upon my dignity had escaped her attention. A ragman of the sort you see in cities —rickety handcart piled with old clothes and quilts and other discarded bric-a-brac he collected from one house to try to sell at another—was heading down the street from the north, and all her scorn was directed his way.

The fleeing boys added rude gestures to their mocking laughter now. I just shook my head, brushed at the snow on my back, then turned away and caught up to Diana and Old Red again.

"Did your landlady or her manservant see you?" Diana asked.

"Not Miss Derringer. Her man Claypool did, though."

"Any particular reaction?"

"Nah. He didn't recognize me. Anyone who knows Otto Amlingmeyer knows he'd have been whippin' snowballs right back at those little squirts."

Old Red nodded. "That does sound more like you. Guess a little dignity can be a disguise, too."

I looked over at my brother. "Maybe we should see how dignified *you* are with a couple snowballs down your collar. I can't miss at this range."

"Otto, Gustav—focus please," Diana said. She'd been giving us lessons all morning, but this was the first time she sounded like a disapproving schoolmarm. "We're approaching the corner and need to make a choice quickly. Do you know which way Clay-pool's liable to go next?"

"No," said Old Red, sounding peevish. He didn't have the years of experience I did with disapproving schoolmarms. "I noticed which way he usually goes when he leaves the house with the old lady, but that's it. No idea what the whole route might be."

"All right," Diana said. "Then we'll go left, and there's a two-in-three chance they'll go straight or to the right. Hopefully they'll do one or the other and we'll be able to turn around and come back here. We can't leave the house unwatched for long."

"Why is it so important to stick to the house?" I asked. "What's gonna happen while Claypool's gone? If my brother's canoodlin' theory about him and Annie is right, I mean."

"I told y'all yesterday—that ain't no 'theory,'" Old Red growled. "It was just a damn guess 'cuz certain people insisted I make one." He shot Diana a look that was half-apologetic (for the "damn") and half-annoyed. "I reckon certain other people got a *real* theory, but they're bein' stingy with it."

Diana favored him with a tolerant smile.

"In the absence of more 'data,' as Mr. Holmes would call it, canoodling remains a fine guess, Occam's razor being what it is," she said.

"Feh," my brother snorted. "Stingy."

Diana's expression turned a bit less tolerant.

"And here we go," she said.

We'd reached the corner. The three of us turned left, heading east on 30th Street.

"Don't look back," Diana said. "Leave that to me."

"Right," I said.

Old Red just grunted.

After we passed a few homes much like Miss Derringer's—big

Queen Annes that felt like palaces compared to the little sod
hovel my brother and I grew up in—Diana glanced over her
shoulder.

"We're in luck," she said. "They're staying on Adams Avenue.
Going straight. Another few seconds and they'll be across Thir-
tieth and we can go back."

"I still don't see what watchin' the house'll do when only
Annie's in," I said.

Diana shrugged. "Perhaps nothing. Let's find out, shall we?"

A moment later we were turning back onto Miss Derringer's
block—just in time to spot someone we recognized doing the
same.

"Well, I'll be da— darned," Old Red said.

Mortimer Gore was coming up Adams, returning to the house
he'd left not ten minutes before.

"Don't stare," Diana warned us even though Gore was forty
yards off and showed no sign he'd noted the threesome eyeing
him from the opposite side of the street. "We know where he's
going, so there's no need."

"And I guess we know why he's goin' there, too," I said. I
shook my head in disbelief. "Annie and *Gore*. Criminy."

"Makes sense, though, in a way," said Old Red.

"I suppose. They're both bony little runts, ain't they? I guess
birds of a feather do more than flock together."

My brother glowered at me. "I meant Annie didn't even have
to steal that watch from him to make like you took it. He just gave
it to her."

"Oh. Right," I said. "So what do we do now? Let the two of
'em...you know...*commence*..." I shivered. "...then fetch back Miss
Derringer so she can see how things are?"

"I'm not convinced that would work," Diana said.

"Why not?" I asked.

We passed in front of Miss Derringer's house just as Gore
disappeared inside.

"Come on," Diana said.

She turned and started hustling across Adams Avenue.

"Oh, dear god, tell me we're not gonna peep in the windows," I said as Old Red and I followed.

"Not unless we have to," Diana said. "It's a bit inelegant as surveillance techniques go."

We reached the other side of the street. But instead of carrying on to the house, Diana turned again and headed for the corner.

"I assume the kitchen's at the back of the house...?" she said. "And an alley, as well?"

"Yes and yes," I said.

"Whatever's goin' on in there, it ain't got nothin' to do with canoodlin', does it?" my brother asked Diana.

She shook her head. "I don't think so."

"Well...?" Old Red prompted.

We reached the corner of Adams and 30th and went right. The entrance to the alley running behind the homes wasn't far off, and soon we were turning right there, as well. Diana slowed and lowered her voice as we drew closer to Miss Derringer's backyard.

"It was the odor on your things that pointed my suspicions in a certain direction," she said. "The fact that they were stored in the basement but smelled of pungent chemicals rather than mildew and mold. When I worked for the Southern Pacific, one of the things I was taught to watch for was...hel-lo."

Diana stopped and pressed herself close to a coach house belonging to one of Miss Derringer's neighbors. Old Red shot her an irritated look as we joined her in taking cover, partially because of the way she'd cut off her explanations, partially because she'd purloined one of his pet phrases. "Hel-lo" is how *he* likes to greet clues.

He didn't glare at our friend long, though. There was her clue to focus on.

The ragman we'd seen on the street a few minutes before had come around to Miss Derringer's back door—and Annie was talking to him with an armful of dented tin cups and plates and what looked like a child's toy elephant.

We hopped back out of sight and looked at each other.

"So Annie's sellin' Miss Derringer's kitchen things and what-all to the ragman?" I whispered.

"That'd explain the missin' punch bowl," Old Red replied quietly. "Maybe the boxin' trophy, too, though it don't seem worth the risk. All she'd get from the likes of him for the likes of that would be pennies." He rubbed his chin. "Don't seem like Miss Derringer to even *have* tin cups and plates."

"Or a tin elephant," I added.

"*Watch*," Diana said.

Implied in that one word were two more: Shut up. Which we did—though my brother didn't look happy about it.

The three of us leaned out for another peep around the coach house in time to see Annie walk the cups, plates, and elephant inside. Apparently she was busy baking again, for black smoke was puffing from the kitchen chimney. Though we were thirty yards off, I took an experimental sniff to try to catch the aroma of fresh pastries or pie. (Please recall I'd had no breakfast.) But we were too far off, and all my sniff yielded was a glare from Old Red.

When Annie returned a moment later, she handed the ragman a single large, shiny coin and a couple biscuits (the lucky so-and-so). He tipped his tattered hat and turned to go.

We drew back from the coach house corner and tried to arrange ourselves in some casual fashion. You know—as respectable folks do when lurking in alleyways.

"Now I'm really confused," I said under my breath. "Annie's not sellin' tin cups and plates but buyin' 'em?"

I heard Annie close the back door, then the sound of squeaky wheels and footsteps drawing closer.

"I'd convert the coach house into servants' quarters," Diana said, voice at full volume. "It's not like we're going to have a buggy and a mare to pull it…unless there's something you're not telling me, Cornelius. A birthday surprise, perhaps?"

She coiled her arm around Old Red's and pulled him close in case he'd forgotten he was Cornelius.

"Yes…servants' quarters. Yes," he said stiffly.

"Don't put the buggy before the horse, Bedelia," I said. "You have to make your offer on the house first, and you don't know it'll be accepted."

The ragman pushed his cart out into the alley. Diana/ "Bedelia" gave him a seemingly distracted, dismissive glance while I offered him a curt nod. My brother just stood there so still and rigid he could've been a cigar store Indian in an overcoat and bowler.

The ragman returned my nod as he went on his way south toward the street.

"Oh, Corny!" Diana exclaimed, startling us all. She pointed at the ragman's cart. "Do you see that old quilt? It's just like one Aunt Bess used to have."

"Uhh…you don't say," Old Red said.

"Oh, the pleasant nights I spent beneath it when visiting Walla Walla," Diana went on. "I simply must have it, Corny. I must!"

Having heard all this, the ragman had stopped and turned back toward us with a grin. At least it seemed like he was grinning from the crinkling of his eyes. His mouth was hidden behind a mass of beard so impenetrably bushy-brown it could've been a muskrat stuck to his face.

"Ten cents, and it's yours, ma'am," he said in the gravelly voice of a man who's either over-varnished his tonsils with rotgut or acquired the habit of gargling with broken glass.

Diana lifted the purse she carried from a drawstring around her wrist and opened it to look inside.

"Oh, dear…I don't seem to have any small change," she said. She glanced up at my brother. "And I know you and your cousin gave all of yours to that beggar outside the hotel."

"Yes…yes, we did," said Old Red.

He isn't much of an actor, but he can recognize a cue when he gets one.

"I'm afraid all I have is this," Diana said.

She fished a single coin from her purse. It gleamed gold in the morning light—but not half as bright as the gleam that came into the ragman's eyes at the sight of a half eagle worth five dollars.

"Oh, ma'am…I don't have much change myself," he said. "Three or four dollars' worth at most."

"Well, just give me what you've got, and we'll call it a trade," she said. She batted her eyes at my brother. "I hope you won't think your bride a spendthrift."

Old Red cleared his throat. "No…no, not at all."

Diana handed the coin to the wide-eyed ragman. He whipped off his droopy-brimmed slouch hat, deposited the coin on the top of his head, slapped the hat back on, then jammed his hands into the pockets of his frayed trousers. He looked anxious to seal the deal fast lest the lady change her mind.

"Here you go, ma'am!" he said, pulling out twin fistfuls of pennies and nickels.

He dumped the change into Diana's upturned palms. It looked to me like a heck of a lot less than "three or four dollars." More like about sixty-seven cents. Maybe sixty-eight. But then Diana gave the coins a little shake that rearranged them in her hands, and my estimate more than doubled.

Mixed in with the smudged brown and dull gray of the coins was one little flash of brightest silver. A single Morgan dollar.

As Diana started working the coins into her purse, the ragman turned away, grabbed up the quilt, and seeing the lady not ready for it, shoved it into *my* arms.

"Pleasure doing business with you!" he said as he hustled around to the back of his cart and grabbed the handles. "Enjoy your new quilt!"

I gazed down at it as the ragman rushed off toward the street. There was nothing "new" about it. It looked like your usual patchwork of faded calico and dingy muslin ornamented here and there with rips, holes, and stains of the sort one tries not to linger on long. Approximate value, in my learned opinion: half a cent. Diana must have been paying for something else, I figured, and when I looked up again, I saw what it was.

She'd stowed all her new coins away except one—the silver dollar Annie had given the ragman a few minutes before. Diana held it up betwixt thumb and forefinger, brought it to her lips, opened her mouth, and gave the coin a good, hard chomp.

"I don't believe it," I said when she held it up again so all three of us could get a close look at it—and the little dents she'd just bitten into it.

"Tin," said Old Red.

Diana nodded. "Probably some lead and pewter, too. All softer than silver and so easy to melt you can do it on a stovetop."

"*That's* where the trophy went!" I said. "And the punch bowl!"

Diana nodded again.

"We've probably got part of one or the other right here," she said, giving the coin a little waggle.

My brother still had his muffler up over the bottom half of his face, but from the hard squint of his eyes I could tell he was scowling.

"Dammit, I shoulda seen it…"

"It was the smell of chemicals on your things that made me suspect something of this sort," Diana said softly. "It's from the nitric acid used to give the coins a silvery finish. How could you have known that? I only knew because watching for this kind of thing used to be part of my job."

"I still shoulda known that stink meant something." Old Red snapped his fingers. "And Annie suddenly bakin' all the time the last few weeks. She was tryin' to cover the stink up, I bet. That's a deduction I coulda made."

Diana shook her head—but did it with a reassuring smile. "Even the keenest natural intellect won't get the job done every time. Not by itself. Sometimes it's experience that makes the difference. Acquired knowledge and instincts and skills. You've already accomplished amazing things, and you're sure to accomplish more. But you're still learning, Gustav."

"Yeah…I guess I am," Old Red muttered.

"Indeed. *We* are," I threw in. (As is sometimes the case when Diana and my brother get to talking deductions, I felt that there was one key piece of data—that fact that I was still alive and present—they were ignoring.) "The question now is what do we do about what we just learned."

"Well…first off, we need to find a telephone we can use, I figure," said Old Red. "Then…"

He heaved a sigh.

I knew what it meant. There was a difficult conversation coming up—one he'd thought he was looking forward to but now wasn't.

"Mi mi mi miiiii…la la la laaaaa," I sang.

It was time to warm up my vocal cords again.

Ten minutes later, we were waiting near the corner of 30th Street and Adams Avenue when we saw a pair of familiar figures —one seated, the other, much larger, hunched over behind it— slowly approaching. We weren't trying to hide now, and Old Red wasn't wrapped up in his muffler like a mummy, so not long after Claypool wheeled the old lady back onto her block, he stopped, staring at us.

Miss Derringer swiveled in her seat to look up at him.

"What are you gaping at?" she said.

She followed his gaze and narrowed her eyes.

"Oh! It's you!" she said when she saw us. Diana was standing between me and my brother, and the lady leaned forward and frowned at her. "With some strumpet, I see. Have you come back for my jewelry? Well, you're not going to get it!"

"Every bit as charming as you made her out to be," Diana whispered.

"WE NEED TO TALK, MA'AM," I said.

Miss Derringer slid her withered hands from the chinchilla muff on her lap and flapped them at us, shooing us away.

"I've got no time for your lies. Claypool—go around them."

But rather than push the old lady's wheeled chair out into the street to get past us, Claypool took his hands off the handles and folded his arms across his broad chest.

"Get out of here, or I'll make you get," he said.

Old Red snorted and started toward him. I went along in case Claypool really did try to "make him get"—or just snap him in two. I'd handed off our new five-dollar rag quilt to Diana, so my hands were free to form fists if need be.

"YOU SHOULD LOOK AT THIS, MISS DERRINGER," Old Red said.

He pulled the Morgan dollar from his pocket and—careful not to linger within grabbing distance of Claypool—darted in to give it to the lady. Claypool started to step around her chair, but by then my brother was already backing up a couple steps to line up next to me.

Miss Derringer held the coin up and squinted at it. "You came back to show me a silver dollar?"

"A COUNTERFEIT DOLLAR," said Old Red. "MADE IN YOUR KITCHEN AND YOUR BASEMENT."

Miss Derringer scowled at him. "What?"

I watched Claypool for a reaction, but all I saw on his beefy face was his usual disdain.

"ANNIE'S IN ON IT WITH THAT FELLA CALLS HIMSELF 'GORE,'" Old Red went on. "I GOT NO IDEA WHAT HIS REAL NAME IS, BUT I CAN GUARANTEE HE DON'T WORK FOR NO EASTERN RAILROAD. I RECKON THAT'S WHY HE'S LAST OF THE BOARDERS TO LEAVE EVERY MORNIN'. DON'T WANT THE OTHERS SEEIN' HE DON'T REALLY GO TO NO OFFICE."

"Nonsense!" Miss Derringer declared.

"MAYBE," my brother said. "BUT THE TOOTH MARKS ON THAT COIN—WHICH ANNIE JUST GAVE TO A RAGMAN FOR TIN—AND THE FACT THAT 'GORE' CAME SNEAKIN' BACK INTO YOUR HOUSE TWO MINUTES AFTER YOU LEFT IT WOULD SEEM TO SAY OTHERWISE. WE'LL SEE IF THE POLICE AGREE."

"Police?" Miss Derringer said.

I nodded back at Diana. "OUR FRIEND MISS CROWE'S GOT FRIENDS ON THE FORCE. WORKED WITH 'EM LOTS OF TIMES. THEY'RE SENDIN' MEN OVER TO LOOK INTO THIS RIGHT NOW. WE WANTED TO LET

YOU KNOW SO YOU WOULDN'T END UP IN THE MIDDLE OF ANYTHING."

"COULDN'T LEAVE YOU SURROUNDED BY CRIMI-NALS," said Old Red.

He glared at Claypool, who kept glaring right back.

Miss Derringer noticed.

"Are you telling me Claypool's part of this supposed gang?" she scoffed.

"OF COURSE HE IS," my brother said. "MAYBE SOMEONE COULD HAVE THEIR OWN PRIVATE MINT GOIN' WITHOUT A DEAF OLD LADY NOTICIN'—"

"I am not a deaf old lady!" the deaf old lady protested.

Old Red kept going.

"—BUT A WORKIN' MAN WITH WORKIN' EARS IN THE SAME HOUSE? HOW COULD HE NOT KNOW? HECK, I WOULDN'T BE SURPRISED IF 'GORE' IS CLAY-POOL'S BROTHER OR COUSIN OR OLD CELLMATE. IT HAD TO BE EITHER HIM OR ANNIE WHO TOLD THE MAN ABOUT THE PERFECT SET-UP THEY HAD IN THAT HOUSE...SO LONG AS THEY GOT RID OF THE TWO DETECTIVES THAT WAS LODGIN' THERE."

"Poppycock!" Miss Derringer said. "Tommy-rot! Balderdash!"

Claypool's vocabulary wasn't nearly so broad.

"[EXPURGATED] you, you [EXPURGATED] [EXPUR-GATED]," he snarled at us.

(The EXPURGATEDs were all variations on the same unprintable one-syllable word. The man wouldn't make much as a writer with a stunted imagination like that.)

Miss Derringer craned her neck to gawk up at him.

"What did you say?"

The way the color drained from her wrinkled face made me think she'd caught some of it even without her ear trumpet to help.

Claypool provided no explanations. Not of the spoken kind. He just turned around and sprinted off in the opposite direction.

"Claypool?" Miss Derringer called after him. "Claypool!"

"THAT'S CALLED 'RUNNING AWAY,' MA'AM," I said.

"I'D SAY HE'S DECIDED NOT TO WAIT AROUND FOR THE POLICE," Diana added.

"Claypool?" Miss Derringer said again. It came out different this time, though. Like no words I'd heard from the woman before. Whisper-soft and trembling.

The truth was starting to sink in.

It sank in all the way after Officers Hicks and McGee of the Ogden City Police showed up and the old lady, still atremble, gave them permission to enter her home. They found Annie in the kitchen cooking up a nice big batch of tin while a whistling "Gore," cheerful as ever, got his molds and acid ready in the basement. She and he were the ones that were siblings, it turned out. Real names Betty and Bob Feger—wanted for counterfeiting and fraud. Claypool they'd been paying off with their "silver" dollars. (Dogsbodies, it turns out, don't pull down much in the way of salary.) But all that came out later.

The day the police hauled off the Fegers, Old Red, Diana, and I found ourselves alone in the house with Miss Derringer. It was still just mid-afternoon—hours before the boarders would begin returning from their downtown offices—and it didn't feel right to leave a shocked and despondent old lady by herself. All of her considerable brass seemed to have melted like the tin to make a phony coin, and she sat slumped in her big armchair staring despondently at nothing. She had no relations in town—that's why she relied so heavily on her hired help—so there was no one to call over to join her. Just us.

"I'LL GO MAKE YOU SOME NICE, HOT TEA," Diana said, making her escape from the silent sitting room.

Miss Derringer didn't even have the heart to yell at her that she only took coffee. Instead she waited for Diana to leave, then looked over at me and Old Red and muttered something.

"WHAT'S THAT, MA'AM?" I asked.

"I'm sorry," she said quietly. "I was too quick to believe you were thieves. It was foolish. It was wrong."

"It's all right," Old Red grumbled. "We're used to bein' misjudged."

Miss Derringer straightened up and eyed him reproachfully. It was fine for her to soften her voice, I guess, but that didn't mean the same was true for us.

"THAT'S QUITE ALRIGHT, MA'AM," I said. "ALL'S WELL THAT ENDS WELL."

"But it's not ended, is it? Not until you have a new place to live," the lady replied. "Of course, you're welcome to move back in here…if you want to."

My brother and I looked at each other.

We'd come back to clear our names—and throw our innocence in the old lady's face like a well-aimed snowball. Now that we'd done that, *did* we want to stay?

"I'd started feelin' pretty comfortable here," I said. "And I think you did, too, brother. It was nice havin' a home for a while."

Old Red just sat silently for a moment, brow furrowed and mouth pinched tight, while Miss Derringer watched us expectantly. Then he took a deep breath and turned to the lady.

"THANK YOU, MA'AM," he said. "WE'LL JUST NEED TO RUN OVER TO OUR HOTEL ROOM AND FETCH OUR THINGS."

He was already speaking loudly, of course, but as he went on his voice grew even stronger—so strong I was sure Diana could hear it in the kitchen and Colonel Crowe could probably hear it in the A.A. Detective Agency office eight blocks away and maybe you could even hear it in New York, Mr. Smythe.

"I'M ANXIOUS TO GET MY BOOKS IN PARTICULAR," Old Red said loud and clear. "I'M LEARNIN' TO READ, YOU KNOW."

O.A. Amlingmeyer
2955 Adams Avenue, Room #4
Ogden, Utah
February 20, 1894

A LOOK AT: BLACK LIST, WHITE DEATH
TWO HOLMES ON THE RANGE NOVELLAS

DISCOVER THRILLING WESTERN ADVENTURES WITH COWBOY DETECTIVES BIG RED AND OLD RED AMLINGMEYER!

In "Black List," the Amlingmeyer brothers ride into the Arizona Territory on a quest to unearth a buried secret, coveted by a ruthless cattle baron. Can Old Red's deductive skills, inspired by Sherlock Holmes, solve the mystery and protect them from the cattleman's hired guns?

In "White Death," the Amlingmeyers investigate mysterious deaths at a tuberculosis sanitarium deep in the Colorado mountains. As they search for clues, a sinister figure lurks in the shadows. When a sudden blizzard traps them with the patients, staff, and the killer, the suspense reaches its peak.

As a special treat, enjoy the bonus short story "Expense Report: El Paso," where Big Red embarks on his first solo mission to collect a bandit's head. But what if the head has other plans?

Looking for the wildest detective tales the West has to offer? You'll find them in *Black List, White Death*.

AVAILABLE DECEMBER 2023

ABOUT THE AUTHOR

Steve Hockensmith's first novel, the western mystery hybrid *Holmes on the Range*, was a finalist for the Edgar, Shamus, Anthony and Dilys awards. He went on to write several sequels—with more on the way—as well as the tarot-themed mystery *The White Magic Five* and *Dime* and the *New York Times* bestseller *Pride and Prejudice and Zombies: Dawn of the Dreadfuls*. He also teamed up with educator "Science Bob" Pflugfelder to write the middle-grade mystery *Nick and Tesla's High-Voltage Danger Lab* and its five sequels.

A prolific writer of short stories, Hockensmith has been appearing regularly in *Alfred Hitchcock* and *Ellery Queen Mystery Magazine* for more than 20 years. You can learn more about him and his writing at stevehockensmith.com.